Serenity's Quest

Serenity Inn Series

Serenity's Quest

Kay Rizzo

BROADMAN
& HOLMAN
PUBLISHERS

Nashville, Tennessee

F
R12

© 1998
by Kay D. Rizzo
Printed in the United States of America

0-8054-1674-9

Published by Broadman & Holman Publishers, Nashville, Tennessee
Editorial Team: Vicki Crumpton, Janis Whipple, Kim Overcash
Page Design: Sam Gantt Graphic Design Group
Page Composition: PerfecType, Nashville, Tennessee

Dewey Decimal Classification: 813.54
Subject Heading: FICTION
Library of Congress Card Catalog Number: 98-20316

Library of Congress Cataloging-in-Publication Data
Rizzo, Kay D., 1943–
      Serenity's quest / Kay D. Rizzo.
            p. cm.
      ISBN 0-8054-1674-9 (pbk.)
      I. Title. II. Series
   PS3568.I836W57   1998
   813'.54—dc21

                                                    98-20316
                                                    CIP

1 2 3 4 5 02 01 00 99 98

Dedication

To Beth Hutson,
a faithful and encouraging friend.

Contents

CONTENTS

~*1*~

Rich Little Orphan Girl

SERENITY POWNELL STOOD MOTIONLESS, watching the yellow flames dance against the evening sky. Suddenly, she stiffened. "Mama's Bible!" she gasped, ". . . in the library!" She scooped up her skirts and darted into the fiery conflagration. As she bounded up the front steps of the family manse, her boot caught on the hem of her dress, ripping a portion of the hem and causing her to stumble. Behind her, the deputy sheriff shouted for her to stop. She ignored his commands. She had only one thing on her mind—her dead mother's Bible.

The young woman ran through the smoke-filled foyer and into the flames engulfing the library. The smoke choked her. She covered her mouth with a portion of her skirt. Glancing about, she tried to find her bearings, but everything looked surreal. Blindly, she felt her way along the wall to the brocade chair where she'd been sitting earlier in the day.

She reached down to the chair seat. "No!" she wailed. The book wasn't there. Tears streamed down her face. "Oh, dear God, I must find my mama's Bible. I've lost so much! Please, I can't lose my last connection with Mama. Help me find her Bible and I'll give my life to You, just like Auntie Fay says. I promise, Lord!"

Serenity slid her hands along the arm of the chair to the lamp stand, where her fingers touched the nubby texture of a book cover. The Bible! Her heart leaped with joy. Several of her mother's daily journals lay beneath it. "Thank You, God, oh thank You," she gasped. Finding the Bible would have been enough, but to also rescue some of her mother's diaries? Crushing the books to her breast, she turned to retrace her steps.

A thick curtain of smoke billowed around her. She ran into a wall, then frantically headed in the opposite direction only to stumble over a footstool. *What is that doing here?* she wondered. Flames licked the hem of her skirts. A fiery strip of wallpaper dislodged from the wall and sailed toward her thick ebony hair. Screaming, she pawed at the air above her head, whirling about in confusion. *I don't know where I am!*

Panic gripped her. Which way out? Her mind refused to give her the answers she so desperately needed. Taking a step in the direction she hoped was the door, the toe of her boot caught on a ripple in the carpet. She felt herself falling. She screamed in terror. When she landed flat on her face, the precious books she'd risked her life to save strewed onto the carpet before her.

"No! No!" she cried. "Daddy, help me! Daddy!"

* * *

The bedroom door burst open and crashed against the wall. "Where is he? Are you all right?" Suddenly the silhouette of a man loomed above the foot of her bed. He wielded a Sharp's rifle.

Serenity clutched the bed linens to her chest. Half awake and half asleep, she skittered to the top of her bed and screamed in terror at the figure. Tears streaming down her face, she cried, "Go away! Go away! Help! Someone help!"

A woman, her hair up in rags and her robe aflutter about her, swept into the room carrying a lit lantern. "What's the matter?" She shot a startled look at the man at the foot of Serenity's bed. "Caleb Cunard! What are you doing in my niece's bedroom?"

"I . . . , b-b-but,—" he cast a helpless glance first at Serenity, then at the woman.

"Auntie Eunice!" Serenity leaped from the bed into her aunt's startled arms. "I'm so frightened!"

"As you should be with this wild man charging into your bedroom in the middle of the night, and carrying a rifle, no less!" Serenity's Aunt Eunice sputtered. "This is totally unacceptable behavior in my home, Mr. Cunard!"

"Ma'am, I heard Serenity scream and I—"

His mother, the woman Serenity called Aunt Fay, burst through the open door interrupting his explanation. "What's wrong? What's happening?"

Immediately behind her, the lean, tall form of her husband, Reverend Eli Cunard, appeared in the doorway carrying a fireplace poker. "What's going on here?"

Serenity sobbed into her Aunt Eunice's shoulder.

"There, there," Aunt Eunice comforted the young woman while glaring at Caleb. "I came in to my niece's room to find your son—"

Everyone glared at Caleb and waited for an explanation. "I heard a scream!" he said. "I thought someone had broken into the house and was hurting Serenity!"

Suddenly there was a clamor of footsteps. Everyone turned to see Serenity's Uncle Joel, his sleeping gown flapping and his nightcap drooping over one eye, thunder into the room. He aimed his breech-loading musket at the terrified girl. "Where'd they go? I'll get 'em!" He whipped the barrel of his gun first at one shadow, then another.

"Put that thing away!" Eunice commanded, pushing the barrel of the musket toward the floor, "before you shoot someone."

Eli Cunard stood in the center of the room, the iron fireplace poker poised and ready for use. "Will someone please tell me what is going on here?"

Everyone except Serenity started talking at once, pointing fingers at one another.

"Wait! Wait! Who screamed?" the reverend asked.

Serenity timidly lifted her hand. "I . . . did."

Again, everyone tried to tell their part of the story at the same time.

Reverend Cunard raised his hands. "Let Serenity speak. Serenity, why did you scream?"

"I . . . I . . . ," she hiccuped between sobs. "I'm sorry. I didn't mean to frighten everyone. I dreamed I was trapped in the fire again." She broke into sobs, burying her face in her aunt's shoulder. "I'm so embarrassed!"

"Oh, honey, it's all right. You've a right to a little hysterics after all you've been through." Eunice patted the young woman's head.

"All right, gentlemen. I think we ladies can take over from here." Fay turned her husband around and nudged him toward the door, then did the same with her son.

Reluctantly, the men shuffled through the bedroom doorway into the hall. Fay strode over to the washtable, poured water into the small crystal tumbler, and handed it to Serenity. "Here, honey, drink some water. It'll help."

Obediently, Serenity drank the water. "I'm sorry. I didn't mean to—"

Eunice brushed Serenity's curls away from her sweaty brow. "We understand."

Fay handed a linen handkerchief to Serenity who sniffed a thank-you. "Where's my father? He said he'd contact me once I got to Buffalo. I haven't heard a word from him, from anyone! I'm trying to be good about everything, but . . ." Serenity swiped at the tears streaming down her cheeks.

"And you're doing fine, darling," Fay comforted. "You've been through more in the last five months than some people go through in a lifetime."

"That's right, honey." Eunice brushed a stray curl from Serenity's wet cheek. "The death of your mama, the loss of your home, and now, your father being who-knows-where. It's enough to give anybody nightmares."

Serenity blinked her teary gray-blue eyes at the two women. "Thank you for being so understanding. I know everybody tries; but sometimes, I feel so all alone."

"Honey . . ." Fay straightened the bedding on Serenity's bed as she spoke. ". . . you will never be all alone, no matter what happens. Remember that text your mama underlined in Hebrews? 'I will never leave you, nor forsake you.' That's what your heavenly Father promised."

Eunice glared at Fay. "Really! Talking religion at a time like this."

Fay smiled. "I can't think of a better time to talk about the security found in our heavenly Father than now."

"She's right, Auntie Eunice." Serenity wiped her tears from her face and blew her nose. "I know she's right, and during the day I do fine. It's at night, when the nightmares start that—" She began to weep again.

Fay strode over to the dark walnut dresser and picked up Serenity's Bible. "Serenity, honey, would it help if I sat beside your bed and read to you, maybe from the Psalms, while you try to sleep?"

"Oh, would you?" Serenity's eyes glistened.

"I'd love to. Slip under the covers and I'll make myself comfortable in the rocker." Fay sat down on the carved dark walnut rocking chair while Serenity wriggled beneath the covers. Fay glanced toward the crestfallen face of Serenity's Aunt Eunice and extended the Bible toward her. "If you'd like to read . . ." Fay suggested.

"Of course not. I'm not too religious, I'm afraid." Eunice adjusted the linens about Serenity's neck, then kissed her tenderly on the forehead. "Sleep well, honey. If you need me, I'm in the next room. Just call."

Serenity nodded. When Eunice slipped from the room and closed the door, Mrs. Cunard opened the Bible to Psalm 91: "He that dwelleth in the secret place of the Most High shall abide under the shadow of the Almighty. I will say . . ."

Serenity closed her eyes and recited the familiar words with Fay, her mother's best friend and spiritual mentor. ". . . He is my refuge and my fortress; my God; in Him will I trust." In her mind Serenity could see the words in her mother's Bible, underlined in her own hand. "Surely He shall deliver thee from the snare of the fowler, . . ." Fay continued.

Serenity gathered her down-filled pillow in her arms and sighed as she listened to her Aunt Fay's voice. *Oh, Mama, I miss you so much. I miss you so much!* she thought as she drifted off to sleep.

After the fire that destroyed Serenity's home, her father, State Assemblyman Samuel Pownell, had to flee the state and the bounty hunters who were determined to arrest him for aiding runaway slaves. The assemblyman left his seventeen-year-old daughter, Serenity, in the care of his trusted young friend and neighbor, Caleb Cunard. But because of Reverend Eli Cunard's oldest son's involvement with the Underground Railroad, anti-abolitionists in the area also pressured the Reverend and his family to leave their home in Central New York. The Cunard patriarch chose to head for the gold fields of California. "A lot of missionaryin' to do out there," the circuit-riding preacher declared to his parishioners.

Serenity intended to travel with the Cunards as far as Buffalo, the westernmost city in New York State, where Assemblyman Pownell's brother, Joel, and his wife, Eunice, resided. There, the young heiress was relieved to find a semblance of human comforts at her relatives' home after roughing it aboard the canal barge that brought her and the Cunards and all their belongings west to Buffalo. Her aunt and uncle's home, while not of the former grandeur of her parents' now burned-out mansion, contained the necessary amenities for daily living, Serenity reasoned. Her relatives welcomed her with such open arms that she decided she would stay in Buffalo until she received further instructions from her father.

The night her father had been forced to flee the state, less than a gallop in front of the determined bounty hunters, he'd held her in his arms and comforted her before he left. He'd promised to meet her in Buffalo. Now, lying in her aunt's home, she remembered her father's warnings: "Don't trust your Uncle Joel and Aunt Eunice with your fortune. My brother and his wife tend to get squirrelly when it comes to money. They're good people, mind you, but when it comes to money . . ." He wrinkled his face for a moment, then continued. "I've asked Caleb to be your guardian until you marry or reach your majority, whichever comes first."

"My majority?" she asked.

"Twenty-one, love. Before that, the government won't recognize your right to make your own decisions, being a female and all." Her father nuzzled his face into her soft ebony curls. "Oh sweetheart, what have I gotten you into? How I wish your mama was here."

Me too, Serenity thought so many times since that terrible night. *Me too!*

Her father had directed Caleb and her to a stash of gold bars he had hidden in the dark recesses of a cave by the lake. The cave had been her childhood hideaway; never had she dreamed it also contained a portion of the family treasure.

Once the gold was retrieved from its hiding place, Caleb built a false base inside each of Serenity's two trunks where she could store them. There they'd stayed throughout the trip from Cayuga to Buffalo. Occasionally when the subject of her inheritance came up in her conversations with Uncle Joel or Aunt Eunice, she'd been tempted to mention the gold she carried with her. But, always, she hesitated.

Serenity knew that Caleb's constant attention to her made him suspect in her Aunt Eunice's eyes. One afternoon, during her first week in Buffalo, Eunice took Serenity shopping for clothing "appropriate of your station," as the wealthy matron put it. "When I introduce you to the young people of our social class, I want you to look presentable."

Most of Serenity's own clothing had been destroyed in the fire. Since then, she'd been forced to depend on the generosity of her former neighbors and on the loving needle and thread of Aunt Fay.

Standing in her stocking feet and slip on the dress-maker's green velvet footstool, Serenity listened to the prat-tle between her Aunt Eunice and the dressmaker. Mostly they talked about Serenity as if she weren't present. "Beautiful bone structure," the woman said, wrapping the tape measure around the girl's hips. "Needs a little meat on her bones, of course, but give her a few years and this little lady will set polite society back on its heels."

Serenity rolled her eyes toward the ceiling. She'd never appreciated the fawning many skilled artisans did at the smell of wealth. Her mother had had a way of making light of the comments and easing the discomfort of the moment until the presumed social barriers fell. *One of the many skills from my mother that I failed to inherit,* the young woman reasoned.

Eunice looked up from the bolts of fabric she'd been examining and said, "Yes, she's going to set the young men's hearts spinning, that's for certain. If she can only keep her heart for an appropriate suitor and not fall for some lesser individual out of gratitude." She gave Serenity a pointed glance. "She'll make a young man of substance a remarkable wife. You do play the piano forte, don't you, dear?"

"Yes, ma'am, a little." Serenity groaned to herself. Another jab at Caleb. The battle for her affections had begun the moment they'd arrived at her relatives' home. As Reverend Cunard and his family made preparations to con-tinue their journey west, Uncle Joel and Aunt Eunice pres-sured her about staying with them.

One evening after a meal of disparaging remarks about the Cunards, Uncle Joel announced to his wife, "Do you know that the young Cunard told me that my brother made him guardian of our niece? Can you imagine?"

Eunice gasped. "What? I've never heard of such a thing. He just wants to marry a rich orphan, that's all."

Serenity slammed her napkin down on the linen-covered table. "Excuse me. I am in the room and I would appreciate it if you wouldn't talk about me as though I'm not."

"Oh, of course, my dear." Uncle Joel reddened. "I am so sorry. I keep forgetting that you are hardly a child anymore."

"No, I'm not a child. And yes, my father did ask Caleb Cunard to take care of me until I marry or 'reach my majority,' as he put it. I was present at the time."

"Tsk! But under the circumstances . . ." Aunt Eunice clicked her tongue and said to her husband, "What was your brother thinking? A hayseed straight off the farm managing your father's fortune?"

"Caleb has taken very good care of me since my father left." The words regarding her father's abrupt leaving stuck in her throat. "As to my wealth, Reverend Cunard and Caleb have repeatedly refused to accept any of the payment I received from selling several of my mother's jewels to Josephine Van der Mere."

Eunice eyed the young woman suspiciously. "I thought everything was lost in the conflagration."

"It was, for the most part. My mother's personal maid managed to rescue several of my mother's favorite pieces before the house was destroyed."

"Did she keep any for herself?" Eunice narrowed her gaze.

Serenity gasped. "I certainly hope so. I told her to."

"Your mother had exquisite jewelry, some that belonged to my husband's grandmother in France, for that matter. Giving away such an inheritance just proves you need someone older and wiser in financial affairs to guide you."

"I beg your pardon! The jewels were mine to give. My father took care of everything before he left—"

"Oh? In between his escapades evading the law? Imagine running an underground station right there on the estate! Did your father . . ." Uncle Joel cleared his throat, then continued, ". . . give you much money to live on?"

Serenity closed her eyes. She could see the gold bars hidden in her trunks. *It isn't exactly money,* she thought. "No, Uncle Joel. Papa gave me no money before he left."

"Hmm." Her uncle stroked his beard in thought. "Could he have entrusted Caleb or the preacher with cash? That would explain why they refused to take any of your jewelry money."

Serenity's face reddened with anger. "No! Papa gave no one money, to my knowledge, at least."

Eunice patted the girl's forearm. "There, there. Of course, Mr. Cunard has taken very good care of you. He brought you to us, didn't he?"

Uncle Joel leaned back in his chair. "For that we are grateful." His body relaxed. "But now, you must admit, his job is done; his promise to your father has been fulfilled."

Serenity cocked her head to one side. "I don't think so. I will be turning eighteen in a couple of weeks, not twenty-one, and I certainly do not see a line of suitors at your door, eager to win my hand."

Eunice's lips tightened. "Don't be impudent to your uncle, young lady. You know what he means. Your neighbors were kind enough to bring you safely to us. Now we mustn't be selfish and keep them from continuing their journey to California." A satisfied smile crept across her lips.

"That's right, honey." Uncle Joel nodded and smiled at his wife's wise strategy. "It would be very selfish of you . . .

er . . . us, to keep them here in Buffalo any longer than necessary. As it is, it's too late for them to make the journey safely across the plains and the mountains this winter."

Serenity hadn't thought of that. She certainly didn't want to be selfish. The Cunards had done so much for her. She loved them for it. She stared into her dessert cup. The apple cobbler had smelled so luscious while baking. Now it turned her stomach.

Eunice dipped her fork into the heavy whipped cream topping on the cobbler. "We know you aren't meaning to be selfish, darling, but the truth is, they've lost a lot of valuable time caring for you and your needs. I'm sure they'd never say so, good Christians as they are."

Joel placed his hand on Serenity's shoulder. "Of course, you should be the one to talk with them, explain to them that their responsibility to you has been more than fulfilled. Free them of their obligation to care for you."

Serenity's breath caught in her throat at the thought of bidding farewell to the Cunards. She bit her lower lip. But her uncle and aunt were right. The Cunards had done more than enough for her. She didn't know how she would have survived had it not been for Aunt Fay's comforting wisdom, and of course, Caleb's constant protection.

"It's not that you'll be alone," Eunice added. "Your uncle and I will always be here for you. We're your family, your blood relatives. The Cunards, as loving as they might be, are just friends. They have their own children to worry about. They don't need an additional burden."

Serenity's eyes flooded with tears. She'd never thought of herself as a burden. Onyx, her oversized dog that she'd begged to bring with her on the trip—yes, Reverend Cunard thought of him as a burden at first. But Serenity had been careful to control and care for her four-legged friend all along the way to Buffalo. Every evening Serenity took the dog for a stroll along the banks of the canal where Onyx would disappear into the woods and return with his nightly meal. By the time they reached Buffalo, she could tell Eli had made up to the big friendly mutt.

Since they'd arrived at her uncle's home in Buffalo, Uncle Joel had kept poor Onyx chained in the backyard. Serenity hated that, but she knew that neither Uncle Joel nor Aunt Eunice wanted a dog underfoot. What if the Cunards tolerated her in the same way her relatives tolerated Onyx? What if she'd been so hungry for love that she'd confused love with kindness, the results of their sense of Christian duty?

Aunt Eunice caressed the girl's shoulder. "We're sorry to have to bring up such a painful subject, but you have to face reality. You are an added responsibility to them."

Serenity dabbed at the tears trickling down her cheeks. "I'll talk with Caleb tomorrow. I promise." Rising to her feet, she gathered her skirts in her hands and hurried from the room.

— 2 —

The Trouble with Treasures

THE FIRST WEEK AFTER THEY ARRIVED IN Buffalo, the Cunard family sought out their own living quarters at a friend's house. Serenity's Uncle Joel insisted they were welcome to stay on at the Pownell residence as long as they pleased. Aunt Eunice assured them, "You've done so much for our precious Serenity, the least we can do is put you folks up for the short time you'll be in town." Yet the Cunards chose to stay with a local Baptist preacher and his family.

"They're friends of ours," Reverend Cunard explained. "I knew Butch Bailey when we were students at the seminary." By the stoic acceptance on Fay's face, Serenity knew the Bailey accommodations were not to her liking. And the girl could tell Fay disliked leaving her to face her relatives alone. Before the Cunards left the Pownell home, Fay assured Serenity, "Anytime you need us, darling, we're here for you. Less than a mile away, in fact." As for Caleb, he promised to come by every day to make certain Serenity needed for nothing.

The five new dresses Aunt Eunice had made for her niece arrived the morning Reverend Cunard announced his intentions to resume the family's westward trek. Caleb arrived at

Joel Pownell's place soon after breakfast to find Serenity sitting in the parlor admiring the perfectly stitched frocks. He paused in the doorway, his face drawn and serious.

"Well, hello there!" Serenity bounded to her feet, her spirits lifted from the previous night's dolor by the beautiful new dresses. "What do you think of my new dresses? Aren't they absolutely luscious?" She scooped up a forest green taffeta and held it before her, hugging its waist to hers. "Which do you like the best? This green one, the beige lace, or the peach, or how about the rose, or the blue?" The laughing young woman sashayed over to him and reached for his hand. "May I have this dance, Mr. Cunard?"

He held her hand for an instant, then let it fall.

"Oh, pooh! You're no fun." She tossed the rustling gown onto the sofa with the others. Her ebony curls, caught up in a yellow ribbon, cascaded down her back, defying his somber mood. "Why are you being such a spoilsport? What is the matter with you, Caleb Cunard?"

"Serenity, we need to talk." He indicated for her to sit on the gold brocade sofa. She pushed aside the skirts of her new wardrobe and sat down as instructed. A pout formed on her lips. "Now, what is it? What can be so serious?"

Caleb sat on a side chair, setting his hat on his knee. "My parents are leaving for Missouri next Monday. They plan to winter in Independence; then, come spring, they'll continue on to California."

Serenity's heart sank. "Why can't they stay here until spring?"

He shook his head. "Mama's anxious to move. The Bailey's are great people, but Mama prefers to raise her children her own way."

Serenity frowned. "I don't understand."

Caleb laughed. "The Bailey's are a little overly strict

with their two young 'uns, and it drives my mother crazy to keep silent. Regardless, my dad has been itching to get going ever since we reached Buffalo."

The young woman sank against the sofa back, disregarding her new dresses. "I . . . I'm going to miss you . . . er . . . your family . . . er . . . Aunt Fay." Her words didn't make much sense, even to her.

"My mother will be over to see you later in the week. To her, you're like another daughter, right alongside Becca. She couldn't love you more if you were a blood relative." He glanced down at his farm-boy rough, calloused hands. "I'm here to invite you to go with us, Serenity. And my dad says even Onyx is welcome in the family." Caleb cast her a half grin. "I think Pa has taken to the big old mutt."

Serenity picked at an imaginary spot on the skirt of her yellow gingham dress. *Leave all of this?* she thought, glancing at the elegant dresses strewn across the sofa. Taffeta and silk would hardly hold up living on the prairie or crossing the continent in a covered wagon. "I don't know what to say."

Caleb crossed his arms, leaving his felt hat balanced on his knee. "Certainly you've known this moment was coming."

Her frown deepened. "I tried not to think about it. I've liked being here at my aunt's place. I've been able to forget all the bad things that have happened. Don't think ill of me, Caleb, but, I like being pampered."

Caleb sighed. "Well, it was my job to extend the offer." He rose to his feet. "You'll have until Sunday to decide what you want to do."

A loud bark caused the young man to glance toward the rear of the house. Caleb frowned. "Does your uncle still have Onyx chained?"

Serenity shrugged. "Yes. The poor dog; he hates it."

Without a word, Caleb strode to the back of the house and out the screen door. Serenity rose to her feet, gathered her gowns in her arms, and climbed the stairs to her room. For the rest of the day, she sequestered herself there. A little after noon, Eunice asked if the girl would like to attend a tea at the garden club. Serenity declined.

"Are you feeling under the weather?"

Serenity hadn't told her aunt the purpose of Caleb's morning visit. The girl nodded her head. "I do feel a bit under the weather today. I think I'll spend the afternoon reading in my room, if that's all right with you?"

"Of course it's all right with me." Eunice placed a kiss on her niece's forehead. "Good, no fever. You get some rest. We want you feeling chipper for Thursday evening's musicale at the Duncans. Their son, Ralph, is the catch of the season, you know. He's into pork bellies, so I hear." She chuckled aloud. "Believe it or not, there's plenty of money to be had in pork bellies."

Serenity laughed in spite of herself at the literal picture she had of the Duncan fellow into his pork bellies. "I'm sure I'll feel much better by dinner, Auntie."

"Good! Then I must dress for the tea. I've been trying to decide between wearing the calico dimity or the pink lace. Which would you recommend?"

Serenity shook off her worries for a moment. "On you, the pink lace heightens your complexion." Eunice loved hearing about her flawless, creamy complexion and snapped her head in agreement.

"You're right. The pink lace is perfect for an afternoon tea." The older woman paused before the freestanding mirror near the door of Serenity's room and touched her cheek.

"Yes, the pink is definitely the best choice. Hope you feel better soon, dear."

The girl sighed as the door closed behind Eunice. Listless and lonely, she ran her fingers along the row of books on the bookshelves by the window. Nothing appealed. Returning to her bed stand, Serenity picked up and opened her mother's Bible. As had become her custom, she prayed before opening the Book.

"Heavenly Father, I don't know where to start looking for direction. You promised to give us the wisdom we need when we need it. I know I've read that before, somewhere in the book of James, I think." She riffled through the pages. "I love the Cunards so much." The words on the pages became blurred. A tear dropped, staining an onion-skin page. "Aunt Fay was the first to introduce me to You. My mother treasured her advice and friendship. On the other hand, Uncle Joel and Aunt Eunice are blood relatives. When my father looks for me, this is where he'll start."

Idly, Serenity turned to Psalm 31 and read over the familiar words. She recalled the first time she'd heard them come from Fay's lips: "Whenever I get to fretting, I recite David's declaration of faith. Maybe it'll help you too. 'In Thee, O Lord, do I put my trust; let me never be ashamed: deliver me in Thy righteousness. Bow down Thine ear to me; deliver me speedily.'" Serenity liked the "speedily" part of the verse. King David understood her heart. Her most difficult act of faith seemed to be accepting God's timing over hers.

"Lord, my problem is past the fretting stage. We're into the decision-making stage, if you ask me. And I don't know what You want me to do." She paused to reread the first two verses of the chapter.

"OK, Father, in You I will put my trust." She continued reading the next couple of chapters until her eyelids grew heavy. The Bible dropped from her hands onto the bed as Serenity curled up to go to sleep.

She awoke several hours later to the sound of her aunt and uncle's voices in the hallway. "Is she sleeping?" her uncle asked.

"She hasn't been herself all day. Don't disturb her."

"But it may be important. It's from my brother's fiancée, Mrs. Van der Mere. She's the only connection we have with Sam."

At the mention of Josephine, Serenity bounded off the bed and ran for the bedroom door. Before opening it, she patted her hair into place and tugged at the waist of her dress, then opened the door slowly.

"Good afternoon," she yawned and stretched. "What a delightful nap I had. How did the tea go, Auntie Eunice? Uncle Joel, you're home from the office all ready? My, what time is it?" She glanced down at the letter in her uncle's hand. "Oh—is that for me?"

"Yes . . ." He cleared his throat and handed her the letter. "As a matter of fact it is."

A familiar perfume wafted from the envelope, creating a wave of homesickness. While she'd known Josephine for only a short time, their mutual love for Serenity's deceased mother and their newness at falling in love with her mother's God bound them together. The aroma of the woman's perfume brought it all back.

Tears glistened in Serenity's eyes as she tore open the envelope. "If anyone knows of Daddy's whereabouts, Josephine will, I'm sure! She really loves him, you know."

Joel and Eunice glanced skeptically at one another. Serenity unfolded the linen writing paper, taking time to appreciate the aroma a second time. At the top of the ecru stationary was the Van der Mere monogram engraved in gold leaf.

Albany, New York, August 12, 1850. My Dearest Serenity, It's been some time since we parted that terrible night. So many times I've wondered how you are faring and have lifted you up to God in my prayers. Mr. Cox, your father's former solicitor, informed me that the Cunards have taken you to your uncle's place in Buffalo as promised. The Cunards are godly people; I believe you can trust them.

Mr. Cox also wrote that your uncle sold off your father's estate and the other family assets in and around Auburn. I am sure that he did it with your approval. And as it's turned out, maybe it's for the better. Dear One, it is with a grieving heart that I must tell you what I've learned regarding your father. As I understand it, the ship, *Wayfarer,* that your father is believed to have boarded in Hamilton, North Carolina, sank in a storm off the coast of Cape May. It would have brought him to Albany and to my side. I continue to pray for his safety, but I've received no encouragement from the officials. I am so sorry to have to be the one to tell you this.

I am sending this letter in a canal packet to Buffalo, trusting you are safely ensconced in your uncle's home. Give everyone my greetings, and please, stay in touch. I will always care for you.

Much love, Josephine A. Van der Mere.

Serenity's breath came in short gasps. Her eyes blurred. She swayed and grasped the doorjamb with her free hand while the two-page letter slipped from her fingers and floated to the floor. Joel grasped Serenity's elbow, steadying her, while Eunice scooped up the letter and read it silently.

"Oh, no!" She shoved the pages toward her husband and wrapped her arms around the sobbing young woman. "Oh, you poor darling, I am so sorry," Aunt Eunice said, then helped Serenity to her bed.

After reading Josephine's message, Joel silently folded the letter and returned it to its envelope, placing it on the dresser in Serenity's room. He paused before leaving the room. "Serenity, this may sound crass right now, but don't lose that letter. It's proof of your right to your parents' inheritance."

"Joel!" his wife snapped. "Not now!"

"It's important that she knows."

"Not now!" The woman ushered her husband from the room and closed the door behind him.

Serenity lifted herself up onto one elbow. "Please, Auntie Eunice, I need to be alone for a while."

"Of course. I'll have Cook Ames bring up a plate of dinner for you."

"No, no. I couldn't eat. . . ."

But Eunice would not be deterred. "How about a hot cup of peppermint tea? I've found peppermint tea perks me up even during the worst doldrums."

The girl nodded. "Peppermint tea would be nice. Thank you."

Eunice edged toward the door. "If there's anything else you need, just ask."

"I will."

"Promise?"

"I promise." Serenity's empty gaze swept across the room. The late afternoon sun cast golden hues on the delicate pink and lavender-flowered wallpaper. At the window, lacy panels fluttered in the light summer breeze. The heavy oak furniture lent a sense of permanence to the room. The girl shook her head, burying her face in the bed pillow. *Permanence?* she scoffed. *That's one thing I don't have in my life!* "Lord, I trusted You!" She rolled over and shook her fist at the ceiling. "You could have protected my father. You knew how much I needed him. For that matter, You could have protected my mama too. But instead, You turned your back on me and left me an orphan!" *Orphan*—the word burst through her brain. She remembered one or two orphan girls who had gone to the female finishing academy she'd attended outside of Boston. They always seemed so pitiful and alone.

Alone? Terror filled her heart. Then the words of Hebrews 13:5 entered her mind, soothing and calming her soul. "I will never leave you; I will never forsake you. . . ."

Drawing herself up on her elbows, she covered her ears. "No! I don't want to hear it. God, if You'd done all that You promised. . . Oh, what's the use? I'm talking to the wind anyway." She hauled herself off the bed to answer Eunice's knock at the door. Taking the promised cup of tea, she strode across the room to the dark walnut rocker beside the window.

Rocking aimlessly, Serenity stared out the window onto the sunburnt grass below. She continued to rock long after the sun set and moonlight studded the landscape with silver.

Serenity heard her aunt and uncle retire for the night. The house grew quiet. She opened the second-story window and peered out into the night. She heard a gentle yip. Onyx. She felt an overwhelming need to hug her old friend. Without lighting a lantern, she brushed her hair back into a tail and tied a ribbon around it. She stepped out into the hallway and tiptoed down the stairs. A stair creaked beneath her tread. She paused to listen for an instant. All she heard was the erratic snoring of her uncle. She slipped through the hallway into the kitchen, across its terrazzo floor and out the door into the backyard.

The instant her foot touched the wooden porch, Onyx barked. "No!" she whispered. "You must be quiet or you'll get us both in trouble."

The dog panted and strained at his leash as she moved toward him. Falling to her knees, she wrapped her arms around his massive shoulders. "Onyx, I've missed you and I've neglected you. Can you ever forgive me?"

The dog replied with a chin-to-forehead lick. Tears fell as Serenity laughed and wiped the dog's saliva from her face. "If Aunt Eunice saw that, she'd have a case of the vapors. Of course, if Mama saw you do that, she'd be none too pleased either."

The dog wriggled in her arms and licked her face a second time. She giggled and lunged at the dog, who pranced before her. The two scuffled on the grass in the moonlight. After a few minutes, the girl sat up. Noting the change in his mistress's mood, Onyx whined and laid his head on her lap. Serenity stroked his head, her tears falling again and moistening the dog's sleek black coat.

As she sat there on the damp grass, she listened to the sounds of the night and thought of home, or what had been her home. Would she ever see the banks of Cayuga Lake again? Would she and Onyx ever run along the shoreline? "The lake—," she said, her mind returning to Mrs. Van der Mere's letter. *Uncle Joel sold the property on the lake! I wonder why he didn't tell me about that? And what's he done with the money?*

She rolled onto her stomach, propping her head up with her elbows. *What about the townhouse in Albany? And*

Daddy's other assets? Serenity bolted upright. The dog jerked awake. She patted his head. "What else has Uncle Joel done without my knowledge or my father's permission?" Her words carried in the night air. The dog nuzzled her hand, begging for more caressing.

Forgetting her anger, she prayed, "Lord, I can't believe what's happening. Please help me to sort this all out." She heaved a broken sigh. "Oh, and by the way, I'm sorry I yelled at You before. Don't give up on me."

-3-
Time to Decide

"SERENITY!" CALEB DREW HER INTO THE Bailey's house. Onyx nosed his way in as well. "What are you doing out at this hour?" Caleb shined the hurricane lamp near her face. "You've been crying. What's wrong?"

Serenity had been uncertain of the Bailey's address. She'd only visited the Cunards once since they arrived in Buffalo and she hadn't paid attention to the route her uncle's carriage driver took. She had no idea how long she and Onyx had been walking, nor exactly when the idea came to her to find Caleb, but it did. And once it did, nothing else would satisfy. She needed to talk with someone who understood her. She knew she should wait until morning, but she needed someone immediately.

Reaching her destination, she walked around the house until she found herself under the second-story window where she knew Caleb and his brother, Aaron, were sleeping. She picked up a pebble from the ground and threw it at the open window. When she received no response, she threw a second, then a third.

Finally the groggy face of the younger Cunard peered out at her. "Hey, what's going on?"

"Aaron, I need to speak with Caleb!" she hissed. "It's important."

"Can't it wait until morning?"

"No," she whispered loudly. "I need to talk with him now."

The boy growled, then disappeared inside the room. After several seconds, Caleb appeared in the window. "Serenity? Is that you?"

"Yes, I need to talk with you. Can you come down here?"

"Go around to the front door. I'll meet you there."

Onyx trotted behind her as Serenity hurried to the front door. The door opened and Caleb drew her into the entry-way. A lantern sat on the small mahogany table at the foot of the stairs.

The instant she saw Caleb, her tears began to flow once more. "Caleb," she sobbed, "my father—"

Caleb grasped her by the upper arms. "Your father? What about your father?"

"Josephine wrote." As the words escaped her lips, she melted into Caleb's startled arms. "Daddy has been report-ed lost at sea."

"What?" Caleb held her awkwardly, uncertain as to what he should do next. Turning to the stairwell, he called, "Mama! Mama! Wake up!"

A gruff and unfamiliar voice boomed from the top of the stairs. "What's all the shouting about?" Preacher Bailey stumbled down the stairs in his partially tied robe and night-shirt. "Do you have any idea what time of the night it is, young man? You probably woke the neighborhood."

Onyx growled as the man strode threateningly toward Serenity and Caleb. "What's that?" the man pointed at the animal. "A dog in my house?" He backed away from the couple and from Onyx. "Get it outside. Now!"

Before Caleb could respond, the tread of several feet clattered in the hallway above their heads. Onyx, worried by the unfamiliar environment, pressed himself against the folds of Serenity's skirts. Caleb shouldered himself protectively between the preacher and Serenity. "Reverend Bailey, I am sorry for the disturbance, but this is Serenity Pownell. She just received word that her father has died."

Serenity heard a gasp as Fay ran down the last few stairs and swept the girl into her arms. "Oh you poor darling. I'm so sorry. I can't believe it."

Before Caleb could repeat the story, the entire Cunard family and the Baileys had surrounded the overwrought girl.

"I'm sorry for interrupting your sleep, Pastor and Mrs. Bailey. I didn't think," Serenity gulped.

"That's all right, dear, preachers' families are accustomed to late-night visitors," Mrs. Bailey assured her. "Do the Pownells know you're here?"

Serenity swung her head back and forth. "I . . . I didn't want to wake them, and I needed to talk to—," she burst into tears.

"Stay the night, then. No good waking them now," Mrs. Bailey said.

"'Oh yes, do!" Ten-year-old Becca Cunard gave Serenity a shy hug. The two Bailey daughters nodded their consent as well.

"Let me fix you a pot of tea. Fay, take her into the parlor where you can speak in private," Mrs. Bailey suggested, waving a finger toward the parlor. "As to you children, back to bed. You can hear all about it tomorrow."

Grabbing a lantern from the lampstand near the door, Caleb led Serenity into the parlor. His parents followed. By now, the reality of what she'd done brought undue color to her face. "I am so sorry for disturbing you in the middle of the night, Auntie Fay. I didn't think."

"Honey—" Aunt Fay slipped her arm around the girl's waist and drew her from Caleb's arms. When he lifted a hand to protest, Aunt Fay sent him a glare. "Where else would you go but to those who love you? You did the right thing coming to us, no matter what time of day or night it might be." She led Serenity to the sofa. "Now, tell us all about it."

Through her tears, Serenity related the entirety of the letter to the Cunards, including the part about Joel selling some of her father's assets. She saw Caleb frown and shoot a worried glance toward his father. The elder Cunard's face remained unchanged.

"My father warned me about Uncle Joel's greed. That's why I haven't told him about the gold in my traveling trunks," Serenity admitted. "He seems so caring, but questions regarding my inheritance do surface in our conversations all too regularly. Maybe his interest is nothing more than concern for my welfare, but—"

Fay squeezed the young woman's arm. "Only God knows the true answer to those questions. Humans look on the outward appearance; only God can see into the heart."

Serenity glanced up into her face. "Then why doesn't He tell me what to do? Caleb told me about your leaving. I don't know what I should do, especially now, with this news about my father." She looked down at her restless hands, then back again at Fay. "And yet, Uncle Joel and Aunt Eunice are family. It makes good sense for me to stay here with them, doesn't it?"

Fay smiled. "Sweetheart, if I've learned anything in my life it's that God is never early with the answers we need; but also, He's never late. He's always right on time."

Caleb leaped to his feet. "Mother, Serenity needs more than promises to get her through this crisis."

Caleb's father placed a restraining hand on his son's shoulder. "There is no better advice your mother could give her than that. Serenity—" He turned his attention to the weeping young woman. "—during the next few days, my family and I will be praying with you that the direction of your future will become clear to you before we head west. In the meantime, you need to be still and trust that He's God."

Fay took Serenity's hands in hers. "We love you dearly and want what's best for you. And no matter what you decide, remember that you will never be alone."

As the Cunards and Serenity knelt to pray, Caleb stared out the window, his face riddled with worry.

When they arose from their knees, Fay gave Serenity a hug. "You'll be all right, darling. The best thing you can do now is get some sleep."

Serenity kissed the woman's cheek. "Thank you. I do feel a little better."

"The girls are in the first bedroom on the left," Fay told her. "Caleb, you put Onyx out for the night."

As Serenity started up the stairs, she heard Caleb say, "You realize, Father, that I must honor my promise to Assemblyman Pownell? If she chooses to stay here in Buffalo, I will stay as well."

In his slow, calm tone, the reverend said, "Son, I don't think Samuel would expect you to carry out your promise if Serenity chooses to stay with her blood relatives. They can take care of her until she marries. Being such a pretty thing, she'll marry within the year, mark my word."

"Son, I don't want you to stay here either," Fay added. "What would you do? How would you take care of yourself?"

"I've been thinking about that. I could go to work for one of the local blacksmiths, thanks to the training I got with Mr. Dodd in Auburn." Caleb paused, a slight grin forming at the corners of his mouth. "Remember what you told Serenity, Mama. The promises apply to me as well. God will take care of me too."

The conversation over, Serenity, who had stopped on the landing to listen, tiptoed into the girls' room. Instead of climbing into the massive four-poster bed next to Becca, she took an extra quilt from the foot of the bed and curled up on the floor in front of the tall, narrow window. *How can I make an intelligent decision now? No matter which way I choose, I'll be hurting the most important people in my life. Oh, Daddy, what should I do?*

Strong and decisive, New York State Assemblyman Samuel Pownell had been her mighty oak throughout her childhood, but even more so since her mother's death. She'd clung to him with a tenacity of fear mixed with love and a touch of hero worship. Curled up on the floor, Serenity began to shake. She clasped the quilt in her hands and wept. After the death of her mother, Fay explained that the day would come when Serenity would see her mother again, in heaven. But her father? Serenity sat up and leaned her forehead against one of the window panes. "Will I ever see you again, Papa?" she said aloud. What troubled her is that she knew her father didn't believe in the loving God her mother worshiped. Being the descendant of persecuted Huguenots who were forced to flee France because of their faith, he'd seen the ugly side of religion. And while he tolerated his wife's interest in spiritual things, he had never seen the value of religion for himself and often said so. "All it ever brings people is trouble. The bloodiest wars in the world have been fought in the name of religion!" he declared whenever anyone would listen. "A bunch of hocus-pocus, that's all it is. I believe that a person needs to live a moral life, treat his brothers with kindness, and work hard." No he didn't share her mother's faith, and if everything Fay said was true, he might not be in heaven either.

The next morning Fay and Caleb escorted Serenity back to her uncle's home. Unaware that the girl wasn't still asleep in her room, Eunice gasped at the sight of the disheveled Serenity standing at the front door still dressed in yesterday's yellow gingham. Joel met them at the door with thunder in his eyes.

"I'll be back this evening to make certain you're OK," Caleb said as he and Fay mounted the wagon, taking their leave.

Serenity smiled up into his solemn face. "Thank you." On tiptoe, she tenderly kissed his cheek. "I really appreciate you, Caleb Cunard."

Embarrassed by her kiss, he stammered his good-bye, then clicked at the mule. Watching from the shadows, Joel and Eunice were not impressed by Serenity's unprecedented kiss. Their lips tightening into narrow lines, they wished her good rest, promising to discuss her improper behavior when she awakened.

Serenity kissed her aunt and uncle on the cheek and headed for the stairs. As she hurried, her skirt brushed against the heavy gold velvet draperies tied back on each side of the doorway of the sunroom. A pouf of dust made her give a cough. At the base of the stair, she coughed again. Realizing how thirsty she was, Serenity started back to the breakfast room. She paused on the stairs when she heard her aunt and uncle discussing her situation.

"What are we going to do?" her Aunt Eunice asked. "We can't have the girl gallivanting about town in the middle of the night. It's unseemly."

"A better question is what are we going to do with that young man she fancies? Caleb could ruin everything for her and for us."

"She certainly can do better for herself." Eunice clicked her tongue. "What was Samuel thinking, entrusting his daughter to that young ne'er-do-well's care? Does the man even have a profession or skill of any kind?"

"I understand he apprenticed with a blacksmith," Joel drawled.

"A blacksmith! What every proper family needs—a blacksmith in the family!"

"And all the Pownell money! The boy is hardly old enough to tie his own shoelaces let alone manage Samuel's estate! Why did my brother make a stranger Serenity's guardian?"

"I don't know about you, but I smell a rotten fish in the net," Eunice agreed. "When we were visiting after dear Charity's death, he asked us to be Serenity's guardians. Then to draft a codicil to his will like he did? I don't understand."

"I intended to invest my brother's money in pork bellies. Do you know the money to be made in such a venture? And as his executor, I could legitimately charge my administration fees—a hefty percentage of the profits, I might add."

Around the corner of the sunroom door, a tickle formed in Serenity's throat. She buried her face in the skirt of her dress to keep from coughing aloud.

"Well, darling," Aunt Eunice soothed, "we haven't lost her yet. The maid overheard that Cunard boy tell Serenity that the Cunards will be heading west in a few days, so I believe everything will be fine."

Joel heaved a deep sigh. "I miss my brother, of course, but my mourning will have to wait until we get his finances in order. And I won't let all that money go outside of the family. The law is on our side, I'm sure. I will certainly challenge the legality of the so-called change in Samuel's will."

"Get everything in writing," Eunice reminded. "You know how persnickety inheritance laws and lawyers can be."

Serenity heard the discussion breaking up and, forgetting the water, headed toward the stairs. Tears brimmed in her eyes. If she didn't hurry, they'd hear her and realize she'd been eavesdropping. Losing trust in the only family she had left caused her to tremble. And all because of money? *They can have Daddy's money,* she thought. *All of it, for what I care! Money's not important. If only I could have Daddy back.* Careful not to make a noise on the hallway floor, Serenity tiptoed up the stairs to her room.

She closed the door behind her and stood, lost and alone, in the familiar guest room that could be hers if she decided to stay with her family. She glanced about the room. Early morning sun splayed across the Oriental carpet and onto the draperies, the rich mauve slubbed satin brocade bedspread, and the comfortable furniture. *Any young woman would relish such comfort and luxury,* Serenity thought. But could she stay after overhearing her uncle and aunt's conversation? Falling to her knees beside the window, she prayed, "Oh, Lord, here I am again. I'm so confused. I thought they loved me, but what they really love is my daddy's money."

She rose to her feet and slipped out of her dress and crinolines, letting them fall to the floor as she walked toward the bureau. Her stiff and tired muscles ached. "I can't live without Daddy, Lord. I can't. I need him—certainly You can understand that. You must have missed Your Son when He left for earth." The thought failed to comfort her. After all, God was God, not a simple girl suddenly finding herself lost in a maze of impossible circumstances.

Flopping face down onto the downy mattress, she wept. "Oh, dear Father, I hurt so badly. Will the pain ever go away?"

~4~

On the Trail

"THIS IS RIDICULOUS! I'VE NEVER HEARD OF anything so preposterous in my life!" Joel Pownell paced across the parlor to the fireplace, then back again. He looked out the window at a star-studded sky, then turned abruptly toward Serenity. "You are a mere child of seventeen. I won't have any niece of mine gallivanting across the country with some strange man, even if his family is along!"

Serenity's lower lip quivered. She'd been dreading this moment since she first decided she would not be staying in Buffalo with her aunt and uncle. After a great deal of thought, she had no doubt that her father would have agreed with her decision. *Now I understand what Daddy meant about Uncle Joel and Aunt Eunice,* she realized.

"And what is that beast doing inside my house again?" Joel pointed at Onyx cowering behind the sofa. "Serenity, take that dog to the backyard and tie him up. And get this scandalous idea of yours out of your head as well!"

Eunice watched the exchange between her husband and their niece. As Serenity headed outdoors, Eunice sniffed into a linen handkerchief. "I've tried to be a good aunt,

Serenity. I had the new dresses made for you, and I've tried to make you feel at home with us."

"Come on, boy," Serenity coaxed Onyx out from behind the sofa. "Thank you, Aunt Eunice, for all you've done. I really do appreciate both of you."

"Well, you've a strange way of showing it," Joel snarled.

Onyx growled at the man. Serenity patted the dog's head to quiet him, trying to gather her courage. "Uncle Joel, I know you sold my father's property at Cayuga Lake." She choked back the tears at the mention of her father. "How much money did you receive?"

Joel's face reddened. He tugged at his collar. "Well, there were administrative expenses, and, of course, I needed to relocate each of your father's servants, and—"

Serenity sighed. She didn't want to hear any more. "I appreciate all you've done, Uncle Joel, for opening your home to me and caring for me. As a thank you, and as payment for the lovely dresses you had made for me, please keep whatever money you received from the sale of my father's estate."

Uncle Joel's mouth fell open in surprise.

"In return," she continued, "I would ask that you sign a release from any future claims on my father's finances and on my inheritance." She handed him a sheet of parchment paper, authorized by a local judge, Judge Wareham. "You are aware that my father changed his will before he left?"

Joel stared at the document. "When did you get this drawn up?"

"Yesterday. You will find it is quite legal." Serenity cocked her head to one side and eyed the startled man. For once she felt strong and self-assured.

"Did that Cunard fellow put you up to this?" Joel asked.

"If you mean Caleb, no. In fact, he doesn't know anything about it. He doesn't even know I plan to go with him and his family when they head for Missouri tomorrow morning. Only Aunt Fay and Uncle Eli know my plans at this moment."

"Quit calling them aunt and uncle! We're your only relatives!" Joel boomed. Serenity swallowed the knot in her throat and silently shoved the paper toward her uncle.

"But isn't the boy technically your guardian?" Eunice asked.

"Yes, but I chose to have Reverend Cunard sign the document as a witness. I knew there'd be no question to authenticity and propriety with his name attached." Now that she'd done it, Serenity wondered where she'd gotten the courage and the wisdom to do what she'd done. Even Reverend Cunard hesitated about taking the girl from her only blood relatives until she related to him the conversation she'd overheard between her aunt and uncle.

"Uncle Joel, I realize that you could contest this and tie up my departure in court, but to what end? I have sent to New York for the codicil to my father's will, the one he drafted before fleeing the state. With that in hand, you lose everything you acquired!"

Eunice gazed at her niece with wonder and disdain in her eyes. "My, you are a clever little butterfly, aren't you?"

"More like a busy little bee, if you ask me!" Uncle Joel snarled. The man's surly tone caused Onyx to utter another low threatening growl.

"I said get that mutt out of here!" the man shouted.

The dog curled his lip and bared his teeth.

"He's a threat to society and should be shot," Joel added, taking a few steps behind his massive mahogany desk.

"It's OK, Onyx. Calm down." Serenity scratched the

dog behind the ears. "That's a good boy. Come on, I need to put you outside for the night. If you'll excuse me?" she added with a slight nod of the head toward her aunt and uncle. She led the dog down the hallway to the back door. As she fastened the chain around the dog's neck, she whispered, "Don't worry, boy. This is the last time you'll have to wear this horrid chain, I promise."

Before retiring for the night, the girl carried a lantern to the attic. The shadows gathered about her as she lifted the lid of the first trunk, then lifted one corner of the false bottom. Holding the lantern over the gaping trunk, she smiled. The gold bars sparkled in the lantern light. She ran her fingers across the bars' smooth surface and sighed with contentment. She checked the second trunk and found the last two bars safely intact as well.

Serenity carefully replaced the false bottoms, being certain they fit snugly in place. *First thing in the morning,* she told herself, *I'll have the trunks brought down to my room.* She smiled at the thought of packing up once again. She glanced at her well-manicured nails. *True, my nails won't look like this again, but it will be worth it to be on my own. With Daddy's gold and Mama's God, I'll be just fine.*

Serenity blinked awake at the first sign of daybreak. Opening the door, she was surprised to see her trunks in the hallway. She pulled them inside. The five new gowns rustled as she folded and placed them carefully in one of the trunks. She smoothed the yards of broad Belgian lace on one of the dresses and wondered if she'd ever have cause to wear it while living on the prairie. *Of course, I can always sell them. They've never been worn,* she reasoned. Even as the thought crossed her mind, she knew she'd never do such a thing.

Pausing to admire her mother's jewelry, she studied the intricate design of the silver filigree on one of the Spanish bracelets her mother especially loved to wear. She wiped a smudge of soot from the inside and read: "To CP, with love from SP." A tear spilled onto her hand. "Mama, Daddy—"

The old familiar emptiness welled up inside of her. She forced it down. "No, things could be worse!" she declared to the empty room. "If the jewelry hadn't been rescued from the fires by the kitchen staff, I wouldn't have these to remember Mama by." She placed the jewelry delicately in the rose velvet pouch Fay had made for her during the canal trip to Buffalo.

Serenity bent down to place the pouch in the trunk with the rest of her possessions when she heard a knock on the bedroom door. "Come in," she called. She glanced up to see the door open and her aunt's tear-stained face.

"I thought I'd see if you need anything?" the woman said, timidly entering the room. Her eyes pled for acceptance and forgiveness. "Do you have adequate sewing supplies? A woman can't have too many needles and spools of thread."

Serenity smiled warmly. "How sweet of you to think of that. I'm afraid my need for sewing supplies never crossed my mind."

Eunice handed her niece an elegant little midnight blue taffeta sewing box with a strip of lace and a tiny white satin bow perched on top. "I know it's not much, but I want you to know that I care for more than your inheritance. I care for you, sweetheart. You know, your mother accepted me into the family when no one else would. I always thanked her for that."

Serenity's eyes misted as she opened the lid of the box to see the neatly arranged spools of thread and needles, along with a small pair of scissors and a silver thimble. "This is so sweet of you." The girl hugged her aunt. "I will treasure it always."

The woman embraced her niece, then held her by the shoulders. "I, uh, do you need any cash? I would hate to send you out into the wilderness as a pauper, dependant on the Cunards' generosity."

Serenity smiled, unable to speak. Suddenly the four bars of gold in her trunks felt slightly tarnished. "I will be fine, Auntie Eunice. I have a few pieces of my mother's jewelry and a little bit of gold as a dowry. God always provides."

The woman looked satisfied. "Well, just so you know, your uncle received word that Mrs. Van der Mere sold your father's property in Albany. We don't know what happened to the proceeds, but your uncle will not let it rest until he's tracked it down."

The girl laughed. "If Josephine sold my father's property, I'm sure she did so with his blessing." Serenity laid the pouch on the bed and gave her aunt a quick hug. "Thank you so much for everything. I do love you. I hope you know that."

The older woman nodded as she swiped at the tears trailing her cheeks. Glancing at the jewelry pouch on the bed, she asked, "May I see your jewelry? Your mother always had such exquisite taste. I was heartsick when I thought of it all going up in smoke."

"Of course." Serenity exchanged the sewing kit for the jewelry pouch. As she untied the silken cords that held the pouch together, settings of silver, diamonds, rubies, and opals glistened in the morning light that poured in through the open window.

Eunice gasped and held up a ruby brooch set in silver and surrounded by tiny diamonds. "Isn't this beautiful? I remember your mother wearing it with matching earrings. Did the earrings make it?"

Serenity shook her head. "No, I fear they were lost in the fire."

Eunice returned the brooch to its satin nest. "If I may be so nosy, were you thinking of keeping that pouch in your trunks?"

"Yes, I guess so."

"You might be wiser if you kept it in another location—just in case, you know."

"I don't understand."

"Wait! I'll be right back." Eunice dashed from the room, then returned seconds later with an oval-shaped box, decorated on the outside with preserved flowers, lace, and ribbon. "Here. It's filled with face powder. Bury some of your more expensive pieces in the face powder for safe keeping."

Serenity stared down at the cardboard box resting in her hand. "In here?"

"Yes. And place the box in your portmanteau instead of in your trunks." Seeing the look of confusion on her niece's face, Eunice added, "My mother once told me never to keep all my eggs in one basket."

"That's good advice, Aunt Eunice. Thank you."

Onyx pranced alongside the wagon as it rolled down to the docks where all the earthly belongings of the Cunard family and Serenity would be loaded on the *Linn*, a massive steamboat. The *Linn* would transport them west over Lake Erie, then south on the Ohio River to the mighty Mississippi. At that juncture, they would board a second paddle wheeler that would wend its way north on the Mississippi to the Missouri River. From there, a third riverboat would take them west to the town at the "bend in the river" called Independence.

Independence. Serenity liked the sound of that. Considering the grief and loss she'd suffered during the first nine months of the year, anticipation over her own independence was a refreshing change.

On the wagon ride to the lake, Caleb and his brother talked about the two types of riverboats, the Eastern and the Western built. The *Linn* was an Eastern model. It had a low-pressure engine, a deep hull, and fine lines for speed. The upper-deck cabins were enclosed for the comfort of the passengers. The intermediate deck was designed for strolling and enjoying the view. Four gigantic smokestacks loomed over the steamboat, two in the front and two in the rear.

The *Linn,* a luxurious triple-decker riverboat had been polished until she glowed. She looked more like a regal swan than a mode of transportation, with her carved embellishments and beautiful sweeping lines. Her decks sported graceful gingerbread filigree and brightly painted pictures on the cases surrounding the paddle wheels.

An interesting feature of this particular riverboat was a calliope that played popular tunes when docking or leaving a port. Somewhere above her head, Serenity could hear the ditty, "Froggie Went a Courtin'."

It had been decided that the Cunards would cover Serenity's expenses until they reached St. Louis, where she could get a fairer price for her gold bars. Serenity held onto the makeshift rope collar Onyx wore about his neck as she followed Fay up the gangplank to the ship. They'd barely stepped on board when the port's roustabouts removed the gangplank, untied the ropes along the dock, and tossed them to the ship's crew members.

A shrill whistle sounded and billows of white steam belched from the stacks as the giant paddle wheel began to turn. Onyx pressed against Serenity's skirts and whimpered as the deck beneath their feet rumbled and shook from the immense power of the engines.

The passengers crowded the decks and waved farewell to family and friends. Farmers, businessmen, gamblers, wanna-be cowboys, gold seekers, and pioneers—their adventure had begun. Many would never see their loved ones again. Serenity waved to her aunt and uncle until the boat rounded a bend and she could see them no longer.

As the other passengers wandered off to explore their temporary home, Reverend Cunard called to his family. "Come, let's ask God to bless our journey." Fay drew Serenity into the circle. It comforted the girl to hear Reverend Cunard's low mellow tones invoke the promises of God for their safety. "And keep us forever in Your will, not in ours, Lord. Amen."

After the amen, Caleb and Aaron set out to explore the inner operations of the paddleboat as Eli and Fay strolled along the deck to get acquainted with a few of the other passengers. "Would you girls like to come with us?" Fay asked.

"No, thank you. We're going to—" Ten-year-old Becca Cunard glanced at Serenity. "What are we going to do?"

Serenity laughed. "You tell me. I haven't an idea in my head."

"We could go exploring." Becca grabbed Serenity's hand.

A frown crossed Fay's forehead. "You stay with Serenity, young lady. There are many places aboard a ship like this where proper young ladies don't belong."

"I will," Becca assured her. "Come on, Serenity, let's go see what we can see."

"Let's put Onyx in the cabin first," Serenity suggested. "Your father said we are in cabin 229." The two young women made their way down the narrow iron staircase to the lower deck. Everywhere Serenity looked, her mouth fell open in surprise. The word *boat* couldn't describe this floating palace. And she'd thought Josephine Van der Mere's barge was elegant! With five to six hundred people of all classes on board, it even sported a floating circus. *Cleopatra, Queen of the Nile, would have envied this splendor,* Serenity thought. They hurried past a hawker urging them to attend a melodrama being held in one theater and a minstrel show in another. The two girls climbed the staircase to the first-class section and peered through the etchings on the leaded-glass doors into the mirror-lined dining room and social hall, where rich, red velvet pile carpet covered the floor.

"Aaron said that the carpet alone cost almost a thousand dollars," Becca whispered in awe. "Can you imagine?"

Serenity stared, dumbstruck at the beauty. Cut-glass chandeliers hung from the ceiling. Matching sconces lined the wall. Tables and chairs of deep mahogany and rosewood filled the long narrow room. A waiter dressed in white linen moved along the long table, setting out silverware and crystal goblets.

"Aaron says the dinner menu offers ten choices of meat and at least fifteen desserts!" Becca licked her lips at the thought.

"That's impossible. I can't even think of that many different kinds of dessert!" Serenity hissed. Yet the longer she gazed into the magical room, the more she believed Aaron's tales.

At the far end of the room, several men sat drinking and smoking at a well-stocked bar, or, at least, Serenity assumed it was well-stocked. Behind the bar was the largest mirror either girl had ever seen. The candlelight from the massive crystal chandeliers reflected off the mirror, causing the entire room to become a virtual fantasyland.

Suddenly a smooth, deep male voice startled the two girls from behind. Onyx growled. The man shot a glance at the dog, then returned his attention to Serenity and Becca. "Good day, ladies."

Serenity quieted Onyx, then found herself gazing into the bluest eyes she'd ever seen. For a moment she couldn't speak, only stare. The carefully dressed young man, in his late twenties, gave her a crooked grin and winked. The wink brought back her voice.

"Er, excuse me, sir," Serenity said, sidestepping past the stranger. "Come on, Becca, let's be going."

Becca glanced at the well-dressed young man, then at Serenity.

"That's right. Mama warned us not to talk with strangers," Becca said.

The man smiled. Turning to a passing crew member, he called, "Yeoman? Could you please do me a favor? My name is Felix Bonner, attorney-at-law. I would appreciate it if you would introduce me to these lovely young ladies."

The yeoman smiled and asked Serenity her name.

Serenity cleared her throat. "This is Rebecca Cunard and I am Serenity Pownell."

With all the formality found at a formal ball, the yeoman made the introductions.

Serenity giggled and turned to the attorney. "My apologies, sir, but I'm afraid this kind gentleman's introduction won't do." Serenity urged Onyx forward. "Now, my young friend and I must be going."

"Wait! I know your name and you know mine. Isn't that good enough?" The young man grinned.

Serenity chuckled. "I don't think it works that way, sir. If you will excuse us?"

"But, of course." Mr. Bonner swept back dramatically, gesturing with his hand. Removing his beaver-skin top hat, he bowed dramatically at the waist. "Pleasure meeting you, Miss Cunard and Miss Pownell. I do hope I'll have the pleasure of seeing you again in the near future."

Serenity nodded graciously, while Onyx looked suspiciously at the man.

When they were out of earshot of the two men, Becca suggested, "Maybe we should keep Onyx with us."

"Oh, I don't think so. Mr. Bonner was just flirting, that's all."

Becca huffed, "Well, I didn't like him much. Neither did Onyx."

Serenity laughed. After depositing the dog in the cabin, the two girls wandered back up onto the deck. Finding a bench, they sat down.

"Now what are we going to do? There's not much to do until lunchtime."

"We could watch the world float by." Serenity straightened her skirts about her ankles.

Becca groaned. "I wonder where Caleb and Aaron disappeared to?"

"Hey, I'll tell you what. Let's have a race. Let's see which of us can spot the most, uh . . ." Her gaze swept the shoreline. ". . . birds."

"Birds? Ugh! There are too many birds. How about we count donkeys or sheep."

Serenity scratched her head. "I know. Let's count the number of shanties we see along the shoreline."

"I guess."

Serenity scanned the shore. "If the shanty has children playing around it, it's worth one point per child that we see."

Becca sighed. "Oh, all right. We have a lot of miles to go before we reach Missouri."

They'd been riding for only a short time when Becca turned to Serenity. "I like having you for my big sister. I missed you when we were at the Baileys."

"Thank you. I missed you too."

The child frowned. "I was afraid you were going to stay with your family in Buffalo. If you had, I would have lost my big brother too."

Serenity glanced down at her. The child continued.

"Did you know that Caleb had already found a job with a blacksmith in Buffalo? Even Daddy couldn't talk him out of it."

The young woman frowned. "No, I didn't know that."

"Caleb said he'd not break his promise to your father by leaving you alone in Buffalo." The girl looked up into Serenity's eyes. "Caleb's like that, you know."

"I'm beginning to discover that."

They counted shanty rafts and barges until the hot sun sent Becca inside the cabin for cover. Serenity leaned her elbows on the shiny oak railing and watched the ship cut through the water. A small boy waved to her from shore. She returned the wave. *Was it so long ago that she waved at passenger boats passing by her home on Cayuga Lake?* she wondered. Oh well, no sense living in the past! She shook her head to clear it.

～5～

Down a Lazy
River

BEFORE THE LUNCHEON BELL CLANGED, THE passengers gravitated to their assigned dining areas. Serenity's ticket didn't qualify her for dining on the upper deck with the captain and society's elite. Nor did it remand her to the common deck where the passengers and lowest members of the crew ate on long scarred oak tables and benches. She and Becca caught up with the rest of the Cunard family as they followed a crowd of two hundred other passengers into one of the splendidly furnished saloons. Three long tables ran the entire length of the room, groaning with the weight of everything beautiful and delicious. Serenity had never seen so much food in one place. It even outshone Josephine Van der Mere's glorious banquets.

The toes of Serenity's pointed slippers sank into the cushiony deep blue velvet carpet, bringing back memories of her father's library in Albany. She swallowed hard, determined not to begin crying again. A tall, swarthy-complexioned gentleman, clothed in a white linen suit, met them at the entrance. As they crossed the bar in the darkened dining hall to one of the individual tables, Serenity shot a quick glance at Reverend Cunard. His drawn and narrow lips told her he wasn't happy taking his family into an establishment that served alcohol—even if the bar was closed during the afternoon meal.

The table sat eight. As Caleb held her seat, Serenity positioned herself in front of the chair and glanced at the empty chair beside her. She hoped it wouldn't be filled by some dyspeptic old man who drooled his food on his ascot. Immediately she scolded herself for harboring such thoughts. They'd barely gotten comfortable when the well-dressed maitre d' told them to serve themselves at the food tables. Passing through the buffet line, Serenity filled her plate with exotic delicacies, including nuts from Brazil and olives from Spain. Twenty-four stewards buzzed about the room, meeting the passengers' needs and wants. Of the fifteen different desserts, she limited herself to a peach melba.

Munching on her hors d'oeuvres, Serenity noted the passengers dining at the other tables: Englishmen, Irishmen, Germans, Scots, Danes, Santa Fe traders wearing striped blankets, Broadway dudes wearing silk suits woven with pin stripes of gold, Kentucky boatmen, Quakers in full garb, United States soldiers in uniform, Spanish Creoles, Mormons, Baptists, Jews, jesters, clay-eaters (Southern "poor whites"), and solemn-faced Sioux chiefs in full regalia. She had never seen so many interesting-looking people in her life!

Caught up in the excitement of the moment, Serenity hardly noticed when the maitre d' escorted two additional guests to their table.

"Reverend Cunard, let me introduce you to one of your dining companions, Mrs. Felicity Rose. She will be meeting her husband in Independence."

Serenity stared at the strikingly beautiful woman with the sunlight-blond hair and sparkling blue eyes as Eli, Caleb, and Aaron rose to their feet. The maitre d' seated the young woman in the empty chair beside Aaron. Serenity was marveling at the woman's exquisite beauty when the maitre d' added, "And this is Felix Bonner, attorney-at-law. Mr. Bonner resides in Independence."

At the mention of his name, Serenity looked at him in surprise. He smiled and bowed his head, but not before she caught the mischievous smile on his face. The maitre d' seated Mr. Bonner in the empty chair beside Serenity. Before the family continued with their meal, Eli introduced each of his own family members, then Serenity. Felix Bonner courteously greeted each person being introduced. When he reached for Becca's hand and Serenity's, he acted as if he were meeting them for the first time.

"Well, Miss Pownell, it looks like we're going to be neighbors, here on the boat as well as in Independence."

"For a short time, it seems."

The man winked at Serenity. "A lot can happen in a short time."

Caleb tensed, then returned to his food.

Throughout the meal, Felix entertained Serenity and the others at the table with tales of living at the "doorstep of the frontier."

Serenity found herself laughing at the humorous word pictures he drew of the people in the area, and Eli asked numerous questions. Mrs. Rose fluttered her eyelashes and simpered over her succotash, or so Serenity thought. As for Aaron, his attention never strayed from the illustrious face of Mrs. Rose. Married or not, the woman held him captive.

At the end of the meal, Caleb escorted Serenity from the dining salon. "You certainly found Mr. Bonner entertaining," Caleb growled.

"He seems to be a friendly sort."

"Like a wood rattler."

"He is good-looking, wouldn't you say?" Serenity glanced up at Caleb. His firm jaw jutted forward; his lips tightened to a thin line.

"I wouldn't know," he replied.

In midafternoon, the boat docked in a small town east of Erie to take on passengers and let off cargo. Serenity took advantage of the opportunity to walk Onyx on shore. As she tied the leash to the dog's collar, Becca popped into the cabin they shared. "Mama wants me to come with you. She says that neither of us should wander off alone. It could be dangerous."

Serenity rose to her feet. "She's probably right, especially with cads like Felix Bonner around."

Becca laughed. "I didn't think he was such a cad. For that matter, I think he's gorgeous."

"Gorgeous! Hummph! Only women are gorgeous." Serenity led the dog out onto the deck.

Becca skipped after her, closing the door to the cabin as she left. "You may be right. He's too good-looking to be believed."

Serenity huffed. "Beauty is as beauty does, so my mother used to say."

Becca linked her hands behind her back and sashayed along beside Serenity and the dog as they walked the gangplank to the dock. "Caleb didn't much like him, I can tell you that."

"What do you mean?"

"I mean, if Caleb left the luncheon table with anything less than an upset stomach, it would be a miracle. He was so angry, I expected to see steam puffing out his ears."

"I knew he was upset, but not that upset."

Becca's eyes widened. "You don't know my brother. He's like Papa. Most of his feelings he keeps inside, but I can tell." The ten-year-old chatted on as they strolled the edge of some woods, while Serenity paused to think of her father. She remembered times when he would be glad-handing potential voters and never let on behind his broad smile the frustrations he felt. Her mother used to encourage him to open up more, let out his anger once in a while. Remembering her mother and father brought tears to Serenity's eyes.

"Did you hear me?" Becca asked.

"Huh? What? What did you say?" Serenity sputtered.

"I think we'd better head back to the boat. The warning whistle blew."

"It did?" Serenity couldn't imagine being so lost in thought that she missed hearing the blast of the steamboat whistle.

The two girls rushed toward the docks with Onyx leading the way. A block from the dock, Mr. Bonner stepped out from behind a wagon and collided with Serenity. In the process, his feet got entangled with Onyx's leash, sending the two of them to the ground. Becca turned and started laughing.

"Oh, I'm so sorry, Miss Pownell!" He climbed to his feet and held out his hand to help her up.

"No, it's as much my fault as it is yours, Mr. Bonner. I should have been watching where I was going."

"You're all dusty. Let me help you." Before Felix Bonner could brush any of the dust from Serenity's skirts, Becca stepped between them. "I can help Miss Pownell. You tend to your own dusting, Mr. Bonner."

"Becca!" Serenity scolded under her breath.

The second blast from the ship's whistle sounded. The young lawyer took each of the girls' arms and started toward the docks. "We'd better hurry or we'll miss the boat." Onyx ran ahead of them, dragging his leash behind.

As they stepped up onto the gangplank, Caleb strode down the plank toward them, his face angrier than ever. Serenity laughed nervously. "You wouldn't believe what happened—," she began to explain.

"You two almost missed the boat. Then where would you be?" While he talked to the both of them, he was staring at Mr. Bonner. "Mother was worried that something terrible had happened to the two of you."

"I'm so sorry, Caleb. You're right. We strayed too far from the dock. It won't happen again." Serenity reached out to the young man, but he turned and stormed back onto the boat.

"Don't mind him," Becca whispered. "He's just jealous."

Mr. Bonner pursed his lips with satisfaction. At the top of the gangplank, he doffed his hat and bowed. "From here on, I will leave you lovely young ladies to fend for yourselves."

Serenity smiled and nodded politely. Once he disappeared from view, Serenity grabbed Becca's arm. "Jealous? What do you mean, jealous?"

"Jealous! Don't try to tell me that you had no idea Caleb has a crush on you." Becca clicked her tongue.

"Don't be ridiculous; honestly, Becca, sometimes you are irksome!" Serenity hurried to their cabin, refusing to discuss the subject further with the child.

"So, this is how it is to have a big sister." The girl rolled her eyes heavenward and tagged along.

That evening at the dinner table, Caleb sat mute while Mr. Bonner entertained the family and Mrs. Rose with anecdotes about his law school days. Serenity noticed the worried glances passing between Fay and Eli as they watched their younger son, Aaron, flirting with the lovely Mrs. Rose. When Mr. Bonner mentioned that the boat would be stopping for several hours at a nearby town to take on fuel, Mrs. Rose asked Aaron if he would escort her into the town as she needed to pick up a few things at the local general store.

"Caleb, why don't you and Serenity go along?" Fay urged. "Onyx will need to be walked anyway, and it will be good for you young folks to get off the boat for a while. Becca? Would you like to go along as chaperone?"

The girl's eyes brightened. "May I? Ooh, that sounds like fun."

Aaron and Mrs. Rose exchanged looks of exasperation. Caleb grunted his grudging approval and Serenity turned to the young attorney. "Mr. Bonner, would you care to join us?"

"Why, I can't think of anything I would rather do, Miss Pownell. I've been dying to ask you questions about your famous father."

Serenity's eyebrows shot up in surprise.

"Oh, I know all about the famous New York state assemblyman. His heroism was written up in last month's law journal. You were even mentioned as his only living heir."

The smile on Serenity's face faded at the mention of her father's demise.

"Oh, I'm so sorry. I should have known better, mentioning your father at such a time. Please let me make it up to you tonight. There's a fabulous little bakery just off the wharf where they bake the best cinnamon rolls." With an expansive wave of his hand, he included the others. "For that matter, I'll treat you all."

Serenity could see irritation building in Caleb's face with the attorney's every word. How she wished she'd never asked Mr. Bonner along on the excursion. But what was done was done, as her mother often said. She couldn't back out now.

When the boat docked, they all gathered at the railing waiting for the gangplank to be lowered into place. Onyx pranced about Serenity's skirts, as eager for the adventure as Becca and Mr. Bonner, the only two who seemed truly excited to go.

"Serenity," Caleb said, "let me take Onyx for you. You can't take him into a bakery, and I'm not in the mood for cinnamon rolls."

"Are you sure?" Serenity frowned. "I hate to have you miss out on the rolls. Mr. Bonner says they're packed with pecans from Georgia."

"I'm sure. You go and have a good time. Onyx and I'll be waiting here on the wharf when you return." He avoided looking into her gray-blue eyes.

The passengers surged forward to be the first off the ship. Gathering her courage, Serenity turned toward Caleb. "Caleb, have I done anything to offend you? You haven't been the same since we left Buffalo."

"No, nothing's wrong." He glanced toward the rest of the group making their way down the gangplank. Only Mr. Bonner hung back, looking over his shoulder at Serenity. "You'd better hurry or you won't be able to catch up."

Serenity glanced over her shoulder at Mr. Bonner, then back at Caleb. "Let them go. Your good opinion of me is more important than any sweet roll."

"I'm glad you feel that way, Serenity. I guess I sometimes forget that I'm your guardian. I don't own you.

Sometimes I might come across as too possessive. But, after all, you're going to be eighteen on your birthday soon." He gazed down at the ship's railing. "So, you go and enjoy yourself. Onyx and I will be fine right here."

"All right. If you insist, but I think your mother wanted you to go along because of Aaron."

Caleb smiled. "Aaron is going to be all right as long as you and Becca stick with him. He doesn't need an extra chaperone."

Serenity bent down and kissed the eager dog's head. "You behave, you hear?" Onyx wagged his tail and gave a yip.

While Felix continued to seek her company, Serenity managed to keep Becca between them. At the bakery, Serenity purchased a creamy French pastry to take back to Caleb.

The days on board the *Linn* as it steamed its way down the Ohio River toward the great Mississippi, took on a distinct routine, including the two stops for fuel that allowed Serenity time to walk Onyx. On the evening stops, Aaron, Mrs. Rose, and Mr. Bonner turned the routine into a party. The closer Serenity's friendship with Mr. Bonner grew, the more distant Caleb became. Caleb remained in the shadows, or so it seemed to Serenity.

One noon stop, Serenity put on her sunbonnet, called to Onyx, then went to the Cunards's cabin to find Becca. She knocked on the cabin door, but no one answered. "Hmm, she said she'd be here," Serenity thought aloud. The dog fidgeted impatiently. Serenity patted his head. "Well, it looks like it's you and me today." Onyx led the way up the stairs, along the deck, and down the gangplank.

As she stepped off the gangplank onto the wharf, Serenity caught a glimpse of Aaron rushing away from the ship. She shouted to him, but the crowd quickly swallowed him up. The girl frowned. This wasn't the first time she'd spotted Aaron behaving mysteriously. *He must be on an important errand,* she thought, brushing the thought from her mind.

"Go, Onyx," she called, "do your business." The dog bounded to the end of the pier, then disappeared to the left, into a clump of bushes and prairie grass. Spotting a narrow pathway running through a grove of young trees growing alongside the Ohio River, she decided to follow it for a while. It would be at least a half hour before the ship's whistle would call the passengers back to the riverboat.

The midday sun beat down on her shoulders and back as she made her way to the small grove of trees. The sunlight sparkled off the surface of the deep blue water of the river. As she stepped into the shaded grove, Serenity remembered her days along Cayuga Lake. It took but an instant for her to decide that what she needed most was to go wading. Making her way to the riverbank, she located a secluded spot where she could safely remove her shoes and stockings. On a whim, she untied the ribbons on her sunbonnet and tossed it onto the ground beside her shoes. She removed the pins from her hair and shook it out, allowing the ebony curls to cascade around her shoulders and down her back.

Hiking her skirts about her thighs, she stepped into the cool water. She shuddered as mud and slime oozed between her toes. A wriggly water creature nibbled at her ankles. "Eeek!" she giggled.

Onyx paced the shoreline nervously and whimpered.

"Come on in the water," Serenity coaxed. "It's OK, boy."

The dog wagged his tail, barked, and sniffed the water, then leaped into the shallows, splashing Serenity's bodice and face. The girl squealed with delight. Caught up in the spirit, the dog paddled out into the current of the river, then back again.

When a man on a passing pole raft waved and whistled, Serenity blushed and headed for shore only to hear someone chuckle. She whirled about to see Mr. Bonner standing on the shore holding her bonnet, stockings, and shoes. "My, my, Miss Pownell. And how is your day? Need I ask?"

"Mr. Bonner! What are you doing here?"

He laughed. "The same as you, I suppose, enjoying the sunshine and the view. Nothing like a pretty girl cavorting in the river."

Serenity straightened, indignant at his laughter. She made her way to shore. "I am not cavorting, sir."

Mr. Bonner laughed again. "You are so pretty when you're angry."

"I am not angry either." She reached for her shoes and stockings only to have him snatch them back out of her reach.

"Say please," he teased.

Her gray blue eyes snapped with fire. "Give me my clothing, sir." She forced herself to add as she reached a second time for her shoes, "Please."

He took a step backward, keeping the shoes and stockings tantalizingly out of her reach. "That wasn't sincere enough. How about a 'pretty please'?"

She tightened her lips and glared. "Pretty please," she uttered between clenched teeth.

He stretched out his empty hand toward her. "Let me help you up the bank."

With one hand clutching her skirts and crinolines and the free hand holding his, she grudgingly allowed him to assist her up the bank. As she stepped onto the mossy grass, Onyx bounded out of the river and up the bank, cutting between them. Caught by surprise, Mr. Bonner released her hand, lost his own balance, and fell backward into the water. Her shoes and white cotton stockings fell with him.

Serenity gasped, then burst into laughter—only to have the giant black dog shake his coat free of the river water, dousing any dry areas left on the girl. "No! No!" she squealed, backing up to get away from Onyx's spray.

She lost her footing on the slippery bank and landed in the river beside the young attorney. Sputtering and struggling to her feet, she shouted, "Laugh will you!" She splashed him with more water.

"Oh, is that the way you want to play!" He filled her shoe with water and dumped it over her head. She screamed and scrambled up the bank. Her hair had tumbled down over her face. She brushed it back from her forehead.

Mr. Bonner pointed and laughed. Mud streaked down her face. Her dress and crinolines hung limp about her body. She peered down and discovered that mud coated her ankles as well. Grabbing the hem of her outer skirt, she wiped the mud from her forehead, spreading it across the rest of her face.

The young attorney climbed out of the water and handed Serenity her shoes and dripping stockings. She wrung out the stockings and poured the river water from the shoes, then draped the stockings on a bush. "Where's my sunbonnet?" She glanced about the clearing.

Mr. Bonner cleared his throat. "Er, I think that might be it out there." He pointed to the main current in the river.

"No! How am I going to get back on the riverboat looking like this? Onyx! Go fetch! Onyx?"

She looked for Onyx, but he'd disappeared. "Great! Now what do I do?"

In the distance, the riverboat whistle sounded. "We have five minutes before the boat leaves!" she shouted. "Where's Onyx? I can't leave without my dog!"

Calling Onyx repeatedly, she stuffed her wet stockings into a pocket in her skirt and struggled into her soggy leather slippers. Mr. Bonner shouted for the dog and whistled.

"We've got to go back. The boat will leave without us," he warned.

"No! Onyx! Onyx! Where are you?" She brushed her curls away from her face once again. Tears coursed her mud-stained cheeks. "I can't leave him behind! I can't!"

Mr. Bonner grabbed her wrist. "Come on! You have to leave him. You have to. The boat is leaving."

"I can't! I can't!" she wailed, allowing herself to be dragged along the narrow pathway back to the wharf.

Stumbling and falling, they arrived at the wharf as the riverboat pulled away from the shore. Serenity could see Onyx standing beside the railing, his two front paws resting on the bottom rail and his eyes searching the wharf for her.

Feeling like the lost sheep in Jesus' parable, Serenity crumbled down onto a wooden crate and cried, "Now what do I do?"

Mr. Bonner stroked her muddy hair gently. "You sit right here for a few minutes. I'll see what I can do."

Serenity buried her face in her arms, ashamed and alone. *How could such a beautiful day end so miserably,* the girl wondered as she sat drying out in the sunshine. Her only thought was, *What will Caleb think of me now?*

~6~
Moonlight Intrigue

THE SUN BEAT DOWN ON HER BARE HEAD. A breeze blew her loose curls about her shoulders and back, but Serenity didn't care. She figured she couldn't look much worse than she already did. The hairpins she'd stuffed into her bonnet were on their way to the mighty Mississippi. "More than I could say for myself," she mumbled.

As she wiped a streak of mud from her hand and onto her crinoline, a giant shadow fell on her, blocking the sun. Fear skittered up her spine. The girl looked up into the furious dark eyes of Caleb Cunard. Arms folded and legs spread, he glared down at her without speaking. She leaped to her feet. Conscious of her disheveled appearance, she attempted to brush herself off. "Caleb? What are you doing here?" She knew she was fluttering, as her school friend Eulilia often told her, but Serenity had no idea how to stop.

"Looking for you, Miss Pownell! What are you doing here?"

"Aren't you going to ask me if I'm all right?" she demanded.

"Are you all right?"

"Yes." She brushed the caked-on mud from her skirts.

Caleb did nothing to ease her nervousness. "Don't you think an explanation is in order?"

"Well, he fell into the river, then I fell into the river, then Onyx ran away, and then we missed the boat." She rattled out her story like a child of seven caught with her hand in a cookie jar.

Caleb's gaze darkened. "He? Who's he?"

Serenity stepped back defensively. "Mr. Bonner, of course."

"You went off with Mr. Bonner?" Caleb's voice raised from bass to tenor.

"No, I didn't go off with anyone except Onyx."

"Then how did the illustrious Mr. Bonner get into the story?"

Serenity clasped a portion of her skirt in one fist. "He came up while I was wading in the river with Onyx. It's a long story."

Caleb waved one hand toward the river. "By the looks of things, we have all the time in the world, so please tell."

She tried to explain, but everything seemed to come out different than she intended. "I am sorry. I didn't intend to—"

Caleb's eyes narrowed.

"He didn't intend to—"

His eyes narrowed further.

"You have to believe me! I looked for Becca before I left the boat, but poor Onyx was impatient."

"Blame it on a dog."

"Well, I hadn't planned to walk so far down the pathway. And I didn't plan on—"

"Come on," Caleb interrupted. He took her wrist and headed across the wharf. "A mail boat is ready to depart and will be meeting the *Linn*. We can catch it if we get moving."

"But what about Mr. Bonner? He told me to wait here."

Caleb gripped her wrist a little tighter. "Mr. Bonner can fend for himself."

"But I told him I'd—"

Caleb snapped about to face her. "You can apologize to him later if you like. But right now, you're going with me, do you understand?"

"You can't do that!" She tried to pull her hand from his grasp, but to no avail. His grip held.

"Yes I can, and I will." Arriving at the mail boat, he released her wrist long enough to lift her over the gunwale.

"I still think we should wait for—"

"If I ever get my hands on Mr. Bonner, I'll mop the floor with him!"

Serenity's feet settled on the wooden deck, she whirled about like a cat ready to pounce. "Caleb Cunard, you are a bully! You leave Felix alone! He only tried to help me."

"Felix is it now?" As the little boat pulled away from the dock, Serenity glanced to shore in time to see Mr. Bonner run to the edge of the wharf and stare after her. Caleb found a large wooden crate on which to sit and stared downriver as if the girl was nowhere in sight. Furious, Serenity stormed over to where he sat and hissed, "Just who do you think you are? You may be my guardian, but you're not my father! If you think I'll stand for this kind of barroom behavior, you are mistaken."

One of the boat's crewmen who had been watching the exchange between the couple, sauntered across the deck and asked, "Is this man bothering you, miss?"

Caleb bared his teeth. "Mind your own business."

The boatman flexed his muscles and glared at Caleb, then up at Serenity.

"No, no, I'm fine. He's a relative, of sorts." The last thing Serenity wanted to end her miserable day was a brawl.

They caught up to the *Linn* in less than an hour. The smaller, sleeker mail boat could dart about the river with speed and agility the larger riverboat could never manage. Caleb disappeared as soon as they were safely on board. Meanwhile, Serenity endured Fay's mothering and Eli's dour silence as she walked to her cabin to change her clothing. Onyx greeted her with a delighted bark and an extra wag of his tail.

"Great friend you are!" Serenity scolded.

Fay offered to help her scrub up, but the girl begged off. "I have to wash this mud from my hair. It will take hours to dry."

"Well, let Becca fetch water for you," she said.

Becca filled basin after basin of water so Serenity could wash away the mud from her body. Her hair squeaked with cleanliness as she dried it on a thirsty Turkish towel. Finally, she slipped into her flannel nightgown and wrapped the towel around her hair. Onyx found his own little corner and snoozed through it all.

"The dinner bell just sounded, Serenity," Becca announced as she scooped up the discarded clothing.

Serenity shook her head. "I'm in no condition to be seen in public this evening. You go and enjoy yourself. I'll be fine."

Becca frowned. "I hate leaving you alone."

"Nonsense. I'll read a book or something."

The younger girl's face brightened. She knew how much Serenity loved to spend time lost in a book. "Can I bring something back for you? Maybe one of those little meat pies they always serve?"

Serenity's stomach growled. "That does sound good," she admitted. The truth be known, Serenity knew she could have pulled herself together in time to dine with the family. Her stomach rumbled again, and she wondered if her wounded pride was worth the sacrifice.

Before leaving Buffalo, Eunice had given her a five-volume set of English classics. Serenity especially enjoyed reading aloud the Shakespearean sonnets, something she could never do when Becca was in the cabin.

Settling down on her berth, she opened the leather-bound book and inhaled the familiar aroma. She turned to her favorite, *Sonnet XVIII:* "Shall I compare thee to a summer's day? Thou art more lovely and more temperate."

Serenity giggled. Her summer's day had been anything but lovely. She continued reading. "Rough winds do shake the darling buds of May, and summer's lease hath all too short a date." A knock sounded at the door. Onyx lifted his head, then settled back to his nap. Wrapping the towel more securely about her head, Serenity skipped across the small cabin.

"Who's there?"

"It's me—Fay."

Serenity unlatched the door. "Come on in."

"I thought you might be hungry, so I asked the steward for an extra plate of food." The woman handed the silver-domed plate to the girl. "You are feeling all right, aren't you? No sniffles or anything?"

The girl grinned. "Just a bruise on my pride. I am embarrassed for all the trouble I caused."

"Pawsh! Things happen." Fay gave the girl a hug. "I was just relieved that you were safe."

Serenity set the hot plate down on the small side table.

"So am I. When I saw that boat sailing off without me, I utterly panicked."

"You should have seen Caleb when Onyx returned without you. He literally leaped over the barrier and onto the gangplank, startling the roustabouts untying the ropes."

"I'm sorry."

Fay moved toward the cabin door. "He really cares for you, you know."

"Yes, I know—his vow to care for his little charge!" A slight pout spread across Serenity's face.

"That too," Fay said as she left the room.

The hot tray of food smelled heavenly as Serenity lifted the dome from the plate. After a hasty blessing, she unwrapped the silverware from the linen napkin and helped herself to a mouthful of mashed potatoes. "Mmm. So much for Shakespeare." The pot roast and the broiled vegetables melted in her mouth. She ate until she had to loosen the belt to her plissé robe. Finally the last mouthful of peach pie disappeared from the plate. She replaced the silver dome and returned to her berth, feeling like a beached sea lion.

Idly turning a few pages, she began to read one of her favorite plays, *Much Ado about Nothing*.

She'd barely gotten past the introduction when she heard another knock on the door. Thinking Fay had returned for something, Serenity swung open the door. It was Eli holding a small package wrapped in a linen napkin. He looked distinctly uncomfortable.

"Er, I thought you might be hungry." He shoved the linen-wrapped package into her hands. "Sleep well," he said, bowing slightly.

"Thank you," she called after him. Surprised, she closed the door slowly. Unwrapping the napkin, she found a slice of apple pie. She smiled to herself, suspicious that Eli had sacrificed his own dessert for her.

She forced herself to eat the pie. The last bite had barely entered her mouth when she heard another knock at the door. This time it was Aaron. He brought her a roll and butter. Becca returned to the cabin several minutes later with several fancy pastries.

"I'm going to attend a minstrel concert tonight with my folks," she announced. "I hope I brought enough."

Serenity laughed. "Believe me. You brought plenty. I don't know how I'll ever finish them!"

"Maybe you'll get hungry later this evening," the younger girl suggested.

"Maybe so." Serenity set the napkin full of goodies next to Aaron's roll and pat of butter.

Becca wrapped her shawl about her shoulders. "I'm supposed to meet Mama and Daddy at their cabin. See ya'."

"Have fun." Serenity returned to her book. The room grew warm despite the setting of the sun. *A few minutes on deck would feel so good,* she thought. Restless, she dressed in her rose silk gown, one of the five Aunt Eunice chose for her, and pulled her hair back into a bow. Slipping into a pair of linen slippers, she peered out the cabin door. The hall was silent and empty. Onyx trotted to her side.

"No, you stay here this time. You get me into too much trouble."

The dog whined as the door closed between them. She scurried down the long corridor and out onto the deck. Seeing a couple silhouetted in the moonlight, she decided she should return to her cabin—until she heard Aaron's voice.

"Felicity, you are so beautiful." Aaron kissed Mrs. Rose on the lips, then buried his head into her neck.

"Oh, no, what should I do now?" Serenity glanced about for a place to hide. Dropping behind a wooden bench, she prayed that the shadows would hide her, then stared in disbelief at the love scene. Before long, Aaron and Mrs. Rose strolled away. Heaving a sigh of relief, Serenity began to rise to her feet.

"Hello. What are you doing down there?"

Serenity jumped. It was Caleb.

"I thought you might be hungry, so I brought you a piece of pie. It's apple, your favorite." Embarrassed over what she'd just witnessed, Serenity awkwardly accepted the linen-wrapped pastry. "Thank you. I'm going to feel like a stuffed turkey by the end of the night."

"What do you mean?" Seeing Serenity's silk gown, his face hardened. "Bonner isn't back on board, is he?"

"Oh, no, but every member of your family has been in to see me, each bearing an offering of food so I wouldn't go hungry tonight. Isn't that sweet?"

Caleb chuckled, then grew serious. "But that doesn't explain what you were doing beside that bench."

"No, I guess it doesn't." Serenity searched for something to say. "I'm in the mood for a stroll along the deck. Would you be kind enough to escort me?"

Caleb looked at her, his face full of questions. Instead of pursuing his train of thought, he offered her his arm. "All right. I would be happy to escort you, Miss Pownell. But don't think this little diversion will get you off the hook. I still want to know."

Serenity's delicate laughter filled the evening air. "You are one persistent gentleman."

"More than you know," he muttered.

They strolled the length of the deck and paused at the

railing. A harvest moon shone on the ripples of the river, forming a golden pathway. "Isn't it beautiful?" Serenity sighed.

"Yes, you are."

"Not me, silly, the river. It's magical." She glanced
toward him, expecting to see a sarcastic grin on his face.
Instead, his deep brown eyes gazed into hers.

"You are so beautiful it scares me."

Serenity stared in surprise. Her gaze wandered from
Caleb's eyes to his lips. Her heart skipped a beat. For an
instant she couldn't breathe. "Caleb? Remember the night
at the lake?"

Caleb nodded slowly, returning Serenity's gaze.
Unbidden, the young woman stood on her tiptoes and
touched her lips to his. "I've missed you," she sighed.

"But I've been—"

She touched her finger to his lips. "No, you haven't
been here and you know it. You've treated me like a pesky
little sister."

"I'm sorry." His words came out husky, filled with emotion. He placed his hands lightly on her upper arms. He
focused his eyes on the lace ruffle at the neckline of her
gown. She felt the warmth of his hands through the gown's
silk sleeves.

"Is that how you think of me, as a little sister?"

He looked up in surprise. "No! Of course not."

"Then, tell me, how do you think of me?"

Caleb cleared his throat and brushed a curl away from
Serenity's neck. "I think of you all the time. And hardly as
a sister."

"Because my father made you responsible for me?"

"Partly."

Serenity gazed up into his face. "And the other part?"

He bit his lip and looked out onto the shoreline, lost in the shadows of night. "I don't think this is the time nor the place to discuss—"

"I disagree. I can't think of a better time or place for such a discussion," she whispered.

"You're hardly more than a child," he argued, more with himself than with Serenity. "You don't know your own mind."

"I'll be eighteen tomorrow, Caleb. Both my mother and yours were married soon after their eighteenth birthdays and pregnant before their nineteenth."

Caleb stiffened. "It's unseemly for a single woman to speak so openly about such things."

Serenity chuckled. "Why Caleb, I think you're embarrassed."

"That's ridiculous, I—"

She peered up into his face. "You are embarrassed."

"All right, I admit I'm uncomfortable speaking of such intimate—"

"So openly? Have you forgotten how outspoken my mother used to be?" Tenderly, she ran her gloved finger along his jaw line. "So, dearest guardian, what are you giving me for my birthday?"

As he stared down into her eyes, he flexed and unflexed the muscles in his jaw. "Are you playing games with me, Serenity? Do you play the same games with Felix Bonner, attorney-at-law?"

Serenity's eyes clouded with pain and anger. "No, Caleb."

Undeterred, his grip tightened on her arms. He drew her to his lips, kissing her soundly. "There! Happy birthday! That's what you came out here for, wasn't it?" Releasing her arms, Caleb turned and stormed down the deck.

Serenity's hands rushed to her face. Mortified by his

retreat, tears sprang into her eyes. Finally she wiped the back of one hand across her lips. "There! That's what I think of your birthday present, Caleb Cunard! I hate you!" Grasping her skirts in her hands, she dashed into the corridor leading to her cabin. In her haste, she ran into a man coming out of one of the cabins. "Oh! Excuse me," she cried before she realized the man with whom she'd collided was Aaron, and the compartment, Mrs. Rose's. Aaron mumbled an apology and fled down the corridor toward the dining hall.

~7~

The Mighty Mississippi

THE AIR HUNG HEAVY WITH MOISTURE AS THE Cunards and Serenity rested on board a new Mississippi paddle boat, the *Liberty*. The "soul of America," the great Mississippi River, looked muddy and sluggish, like the night air felt.

Serenity and Becca moved slowly along the brass railing, putting off the moment they'd have to turn in to their cabin for the night. Over their heads the moon hung high, producing a gray white glow. Raucous music and laughter poured from taverns lining the shore. A banjo strummed a mournful tune on the opposite shore. The steam-powered calliope in the ship's gaming room played "Oh, Susannah," to the late-night passengers' enjoyment and the gamblers' and card sharks' delight.

As Serenity watched the river life flowing about her, she supposed Felix Bonner had found his way on board the *Liberty*, though she had studiously avoided looking for him. He had made his way back to the *Linn* somehow because he'd shown up at her birthday party the night before, but so far she hadn't seen him on the *Liberty*. She had been relieved at dinner when he hadn't been seated at the Cunard table.

Serenity watched as massive steamboats with tall, slender, brass-trimmed funnels churned the treacherous, muddy waters. Pulling a kerchief from her bosom, she dabbed her upper lip. It was breathlessly warm, the kind of night all too familiar to the inhabitants of the river towns. To Serenity, however, it was unbearable.

"I could get used to this life." Becca trailed her fingers along the highly polished brass railing behind Serenity. "Don't you just love dining on exquisite china and drinking from crystal goblets? But, of course, none of this is really new to you, is it? Your father being rich and all."

"Hmm—" Serenity stared off into the haze and dabbed her face again.

Further along the deck, a man stepped out of the shadows. His body was silhouetted against the moonlit night. He struck a match and lit a pipe. He bent to rest his elbows on the railing, hunching his broad shoulders forward. When the door behind him opened, the corridor light illuminated his profile.

"Oh, no, that's Mr. Bonner!" Serenity hissed. "I don't want him to see me." Darting through the first door available, Serenity let it slam behind her. Immediately the door swung open, and Becca stormed into the corridor.

"What is going on?" she asked. "You've been acting as weird as my brother."

"I don't know what you mean." Serenity paused to catch her breath.

"Yes you do. First Caleb and now you! Even my parents have noticed."

"Noticed? Noticed what?"

"The way Caleb will hardly carry on a conversation with anyone, the way you run the moment he approaches—"

Serenity laughed. "You're exaggerating!" She strode down the corridor to their cabin. "I have no idea what you're talking about."

"At your birthday party, when Mr. Bonner tried to give you the tiny gold pendant, you refused. I don't understand. We were all having such fun together until you and Caleb began acting so strange."

Serenity frowned at the memory. She'd been so thrilled when the Cunard family arranged to celebrate her eighteenth birthday on board the *Linn*. The riverboat's dessert chef had even honored her by decorating a special cake like the ones her mother had seen while visiting Paris. The dining room staff each stopped by the table to wish her well. It had been a special night, except for Caleb.

For months the young woman had been assuring herself that once she turned eighteen, Caleb would cease treating her like a small child and see her for the woman she really was. And it looked like it might happen until Felix draped a lovely gold locket around her neck and kissed her cheek. "Happy birthday, Miss Pownell."

Serenity touched the locket's cool surface and glanced toward Caleb. The deep frown on his face prompted her to thank Felix for the gift, then to return it. "It's too much, Mr. Bonner. It's lovely, but it's too much."

"Nonsense. It's very little really. You are a beautiful woman. A woman like you is the reason such pretty baubles were fashioned."

She removed the necklace and placed it in Felix's hand. "I am sorry, but I can't take this from you right now."

His eyes brightened. "Does that imply that you might in the future?"

She smiled sadly. "Who of us knows the future, Mr. Bonner? Surely not I."

She heard a chair shift and Caleb left the table. Seconds later, Felicity and Aaron excused themselves as well. Serenity waited until she felt she could leave gracefully, then rushed out onto the deck, but Caleb was nowhere to be seen.

"My mama's worried about those two—" Becca said as she came alongside Serenity.

"Worried?"

"About Aaron and that Mrs. Rose. She's a married woman!" Becca clicked her tongue.

Serenity frowned as she walked towards the cabin. "Your mama has good cause to worry."

"Why?" The younger girl's eyes danced with excitement. "What do you know that I don't?"

"You know too much already for your own good!" Serenity opened the door to their cabin and lit the wall sconce by the door. "Oh! It's hotter than Satan's cauldron in here! How will we ever sleep tonight?"

"Come on, Serenity! You know something about Aaron and that woman and you're not telling. No fair! He's my brother!"

Serenity laughed as she undid the wrist buttons on her sleeves. "You're right on both counts. I can hardly wait to get out of these petticoats! And these shoes! My feet are killing me."

"You're changing the subject." A pout formed on Becca's lips. "The other night I was looking for Mama when I overheard Papa and Aaron arguing. Imagine Papa arguing!" She clicked her tongue. "Papa didn't raise his voice like Aaron did, but I could tell he was mighty angry. They were discussing Mrs. Rose." The girl nodded her head sagely. "When they saw me standing by the open door, Papa sent me to find Mama on the upper deck. Then he closed the stateroom door."

"Hmmph!" Serenity snorted, lighting the lantern on the shelf near her berth. "It won't work, scamp. I still won't say anything. You know that, don't you?" The young woman picked up her Bible. "If you will excuse me?"

Becca grumbled as she shed her soiled clothing and slipped into her cotton plissé nightgown. "This thing is too hot," she muttered. "I'm going to wear my slip to bed."

Serenity giggled. "You'll be in trouble if we have to abandon ship in the night."

"At least I won't have yards of cotton wrapping around my legs when I hit the water." Becca turned down the wick in the sconce by the door, then climbed into her berth as Serenity returned to her reading.

Like the river, the days aboard the *Liberty* flowed on at a steady pace. Serenity spent much of her time alone or with Becca. She knew the Cunards were concerned over Aaron and that they'd be much more concerned if she told what she knew about his comings and goings. More than once when the nights were too steamy to sleep, she and Onyx would slip out onto the deck in time to see the younger Cunard boy disappear into the gaming parlor or to the dance hall, usually with Mrs. Rose on his arm. Should she tell Fay or not? If she'd been on better terms with Caleb, she would have talked it over with him.

One afternoon, Serenity strolled along the railing with Onyx by her side. A gentle breeze cooled her overheated face and neck. Her straw bonnet protected her face from the brutal sun, along with the help of a white lace parasol her Aunt Eunice had managed to slip into her trunk before she left.

After a walk around the deck, she returned to her empty stateroom. Becca was spending the afternoon with Caleb. Serenity wished she'd been invited along; in times past she would have been. She bit her lower lip. So much had changed. *Maybe I should have stayed in Buffalo,* she thought. *Maybe I've made a terrible mistake.* After hanging her parasol on a hook behind the door, she removed her bonnet and tossed it onto the hook as well. Kicking off her shoes, she stretched out on the berth and stared at the wood-paneled ceiling. She opened her Bible and tried to read, but the words on the onionskin sheets made little sense. Her thoughts grew so tangled that when a light tap on the door sounded, she didn't hear it. Someone rapped again.

She sighed and turned from the window. "Come in," she called. The door opened. Caleb filled the doorway.

"Oh." She sat up, straightening her skirts around her ankles. "What are you doing here?"

"I need to talk with you, Serenity. Could you come out onto the deck for a few minutes?"

"Sure. Let me get myself together."

"We're docking in a half hour," he said. "Perhaps we can walk the dog together."

She eyed him suspiciously. He'd barely nodded in her direction for days. "OK. Take Onyx with you. I'll be there as soon as possible."

The instant the door closed, she leaped to her feet and scrambled to put on her slippers. Dabbing her face with rice powder, she doffed her hat, grabbed her parasol from the hook, and darted from the stateroom.

Screeching to a stop at the doorstep opening onto the deck, Serenity took a deep breath, waved her hands to cool her cheeks, pinched them, then with grace and dignity opened the door and stepped through. "Caleb?" she called to the young man leaning against the railing. He turned and smiled.

"There you are. Perhaps we can sit down?" He gestured toward a bench. "I'll get right to the point. I was talking to Becca this morning about Aaron. She told me that you might know something about his recent behavior."

Serenity reddened and shifted her weight. "I'm not sure what I know or don't know, Caleb. That's why I haven't said anything to anyone."

"Like?"

"His leaving Mrs. Rose's cabin in the middle of the night; the two of them spending time in the gaming parlors."

"You've seen this?" Caleb's gaze intensified.

She nodded. "But, I'm sure there could be a dozen explanations—"

Caleb scowled and shook his head. "If it weren't for what your Mr. Bonner has said, that her husband is alive and well in Independence, I'd say she was a widow by her behavior."

"My Mr. Bonner? He's hardly my Mr. Bonner." Serenity's eyes flashed with indignation.

Caleb reddened and glanced away. "Sorry, I didn't mean to—"

"Yes you did. That's exactly what you meant to do." Serenity's lips tightened into a thin line. "For your information, I haven't seen Mr. Bonner for more than a week, except at meals, of course."

He lowered his gaze to his calloused hands. "I'm sorry. You're right. There's no excuse for—"

Suddenly a cheer went up from the opposite side of the vessel. The *Liberty* surged forward. Serenity grabbed her hat with one hand and the bench with the other. "What's happening?"

A second cheer erupted, rattling the ship's rafters.

Caleb sighed. "I suspect it's a river race."

"A race?" Serenity's eyes brightened. Life on board the *Liberty* could be a little tiresome for those who chose not to gamble, drink, or attend the stage plays held aboard ship.

"Yes, I hear it's common on the Mississippi. Very dangerous too. Before you came out, I saw another steamboat, the *Telegraph*, gaining on our port side."

Serenity leaped to her feet. "Let's go watch."

Caleb grabbed her wrist. "It's dangerous."

She shook free her arm. "Is it any less dangerous if we don't watch?"

"Well, no, I suppose not."

She grabbed his hand and pulled him to his feet. "Then let's at least enjoy the race since we can't do much to stop it." Her excitement proved contagious, and Caleb allowed her to drag him to the port side of the boat.

Racing these powerful vessels, many as long as a city block, was a risky game. Their high-pressured steam engines produced as much as two thousand horsepower. In races, the red-hot furnaces forced more steam pressure than the boilers could hold, sometimes resulting in a devastating explosion.

Regardless of the danger, passengers filled the port-side deck to cheer on their captain. The professional gamblers on board began taking bets on which riverboat would win. Along with the shouting audience, loud squeals, clangs, and metallic squeaks burst from the overheated boilers as they strained to meet the demands of the captain and his crew.

Caleb and Serenity found an empty spot along the railing and stood, waving at the bystanders along the shore. When the impromptu race broke out, word of it traveled up the Mississippi faster than the speeding vessels. People in the sleepy waterfront towns crowded along the levee to cheer on the dueling monsters. Muddy islets of water rose dangerously between the two boats and the shoreline as the captain navigated around the deadly tree snags looming up out of the water. When the *Telegraph* pulled ahead of the *Liberty,* its passengers screamed and shouted. Then, with a sudden surge of power, the *Liberty* lunged forward, arousing cheers and catcalls from the *Liberty* passengers. Serenity danced and tugged at Caleb's arm as they wandered further down the deck. "Isn't this exciting?" She bobbed her head around one person, then another, trying to get a better view of the *Telegraph.*

"I can't see too well from here."

"Here." Caleb lifted her onto one of the metal benches. "Is that better?"

Serenity grinned and nodded her head enthusiastically.

"How are you doing, son?" Eli and Fay suddenly appeared from nowhere and sidled up to Caleb and Serenity.

"Isn't this fun?" Serenity asked. "There's room up here if you'd like to join me."

The older woman shook her head. "Thank you, sweetheart, but I can see fine from where I am."

A renewed surge of power rumbled through the floorboards of the *Liberty.* Serenity grabbed hold of Caleb's sleeve for balance. He laughed and reached for her. "Don't worry. I'm right here. I won't let you fall."

Her eyes sparkled as she smiled down at him.

Across the narrow expanse of water, the *Telegraph* again surged ahead to the shouts and laughter of its passengers.

"Go! Go!" the passengers of the *Liberty* shouted.

First one riverboat ahead, then the other; back and forth, the dangerous dance continued for several minutes. The open furnaces on the two boats did their best to keep up as passengers thronged the lower deck, barely above water level.

Serenity realized that they must look much the same to the passengers on the other ship as they did to her. She glanced up at the captain in the keel house. The tough, grizzled-faced, unpolished character knew every twist and turn of the river, she assured herself. He cut a picturesque figure, whether dining in the lounge or, as he was now, competing in a riverboat race.

Suddenly an arm around her waist brought Serenity to the deck. "Come on, Serenity. This is getting too dangerous. Let's get out of this crowd," Caleb whispered in her ear. "I'm afraid the furnace is going to blow."

The words barely escaped his lips when a horrendous boom rocked the *Liberty* and Serenity fell into Caleb's startled arms. He struggled to maintain his balance amid the jostle, as many began shoving to get away from the handrail lest another jolt send them overboard.

Serenity gasped as a sudden blaze of fire erupted from the *Telegraph*. Flames shot into the air, engulfing the throng of passengers on the other riverboat's deck. Screams, shouts, and cries of pain echoed off the silent forests bordering the river as people along the shore watched in horror at the *Telegraph* passengers—set afire by the explosion—leaping into the river. Burning embers shot hundreds of feet into the air, cascading down on the scurrying onlookers as well as the roof of the *Liberty*.

Even as chaos broke loose on the other boat, the *Liberty* raced forward, leaving the wounded craft and the injured passengers in its wake.

"Do something!" Serenity shouted at Caleb as a second boom from the *Telegraph* shook her to her knees.

Caleb grabbed a life preserver and ran for the stern of the boat. Other men followed his lead, including Eli and Mr. Bonner.

"No!" One of the crew grabbed Caleb's shirt. "You can't save them. We can't stop now or we'll all die."

Caleb pointed at a small child bobbing in the water less than one thousand feet behind them. "Let go of me. I have to help that child—"

"By the time you reach her we'll be too far upriver for you to get back on board."

Caleb shook his arm free of the crewman and plunged into the muddy river. Serenity watched as Caleb swam to the child's rescue. Fay rushed to Serenity's side as Eli forced a reluctant crew member to unleash one of the life boats strapped to the riverboat's side. Then Aaron and Mr. Bonner, along with a couple other men, leaped into the boat and began rowing downstream to the *Telegraph*.

The women watched helplessly as the *Liberty* rounded a bend. Ahead, the little town of Cape Girardeau glistened in the sunlight. Before the riverboat docked, the news was out about the explosion aboard the *Telegraph*. Dozens of small riverboats set off down the river to help with the rescue.

Finally the Cunard men and Mr. Bonner returned, wet and coated with mud and ash. They helped a burned man and two women from the little rowboat and onto the dock, where a doctor and several community members took charge of their care.

Serenity ran down the gangplank to Caleb. "The little girl?"

The young man shook his head. "She went under before I could reach her. The river was too muddy, I couldn't find her. I tried. God knows I tried." He closed his eyes as if to block out his anguish.

"Oh, Caleb, I'm so sorry." She wrapped her arms around him and buried her face in his chest. "I'm so thankful that you're all right. When you dived into that water, I was afraid I would never see you again."

With the last of the rescuers on board, the *Liberty* captain sounded the whistle. The gears screeched. The paddle wheel turned and they were on their way upriver once more. A warm evening breeze wafted across the bow of the riverboat. A golden moon rested on the horizon's edge, casting a pathway of light across the river. On the deck, the men still in their soiled clothing, the Cunards and Serenity linked arms, forming a large circle. Eyeing Mr. Bonner standing awkwardly outside the huddle, Fay drew him in by sliding her arm inside his.

Eli, mud coating his beard, gazed about the circle, his eyes misty with tears. "Thank You, O Lord, for today. For this is the day You made. We will rejoice and be glad in it." When he said "we will rejoice," there was no hesitation. Saying it made it so, or so it seemed to Serenity. Around the circle, the group thanked God for His protection, including a brief prayer by Mr. Bonner. Everyone except Aaron muttered a distracted apology. Serenity and Caleb exchanged concerned glances. After the last prayer, Eli's bass voice broke into "Praise God, from whom all blessings flow," and everyone joined in.

"Amazing grace, how sweet the sound . . . ," Aunt Fay's warm alto voice began after the previous song concluded, comforting Serenity as she thought of the hundreds of people aboard the *Telegraph* who didn't survive the disaster. Serenity listened as the others blended their voices with the faithful woman's. Passengers in the area, hearing the singing, wandered out onto the deck and were drawn into the circle. Tears flowed as more than fifty passengers harmonized on the last verse of John Newton's famous hymn: "When we've been there ten thousand years; bright shining as the sun, we've no less days to sing God's praise than when we first begun."

A bond formed among the passengers on the deck. A gray-haired grandmother, her voice quivery and hollow, began the next hymn: "At the cross, at the cross, where I first saw the light . . ." The rest immediately joined her: "And the burden of my heart rolled away. It was there by faith, I received my sight. And now I am happy all the day."

After those strains died away, the group listened with reverence when a large black crewman, who'd been stoking the furnace during the race, raised his deep bass voice: "Were you there when they crucified my Lord?"

The singing finally over, Serenity walked Becca back to their stateroom. Lying in her berth, she marveled at how quickly the music had quieted her, had quieted everyone. That evening, the passengers on the *Liberty* were subdued; even the folks in the gaming halls and the ship's saloon seemed less raucous than usual. As Serenity lay awake listening to the sounds of the night, she could hear the man stoking the furnaces singing, "No . . . more, no . . . more, no . . . more; O Lord, I'm tired, so tired, no more . . ." The haunting dirge wafted through the ship and into the night.

~8~
On to
St. Louis

 SERENITY COULD FEEL THE POWER OF THE Mississippi River beneath her feet as she walked along the riverboat's deck. Along the shore, gracefully arching trees dipped their branches into the fast flowing water. Rolling hills rose behind the small lazy towns lining the causeway. As beautiful as the view was, Serenity was bored. She could barely wait to reach St. Louis where she could go shopping in a real city. And she was eager to convert one of her gold bars into cash to pay for her trip. Thus far, the Cunards had assumed all the expenses and Serenity knew that needed to change.

Since the afternoon of the tragic race, she and Caleb had reestablished communication. He'd agreed to accompany her to the St. Louis bank to make certain she received a fair exchange for her gold and returned to the riverboat safely.

Serenity paused to watch a great blue heron search for food in the murky water. "Shouldn't you be heading south by now, you silly bird?" The bird continued to prod its head in the sludge of the river.

"Who are you talking to?"

Serenity had been so caught up in her reverie she'd been unaware of Becca's presence until she spoke.

"How long have you been standing there?" Serenity asked.

"Not too long," the ten-year-old replied, mimicking Serenity's stance at the rail.

Onyx rubbed against Serenity's skirts. Serenity scratched behind the dog's ears.

"What are you watching?" the child asked.

Serenity smiled toward Becca. "That heron out there. You'd think he'd have flown south by now."

Becca laughed. "There's the town." She pointed. "We're stopping. Do you want company on your walk with Onyx?"

Serenity brightened. "Indeed I do. Have you been as bored as I these last few days?"

The younger girl nodded. "I've read every book I brought along and most of yours, I might add."

Serenity frowned. "I haven't seen you reading in the stateroom."

The girl grinned. "I have a secret cubbyhole up by the stem of the boat where I crawl into when I want to be alone."

"So that's where you've been. You stinker."

Becca smiled. "The only person other than you that I've told about the spot is Aaron. He promised not to tell anyone. You have to promise as well."

Noting the girl's serious face, Serenity promised. As the steamboat eased up to the dock, the two girls and the dog waited eagerly until the crew lowered the gangplank, then dashed across the plank to the wharf and onto a patch of wild grasses growing beside the dock.

"Ooh! It feels so good to walk on solid ground again." Serenity pulled free a stalk of grass and nibbled on the fresh cut end. "Don't you just love it?"

"Let's head downshore to that field we passed. It's not far." Becca headed in the direction she'd indicated. Onyx bounded ahead of her, pausing only to sniff a dead fish rotting beside the narrow pathway.

"We can't go too far," Serenity reminded as she ran after the girl and the dog.

Suddenly, up ahead, Becca screamed, then froze. Terror flooded her face. Her hand shook as she pointed with her forefinger at something in the half-trampled grass five feet from where she stood.

"What? What's the matter?" Serenity studied the clump of grass until she saw it—a rattlesnake, coiled and ready to strike. "Oh, dear God," Serenity gasped. "Don't move, Becca. Stand very still. Don't move a muscle."

Becca obeyed. Beads of sweat formed on her forehead. The terror in her eyes warned Serenity that every fiber in the child's body said to do the opposite, to run.

"Oh, dear God, what should I do?" Serenity glanced about her slowly, searching for a stick or a rock. Her legs trembled as the snake rattled its warning and raised its head, its tongue darting in and out.

At the top of a knoll, Onyx stood looking at the two girls, urging them to follow. "Dear Father," Serenity whispered, "don't let Onyx run back here now. He'd certainly cause the creature to strike."

Seeing a large rock near the river, Serenity took a step backward. The snake hissed and shook its rattle again, poised and watchful.

As she stepped back, Serenity sensed a presence behind her. "Don't move, Miss Serenity. Stand very still," Mr. Bonner hissed. He stood to her right, holding a pistol with one hand and bracing the weapon on his other forearm.

Suddenly Becca jerked her hand up to her mouth to swallow another scream. The snake sprang. Bonner fired. The bullet severed the snake's head from its body, but not before the poisonous fangs sank into the little girl's ankle.

The girl screamed and sank to the ground. Mr. Bonner raced forward and snatched the girl into his arms. "Quick, see if the fangs punctured her skin."

Serenity ran to Becca and ripped the sobbing girl's heavy cotton stocking away from her leg. Serenity gasped at the sight of the poisonous venom bubbling white on the surface of the child's skin. Using the torn garment as protection, Serenity wiped the venom from the girl's leg. Beneath it, the skin was already reddening around two tiny fang pricks.

The ship's whistle sounded. The child continued to scream in pain.

"Hurry, we've got to get her back to the boat," Serenity cried.

Mr. Bonner slipped a hunting knife from his boot. "Not before we remove the venom from her leg."

Serenity stared at the six-inch blade in horror. "What are you going to do?"

"I just told you, remove the venom. You go back to the steamboat and get help. But be careful where you step, rattlers usually travel in pairs."

The snake, though dead, continued thrashing about in the grass. Seeing the snake's body gyrating in the grass, Onyx bounded back, grabbed the body in his teeth, shook it, and dumped it into the river.

Horrified, Serenity ran blindly in the direction of the riverboat. Onyx passed her before she reached the wharf. He bounded up the gangplank, barking as he ran. Tears of relief flowed down Serenity's face when Caleb appeared at the head of the plank.

"What's the matter?" the young man shouted. "This dog's gone berserk, pulling on my clothes and barking. Where's Becca?"

"She's been bitten by a rattler. Mr. Bonner's back there taking care of her." At the mention of Bonner's name, Caleb bristled. Out of breath, Serenity held her stomach and gasped, "Forget Bonner. You gotta help Becca."

"Where is she?" Caleb grabbed Serenity's arms.

"Down that way about a thousand yards or so." Serenity pointed.

As he ran down the gangplank, he glanced over his shoulder and shouted, "Tell the captain what's happened! Tell the folks too. See if there's a doctor on board." Onyx bounded after Caleb.

Serenity stumbled up the gangplank. One of the crew stood shouting orders to a dock worker. "Sir!" Serenity tugged at the man's sleeve. The mustached worker grinned down at the frightened young woman.

"My little sister has been bitten by a snake. They're bringing her back to the riverboat right now. Don't leave without them, please!"

The crew member narrowed his gaze, thought a moment, then signaled the helmsmen. Not waiting to see what the ship's response was to the man's command, Serenity ran to the Cunard's cabin. No one was there. She took the stairs to the dining area, two at a time. Again, none of the family was anywhere to be seen. She dashed to the starboard side of the craft. Spotting Eli and Fay standing at the stern near one of the paddle wheels, she shouted, "Hurry. Becca's been hurt!"

"What?" Eli lifted a hand to his ear to block out some of the noise from the steam engines.

Serenity shouted a second time as she ran toward them. "Becca's been hurt!"

This time they heard her message.

Minutes later, Caleb returned, carrying the injured child. Mr. Bonner followed closely behind. They carried her into her parents' stateroom. "Stand back," Mr. Bonner ordered. "Give the child breathing room."

Curious travelers hovered around the open door, watching as Fay removed the bandage made from the attorney's white cotton shirt while Serenity poured water into the washbasin and set it on the floor beside the berth where they'd placed the injured girl. The child's cries subsided knowing she was safe in her mother's care.

"There's a roll of cotton bandages in the right-hand side of that trunk. Bring it to me, please." Fay tenderly washed the girl's wound with soap and water. Immediately, Serenity did as she was told, remembering sitting on the porch at the Bailey's house beside her mentor, helping her cut the fabric into strips and roll them into a ball.

"Why did you cut her leg?" Serenity asked Mr. Bonner as she handed the roll of fabric to Fay.

"To suck out the poison before it reached her blood stream. My father's a physician in New Orleans. He's had lots of experience with snake bites," Mr. Bonner explained. "Dad discovered that if the snake venom is removed quickly enough, the victim's life might be spared. I hope I got it all."

"I've heard of that remedy." Eli leaned against the wall at the foot of the berth. "My wife and I thank you for your quick thinking, Mr. Bonner."

"Glad I was close by." Mr. Bonner rose to his feet.

Fay looked up from her daughter's wound. "How soon will we know if—"

"I don't know," Mr. Bonner shrugged. "I think the best thing we can do now is leave Reverend and Mrs. Cunard alone to care for their daughter."

"Bonner's right. Becca needs her rest." Caleb gently urged Serenity and Aaron toward the door. "Come on, Onyx." The dog lifted his head, glanced up at the berth that held Becca, then laid back down and closed his eyes.

"Onyx!" Serenity ordered.

The dog ignored her. She started toward the dog, but Fay stopped her. "It's all right, honey. The dog knows Becca needs him more than you do right now. Let him stay."

Serenity nodded mutely, turning back toward the door.

"Wait, let's pray for her," Eli suggested, including the spectators hovering around the door. "There's power in the prayers of many."

Serenity and the others bowed their heads as the reverend prayed. "Dear heavenly Father, I hold up to You my precious daughter Becca, a gift from You from the day of her birth. You have promised to be our Healer. You said You would deliver us from the snare of the fowler and from the pestilence. Father, she is hurting. We lift her up to You today. You've already sent this knowledgeable young man to come to her aid. Now as the Great Physician, complete the job. Make her whole once more. Amen."

A rumble of amens passed through the group. As Serenity and the others stepped from the room, Eli closed the door behind them. Mr. Bonner and Aaron headed toward the lounge.

Taking Serenity by the elbow, Caleb guided her down the hall. They paused outside a stateroom door. Serenity whirled about to face him. "I know what you're going to ask, 'Why was Mr. Bonner with us?' He wasn't. He just happened to be nearby, just happened!"

Caleb looked at the girl in surprise. "I wasn't going to ask that."

"Maybe not, but you were thinking it." She shook her finger in his face. "I know you."

Caleb grinned. "You think so."

"You bet!"

The young man chuckled. "Actually, I was going to ask if you were all right. Obviously, you're in fine fettle."

Serenity gulped. "I'm sorry. It's just that every time—"

"I know. And I need to apologize to you for that. I may be your guardian, but I'm not your father." He glanced over her head at the far end of the empty corridor. He scowled. "Papa says I need to allow you to meet eligible young men, that you are definitely at a marrying age and that I shouldn't inhibit that process."

Serenity swallowed hard. "But I—"

"No, let me finish. Please forgive me. I'm sure Mr. Bonner is a fine man with a golden future. His ambition is to become a U.S. senator. I won't stand in his way, or yours."

Frustration welled up inside of Serenity. She clasped and unclasped her fists before speaking. "Mr. Cunard, you don't understand a thing about women!" Opening the door to the stateroom, she slammed it so hard that it swung back open, which gave her the satisfaction of slamming it a second time. "Of all the arrogant—" Words failed her as she stormed across the small stateroom to the berth, then back again. She paced back and forth across the room like a caged tigress, her body quivering with rage. Suddenly she stopped and glanced about the room. Her breath caught in her throat as her gaze darted from one personal object to another. This wasn't her stateroom! It was Aaron's and Caleb's. "Oh no! Of all the foolish—"

The rap on the door made her jump. She clutched her hands to her chest to slow her rapidly beating heart. Her gaze darted about the room. She considered, then discarded, the idea of squeezing out the narrow porthole. There was no escape. She would have to face Caleb Cunard and his sarcastic grin.

She jerked open the door to find Caleb leaning against the frame, his thumbs hooked in his belt and, of course, a sarcastic grin across his face. "What do you want?" she demanded.

"Uh, this is my cabin. I thought I'd gather a few things, that is, if you don't mind."

"Oh! You are an odious man!"

Sniffing his armpit, he shook his head. "Not any more than usual."

"Oh!" She balled her fists and charged past him into the corridor, looked both ways to establish her bearings, then whipped down the hall to her own stateroom. The door slammed with a resounding crash, then flew open again. Before she could slam it a second time, she heard a click coming from the doorway. She spun about to find herself face to face with Caleb's taunting grin once more.

"What are you doing here, in my stateroom? You shouldn't be in here!"

"You were in mine," he reminded.

"You know that was an accident." She backed up against one of her trunks which caused her legs to buckle. She sat down on the trunk top with a bang. Caleb ignored the girl's moment of indignity.

"Serenity, you baffle me. I thought you'd be happy that I was stepping aside so that your beau, Mr. Bonner, could court you."

Serenity took a deep breath. By the look in his eyes she could tell he truly didn't understand. "Caleb, Mr. Bonner is not my beau. While he's a fine person, and I'm sure an excellent lawyer, I have no romantic feelings for him."

The grin faded from the young man's face, replaced by a look of consternation. "Well, there will be other young men once we reach Independence, I'm sure."

Serenity placed her hands on her hips and glared. "You're a blockhead. Do you know that?"

"What?" He raised his hands in surrender. "I thought I was—"

"You thought! You thought! That's your problem, stop thinking!" She snatched open the door and fled to the stern of the ship. This time he didn't follow her.

There she watched the paddle wheel churn the water for several minutes, hoping Caleb would come find her. When he didn't, she sighed, leaning her elbows against the glossy wooden railing. *Life at eighteen is a whole lot more complicated than it was at seventeen,* she thought. And as had become her habit, she addressed her heavenly Father.

"I don't understand Caleb. One minute he acts like he cares for me and the next, well, You heard what happened back there." She paused for a moment, then remembered Becca. "Here I am fussing about a nonessential problem when poor Becca might be fighting for her life. I'm sorry, Father, for being so self-centered. She's the closest thing to a sister I've ever had. Please heal her. Please?"

Throughout the rest of the day, Serenity wandered about aimlessly, checking every now and then with Fay or Eli regarding the child's condition. Becca had developed a fever, like Mr. Bonner said she might. Serenity hovered out-side the Cunards' cabin, occasionally running back and forth from the riverboat's galley bringing cold water and chunks of ice.

When Mr. Bonner came by and asked about the child, Serenity thanked him for his help. "Becca would have been dead if you hadn't come along. Why did you?"

The young man smiled, a twinkle in his eye. "Honest?"

"Honest."

"I saw the two of you head off that way, and, well, I was hoping to accidentally run into you, an excuse to spend time with you without Caleb lurking nearby. What is his claim to you?"

"Caleb is my guardian, Mr. Bonner, appointed by my late father. That's all."

"Ah, you think that's all? Take it from one gentleman regarding another, there's more to Caleb's interest in you than that."

She shook her head sadly. "I don't think so, Mr. Bonner."

The next day, wherever she went, small clusters of passengers stopped Serenity to tell her they were praying for the little girl. Serenity marveled at how many people knew the Cunards and had heard about the snake bite.

"We've really appreciated Mrs. Cunard, the way she's taken her time during the journey to read stories to the little ones. They get so restless, you know," one woman told Serenity.

A portly man wearing a gold watch fob over his green brocade vest said, "Reverend Cunard is a good man. He was right by my side last week when I received word that my father died of influenza. I was so distraught, I didn't know what to do. Reverend Cunard prayed with me through the night. I know if God will heal anyone, He's gotta heal the daughter of such a righteous couple."

The helmsman stopped Serenity on the way into the dining hall. "Please tell the pastor and his wife I am praying for their little girl." Serenity assured him she would relay his message. The helmsman continued speaking, "I used to love the Lord when I was a little shaver, but somehow I lost track of Him. Pastor Eli helped me find Him again." The man's face glowed. "He's a godly man."

Everywhere Serenity went, someone had good things to say about the Cunards. Where had she been, that she never heard of Eli and Fay's ministrations? Living out her little dramas? Suddenly Serenity felt very selfish and decided she needed to do something to show her hosts some gratitude. She told the head dining steward that she wished to prepare a tray of food for the Cunards, but he shook his head. "No, no, that's all taken care of. Just sit and eat. We would not allow such nice people to go hungry while they care for their daughter."

Serenity smiled to herself as the steward seated her at the family's usual table. No one else had yet arrived. Sitting alone, Serenity considered the impact Eli and Fay had had on her life and on her mother's life, and how their witness touched the life of Josephine Van der Mere, and now, so many people on the riverboat. Bowing her head, the young woman prayed, "Thank You, Father, for the Cunards's witness. Thank You for showing me what sharing Your love is all about."

~9~

A Day in the Big City

FINALLY THE BIG DAY ARRIVED. AN EAGER anticipation throbbed in time with the mighty engines as the paddle wheeler eased up to the dock in St. Louis. Once the ship's whistle announced their arrival, the travelers crowded on the deck and watched as the crew anchored the riverboat and lowered the gangplank. St. Louis was the last major center of commerce before the frontier, and everyone was anxious to make final arrangements before heading west. While there'd been small river towns all along the journey, St. Louis had it all.

Serenity offered to stay with Becca while Fay and Eli shopped in the big city. When they returned, she and Caleb would find a bank where she could convert her gold bars into cash.

"Becca's fevers still come and go without warning," instructed Fay. "Between fevers, she'll probably sleep. Should a fever arise, wash her body down with rubbing alcohol until she relaxes and her skin feels cool to the touch."

"I promise to take good care of your little girl, Aunt Fay," Serenity said.

"I know you will, dear. Becca hasn't had a worrisome fever in the last twenty-four hours, but you never know."

Fay clutched the well-worn leather purse in her hands. "If anything goes wrong, send Caleb to find us."

"I will."

The woman nodded.

"Come on, woman, you're worrying poor Serenity to distraction. She'll do fine. Besides, we want to finish our business so she and Caleb can take care of theirs," Eli reminded as he lead his wife from the room.

Serenity chuckled to herself at the preacher's "woman." Coming from some men it would sound rude and crass, but when Uncle Eli said it, it came out as an endearment. She had to admit that even her mother and father, as much in love as they'd been, didn't enjoy the closeness these two people had. *Could the extra dimension to their romance be the spiritual,* she wondered. *Could a faith in God make a difference even in human love?*

The riverboat grew silent as the passengers and many of the crew members left for their day's excursion. She listened as the water lapped the sides of the riverboat. The distant sounds of whistles, bells, and dock workers reminded her that she wasn't totally alone. And even if she were, she told herself, it felt good to sit and read in peace. She picked one of Uncle Eli's books, *Pilgrim's Progress,* and began reading aloud to Becca as she dropped in and out of sleep.

Serenity read for some time, stopping now and then to give Becca a sip of water before the girl returned to sleep. Once she looked at the girl's bandaged ankle. *Becca was lucky she'd been wearing her heavy stockings or more of the poison would have reached her blood stream . . . that, and Mr. Bonner's quick-thinking surgery.*

Once certain Becca was sleeping peacefully, Serenity ran upstairs to the dining room. "Sir?" Serenity approached the steward. "Could I have a pitcher of cold milk for Becca Cunard when she wakens?"

"Absolutely." He went to the kitchen and returned with a crystal pitcher filled with ice cold milk and a tray of sweet cakes. "Here," he said, "we had these pastries left over from breakfast."

Serenity thanked him and hurried back to her charge. Not watching where she was going, she rounded the corner at the end of the corridor and slammed into a slightly built Negro boy. Milk flew all over Serenity's clothing and the child's baggy pants and patched shirt. The tired, felt hat on the boy's head couldn't conceal the fright in his eyes.

"Please, miss, I sorry." He tried to dab at Serenity's skirt with his sleeve. "So sorry. So sorry."

"It's all right. I'm washable." Serenity laughed and started toward her stateroom. The boy ran to the end of the corridor and let the door slam behind him. "He certainly was in a hurry," she mumbled as she entered the Cunards's cabin.

Stepping inside the room, she glanced down the corridor in time to see the door to Mrs. Rose's cabin snap closed. *Hmm, I'm sure I saw her leave the boat with Aaron.* Serenity set the half-filled pitcher of milk on the travel trunk near the bed, where Fay had placed one of her embroidered tablecloths so they could use it as a table. She caught sight of herself in the wall mirror behind the washstand. She clicked her tongue and strode over to the basin. *What a mess!* Taking a cotton square Fay used to cool Becca's fever, Serenity dabbed water onto the milk stains forming on her blue and white gingham dress.

"Mama?" Becca moaned.

Serenity dropped the cloth into the basin and hurried to the girl's side. "It's OK, Becca. Your mama went into town. She'll be back in a few minutes."

"I'm thirsty."

"Would you prefer water or a cool glass of milk?"

"M-m-m, milk would be nice." A weak smile formed on the girl's face.

Serenity poured some milk into the water glass, then helped Becca sit up so she could drink the milk. While the child only took a sip before she'd had enough, it was a start. Serenity touched her wrist to Becca's forehead. "You're nice and cool. That's the way we like it."

Again the girl smiled and closed her eyes. "I'm sleepy."

"Then you should sleep," Serenity encouraged, making herself comfortable at the foot of the berth. Shortly, the warmth of the morning sun coming in through the small oval window lulled both of the girls to sleep.

Suddenly, a fist pounding on the stateroom door bolted Serenity out of her slumber. "What? Who?" Before she could collect her wits about her, the stateroom door burst open and two burly men stormed in. Behind them a short, wiry man with a bushy blond mustache and goatee strutted into the cabin. "There it is," the man said, pointing to the trunk. "Open it!"

Serenity leaped to her feet as fear darted from her eyes. Her voice shook as she demanded, "Who do you think you are, bursting into a lady's bedroom?"

"Out of the way, girl!" One of the two larger men brushed her aside with one arm like he might a bothersome kitten.

Waking fitfully to find strangers in the room, Becca reared up in the bed and drew her sheet up to her chin. Suddenly she screamed. Serenity rushed to the girl's side and gathered Becca in her arms as she watched the men rip the tablecloth and milk pitcher off the trunk. Serenity gasped in horror as the pitcher slid across the cabin floor and crashed into the wall. "You can't do this! I'm going to call the steward!" she gasped.

As if answering to her beck and call, the head steward peered around the doorframe. "Stop these miscreants immediately," she shouted. "Do something!"

"I can't, miss. They've got the law with them," the steward confessed.

"The law? What kind of law allows them to burst into a lady's chamber?"

The man pawing through the trunk, straightened. "She's not here, sir."

"Who? Who's not here?" Serenity demanded, her body raging with anger.

"A runaway slave. You seen her?" The man's blond goatee bobbed just inches from Serenity's nose.

"Slave?" Serenity's eyes darted toward the steward, then back toward the goateed man. "What slave?"

"If you're harboring my slave girl, I'll skin you alive!" the goateed man snarled.

The head steward stepped between them. "If you know something, miss, you better tell 'em. If they think you know something, they can throw you into jail."

Serenity glared back at the blond-headed man. "I don't know anything about your runaway. I've been caring for this child all morning!"

"She's right, sir," the steward offered. "The Cunards left Miss Pownell in charge of their sick daughter. The child stumbled on a—"

"Oh, shut up!" the man in charge snarled. "I know she's on this boat! My spies tell me that a man and a woman spirited her aboard in Illinois."

Serenity clicked her tongue like an irritated school

teacher. "Did you ever consider that this slave girl of yours might have left the ship by now?"

"Watch it, woman." The blond-headed man glared. "I don't cotton to mouthy females."

Serenity's eyes narrowed. "What? A mighty man, bullying a young lady?"

The man grabbed her arm. "Why, you—"

"Let go of me!" She measured each word carefully. While inside she shook like jelly, outside she remained steady and cold.

"I'd do what the lady says!" All three men turned to see Caleb's form filling the doorway. In his arms he cradled a shotgun. "Now!"

The blond-headed man released her arm and turned on Caleb. "Are you part of the Yankee ring aiding and abetting my runaways?"

Serenity stood transfixed by the fire in Caleb's eyes as he gazed at the intruder. "As you can see, nothing in here belongs to you, sir. I'd suggest you leave my parents' stateroom now." Caleb strode into the crowded cabin and planted himself between the men and the two girls.

Moments later, Fay charged into the room, her eyes blazing. "What is going on here?" She pushed through the cluster of men to her daughter's bedside, then turned on the strangers. "I demand to know who you are and what you think you're doing disturbing my ailing daughter."

The blond man doffed his wide-brimmed felt hat and bowed at the indignant woman. "Beauregard O'Gilvie, Esquire, at your service, ma'am."

"You get out of here this instant!" She drew Becca close to her chest. "My poor baby. How dare you disturb my poor baby."

Serenity looked up to see Eli standing in the doorway observing the action. Aaron stood behind him. The reverend leaned against the doorframe, a lazy grin on his face. "My, my, didn't your daddy ever teach you not to come between a mama bear and her cub? If I were you, sir, I'd hightail it for safer quarters."

Caleb, less amiable, leaned into the man's face. "You heard my father, Mr. Esquire."

Irritated, the man hissed, "It's not Mr. Esquire, that's my title. I'm Mr. Beauregard O'Gilvie, and I own the largest cotton plantation in the county. And if your a' hidin' my girl, I'll getcha, Yankee boy," the man snarled and strode out into the corridor. The other man and the steward followed, brushing past Aaron. The steward circled the younger Cunard carefully.

A smirk creased Caleb's face as he reached out to close the door. "If I were hiding your slave, you'd never see her again, sir," he said under his breath.

Serenity's hand flew to her mouth. "Are they searching all the staterooms? If they go through mine, they're going to find my mother's jewelry, and maybe Daddy's gold. I don't trust them."

"Good thinking. Come on, let's go." Caleb grabbed Serenity's wrist and pulled her to the door. "Why don't you come too, little brother?"

"Mind if I join in?" Reverend Cunard asked, falling into step behind the others.

"Be careful," Aunt Fay called. "Those are dangerous men. No gold is worth sacrificing your life for."

When Caleb swung open the door to Serenity's cabin, the men had the contents of the two trunks strewn across the floor, and one of the men was about to lift the lid to the false bottom. The leader of the group held Serenity's container of face powder in his hands.

Serenity gasped, realizing that a second or two more and both the jewelry and the gold would be uncovered and quite possibly transferred to O'Gilvie's pockets.

Caleb snatched the powder box from the man's hands. "Gentlemen, no child could hide in the places you are looking. I suggest you look elsewhere." With his free hand, Caleb slammed shut the trunk lid. The lid caught the intruder's hands. Serenity winced as the man cried out in pain.

Caleb placed the powder box in Serenity's hands. "My brother's and my cabin is next door. Do you wish to search it as well?"

The injured man nursed his hand while the boss stormed toward the door. "Absolutely. I *will* find my slave girl!"

"Fine, but keep in mind that you are looking for a young girl, not personal items that don't belong to you."

Serenity stayed in her room while the men searched the next cabin, and the next. She knew they had reached Mrs. Rose's stateroom when Serenity heard the woman scream. By the loud shouting in the hall, she supposed the Cunard men were defending the lovely Mrs. Rose's privacy as well. Serenity stayed in her cabin until the intruders moved on to the cabins of the upper deck.

"Serenity?" Caleb knocked on the cabin door and peered into the room. "They're gone, but they might be back. It would be wise to leave your jewelry and the gold bars in my parents' room while you and I are in town."

"You're right." Serenity pointed to the bed where the collection in question was wrapped in a pillow case. "As you can see, I already pulled it out."

In town, Serenity forgot about the altercation aboard

the riverboat. It felt good to be free of the stringent river life and behave like a normal land-loving person again. She clutched her cut-velvet brocade portmanteau, containing one of the gold bars, to her chest. Caleb strode beside her, clutching her arm protectively with one hand while his shotgun rested in the other. "For thieving polecats," he explained when Serenity asked about the weapon.

Walking toward the bank, Serenity decided she'd feel better once the gold bar was safely in the bank. As they walked, the gold bar grew heavier with every step. Her eyes darting one direction, then the other, she was certain that someone, possibly one of Mr. O'Gilvie's simpletons, would jump out from behind one of the painted store fronts. Still, drawing near to a grocery, she paused.

"I need to stop in this dry goods store before we go to the bank," Serenity said, and shot into the store without warning.

"Hey, wait for me," Caleb struggled to keep up.

"I need two yards of cotton flannel. Can you pay the man?" she asked.

Caleb scowled. "Flannel? What for?"

"Will you please pay the man? I'll pay you back in a few minutes."

"Yes, I suppose I can."

"Good." She handed Caleb the portmanteau, picked up a bolt of white cotton flannel, and walked to the counter. The clerk peered over a pair of spectacles at the young woman.

"May I help you, miss?" His heavy gray-brown mustache hid his mouth and most of his chin. Serenity wondered how the clerk managed to eat without biting into his mustache as well.

"Yes, two yards of this flannel, please." Serenity passed the bolt over the counter.

The clerk measured and cut the fabric, then handed the small bundle to the young woman. "That will be twelve cents. Will you be needing thread?"

"No, sir, and thank you." While Caleb paid the man, she turned and strolled over to the window to examine a pink cabriolet bonnet covered with matching lace and satin ribbons. "Ooh, isn't it beautiful?" she asked when she sensed Caleb once again by her side.

"Hmmph!"

She smiled to herself. "Are you ready to face the fearsome bank manager?"

"If you are," he muttered, leading her from the store. "The clerk said the nearest bank is on the corner."

Serenity nodded. Seeing a Negro woman carrying a load of laundry out of a shop, her thoughts shifted to the riverboat. The collision. The young Negro boy. Spilled milk. She gasped. "I think I know who those men were looking for. I think I saw the boy in the corridor!"

Caleb lifted his eyebrows in mock amazement. "Really? But I thought they were looking for a girl?"

"Well, she was dressed as a boy, I think."

Caleb laughed. "In other words, you saw nothing, my dear."

"Don't patronize me, Caleb. The fear in that boy . . . er . . . girl's eyes, I've seen it before—in the eyes of the slaves hidden in my daddy's attic."

"Long ago and far away." Entering the bank, Caleb led her to the caged counter. "Just put it out of your mind." He smiled at the bank teller. "Miss Serenity Pownell needs to make a transaction with one of your bank officials, please."

The clerk behind the bars wriggled his handlebar mustache and called to the portly bank manager sitting at a desk in the back corner. When the man stood and offered his hand, Serenity swept gracefully to his desk.

"My name is Mr. Foote, Mr. Henry Foote. How may I help you?"

Caleb carried the bulging portmanteau back to the *Liberty.* "We must do something with this money. The way the scuttlebutt flies aboard the riverboat, you'll be a target for every swindler and card shark aboard."

Serenity's frown stretched into a grin. "I have an idea. Of course, I'll need your help and your mom's as well."

"Well, are you going to tell me what your idea is?" He shifted the heavy bag from one shoulder to the other.

"First, as Aunt Eunice would say, 'Don't put all your eggs in one basket.'"

"And what does that mean?"

She giggled and skipped ahead of him up the gangplank. "You'll see!"

The family gathered in the Cunards' cabin. None had seen so much money in one place before. While Caleb guarded the closed and locked door, Becca stared at the paper bills and the silver coins, and oohed as if they were a newborn kitten. Even Aaron's eyes lit up when Serenity dumped the contents of the portmanteau onto the berth.

Carefully Serenity counted out the cost of her passageway west and her expenses, then handed the bundle to Eli.

He reddened, tugging at the collar on his starched white shirt. "I wish I didn't have to take this from you, Serenity. It should be kept for your dowry."

"An agreement's an agreement, Uncle Eli." Serenity placed one hand on his arm. "My father planned for my care. And you folks have opened your hearts to me and taken me in. You didn't have to, despite Caleb's promise to my dad."

Fay wrapped her arms about the girl. "And every minute has been a pleasure. We love you like our own."

"I know that. And now, I need to trust you as I would my family,"—she blushed—"not counting poor Uncle Joel, that is. There's no doubt that too many people know about my wealth. If you're willing, I would like you and Uncle Eli to carry some of my money for me, and Caleb, of course. Not in your purse, Fay, but where my mother carried extra money when she traveled, in her corset."

"Corset?" Eli and his two sons laughed.

"Not you three, of course. You will carry little bits of cash in your boots. My mother made a small flannel envelope for my dad to carry extra money in his boot when he traveled from Auburn to Albany."

"And me?" Becca asked, her eyes dancing with excitement.

Fay shook her head. "You're only a child, Becca. And still quite ill."

The girl's lower lip protruded and tears formed in her eyes. "But I want to help too!"

Serenity frowned. "I know. And you will, if you do what I plan."

"And what's that?" the child asked.

"Well, if you gentlemen will excuse us, I will show you."

"Is that what the rest of the yardage is for?" Becca asked.

"Exactly."

—10—

Independence

"THE CITY BEYOND THE RIVERBEND," FELIX Bonner said, extending his hand toward the town of Independence, Missouri. They'd boarded their third riverboat to travel down the Missouri River and now were nearing their final stop. Standing to his left, Serenity leaned against the boat railing trying to catch a glimpse of the town that would be her home for a time. Caleb stood silent on the other side of her, feeling equally as curious about the town on the edge of America's frontier. While they could only see the part of the town that towered over the treetops, Independence was much larger than either Caleb or Serenity imagined.

"The closest Indian village is ten miles that way," Bonner pointed south. "You'll see lots of them from different tribes in town come spring. During the winter, though, they hibernate in their teepees. It gets mighty cold in these parts."

Serenity smiled at the drawl Mr. Bonner developed during the last few miles of the journey. It matched the frontier duds for which he'd exchanged his eastern-style dandies. As "frontier" as his image might be, she thought, his camel brown suede knee britches and matching jacket displayed a refined cut and style not evident on the other frontiersmen she'd seen aboard the riverboat.

"More than sixteen hundred people call this place home, from the Methodist church spire in the north to the Congregational church spire in the south. Come spring, more than five thousand people will pass through here on their way west," Felix added. "We're the second most populous county in Missouri." He pointed to what appeared to be the center of the city. "We have at least thirty dry goods stores, two hotels, five boarding houses and"—he cleared his throat—"at last count, thirty-some drinking establishments."

Serenity rolled her eyes heavenward. She'd heard tales of the wild mountain men's brawls and the Mexican vaqueros' knife fights that began in the town's bawdy bars. "Hardly a place for a lady, Mr. Bonner."

"After all this time, you still call me Mr. Bonner. Surely by now we can consider one another friends?"

She blushed, giving the man a coy grin. "Of course, Felix."

The lawyer smiled with pleasure. "Thank you, Miss Serenity. How about you, Mr. Cunard? Have we reached a first-name basis yet?"

"Many blacksmith shops in these parts, Felix?" Caleb asked.

"Twenty, so they say, the biggest being Ross Camp. Ross runs an extensive smelting operation. Most of the blacksmith shops around here spend their time building covered wagons for the emigrants heading west each spring. Only a few take on the small jobs like shoeing horses and such."

It was evident that Mr. Bonner was proud of his prairie town. "We would have had telegraph by now except the construction slowed down outside St. Louis because of the cholera outbreak that hit the area last spring. S'pect there'll be telegraph service by next summer though."

"Cholera?" Caleb asked.

"Pretty bad in forty-nine. The Noland house had seven deaths alone. At East Bottoms, over three hundred Belgium workers died."

"All from cholera?" Serenity asked.

"Not for certain. Some say it was due to the plowed fields in Palmyra. Others blame rotting potatoes, and still more say it was due to the burning of coal, tar, and sulfur in St. Louis."

"Rotting potatoes?" Caleb frowned. "Isn't that a little farfetched?"

Mr. Bonner shrugged. "Some religionists just chalk it up to an act of God for the sins of the people."

"That's a horrid idea." Serenity knitted her brow. "My God isn't like that."

Mr. Bonner chuckled. "You would know, not me. Personally, I think humans give God, if He exists, too much credit, as if He would be interested in a ragged little community out in this wonderfully God-forsaken country."

"Wonderfully God-forsaken country? That's hardly a badge of honor," Serenity muttered.

"You'll learn, Miss Pownell, that most frontiersmen prefer to put their faith in their shooting irons. Say your prayers, but keep your weapons handy. Take Becca, for instance. Where was God when I shot off the head of that rattler?"

Serenity smiled up into his sarcastic grin. "Where was God? That's easy. He was busy answering my prayer by getting you there in time to shoot the varmint!"

Felix smirked at her quick reply. "You never cease to surprise me, Miss Serenity."

Together, the three of them disembarked the riverboat. "The actual town is two miles downriver," Felix volunteered.

"May I make a suggestion? I have a wagon waiting to haul my purchases to my home in Independence. You can either rent a wagon by the hour here at the docks—an expensive endeavor, I might add—or a couple of you could ride into town with me, look around, then borrow my wagon to move your supplies to wherever you decide to go."

Eli and Fay, along with Aaron who was carrying Becca, joined them on the wharf as Felix waved toward a large wagon being loaded with crates by the roustabouts. "That's my wagon. I need to go check on my purchases. In the meantime, you folks decide what you want to do."

Caleb explained Felix's offer to his father while Aaron placed his little sister on a log beside the wharf.

"He can't take all of us along with our goods as well as his. Most of us will have to stay here and guard everything," Caleb explained.

"How long will it take to make the trip?" Fay asked.

"He said the town is two miles away, but look at the number of wagons lining up." Caleb pointed to the traffic jam forming at the base of the wharf.

"It's very nice of Mr. Bonner to offer," Eli admitted. "I talked with one local merchant onboard the riverboat, and the cost to rent a wagon is steep."

"Being we must pay for housing throughout the winter, it would be wise to economize as much as possible," Fay added. "But I don't like being left behind to wait."

Eli eyed his wife. "I don't blame you, darling, but with Becca's problem—and it's obvious that Bonner won't have enough room for all of us and our goods on his wagon."

"We'll stay," Fay murmured, "but I don't like it."

Aaron, who'd been somewhat distracted during the riverboat's landing, volunteered to let Caleb and his father go with Mr. Bonner. "I want to make certain Mrs. Rose has met her party."

"Her husband, you mean," Becca whispered so only Serenity could hear. "That should be quite a party."

"Sh!" Serenity hissed. "Someone will hear you."

"As if it matters. Everyone knows about her and my brother anyway," Becca snapped. "There she is, Aaron. Look, over there by the station embracing her husband, I presume."

"I see her," Aaron growled, kicking at a stone with the toe of his boot.

"For a ten-year-old," Serenity whispered in Becca's ear, "you are certainly an outspoken little thing."

"I must take after my big sister then." The girl smiled slightly and shifted her leg, her eyes revealing her pain. Serenity stroked the girl's braided hair and watched while Eli and Felix Bonner climbed aboard the Bonner buckboard. The two black mares hitched to the wagon flicked their tales at the pesky flies swarming the area.

"May I suggest that you ladies stroll over to the boat station where you can stay in the shade until we return?" Mr. Bonner called. "They sell the most delicious lemonade. Ice cold."

"Thank you." Fay waved as Caleb hopped on top of the loaded wagon, perching himself on a large wooden crate.

"Be careful, that's my new pianoforte," Mr. Bonner warned Caleb. Felix flicked the reins. The horses strained against the weight of the wagon and the wheels began to turn. The wagon joined the long line of freight wagons and passenger carriages heading for Independence.

Serenity waved until they disappeared in the cloud of dust. Staying behind was not her idea of fun. "If I can't go to Independence right away, I'll explore what I can right here. Come on, Becca, let's try some of that lemonade."

The child glanced down at her leg and over at the riverboat station. "But I can't walk that far."

"What do you think, Fay?"

"I'll get Aaron to carry her." The older woman turned around, but her son was nowhere in sight. "Aaron? Aaron!" Aaron didn't answer. "Where can he have disappeared to? Maybe Becca and I had better stay right here with our freight until he returns." Fay raised her parasol and seated herself on the trunk next to Becca.

Serenity shrugged. "Give me a container and I'll bring some lemonade back for you."

"Good idea." The woman opened her portmanteau and handed Serenity a pewter tankard. "Here's some change." Fay reached into her string purse.

"Put it away. This is my treat," Serenity assured her, holding up her small cream suede purse that matched her embroidered gloves.

"I'd really rather . . ."

"Don't be silly. Remember, grace is no less needed when receiving as when giving." Serenity sashayed toward the riverboat station, her deep mauve cotton skirt swooshing about her ankles from the weight of the coins Bella had helped her hide.

Onyx bounded ahead of her.

"Be careful, honey," Fay called. "We don't know much about this area."

The girl cast a teasing glance over her shoulder. "I know enough about this place for me to stay within clear view of you and Becca." She laughed and broke into a skip. She paused and gazed toward the West. It felt so good to finally be free of the boat. For so long it had been her tether. But now the land would be her home, as far as the eye could see and beyond to the mountains. She tried to imagine the great mountains as she'd heard them described by frontiersmen aboard the riverboat: "Mountains that disappeared into the clouds."

Will I ever see them, she wondered. "For now, Father, I'm just thankful to be able to walk on dry land once again." The young woman swooshed her skirts with her hands, tossed back her head, and laughed. The bow fastening her deep purple closed bonnet untied. Before she could catch the mischievous satin ribbons, a breeze caught the hat and flung it into the air. Serenity squealed and reached for the hat, which tumbled across the clearing like sagebrush on the open prairie. The longshoremen paused from their work to watch the pretty young woman trying to catch her runaway bonnet. Their laughter angered her. One man dressed in buckskin britches, a matching fringed jacket, and a raccoon-skin hat leaned against the corner of the riverboat station, stomped his foot, and hooted with laughter. For some reason his laughter bothered her more than the others.

Serenity chased the hat into the center of a wild berry bush. As she studied the bonnet in the thorny bush and how she could best retrieve it without tearing the ruffled sleeve of her dress, a shadow fell across her. She looked to see a tall, muscular, dark-skinned man, stripped to the waist, his chest glistening from the sweat of heavy labor. He smiled, revealing a shiny gold tooth. He removed his battered felt hat and bowed. "May I help you, miss?"

Serenity brushed a mouthful of hair from her face. "Yes, I would appreciate that. You see, my hat blew into the bushes; and I can't reach it."

"Ned Ward, at your service, ma'am," the man said with a slight bow. Without further introduction, the man reached his bare arm into the bush, extracted the bonnet, brushed it off with his forearm, and handed it to her.

"Thank you so much, Mr. Ward." Serenity looked at his forearm and gasped. A bright red strip of blood oozed from a deep scratch from the bush's briars.

"Mr. Ward, you're injured. Let me help you."

He smiled. Removing a red print handkerchief from his neck, he tied it around the cut. "I'll be fine, ma'am."

Not knowing what to say, she watched the man adjust the bandage over his wound. "Er, thank you for rescuing my bonnet. I'm sure my Aunt Fay wouldn't mind putting some salve on that cut."

The man shook his head, bowed once again to the young woman, then put on his own sweat-stained hat and strode behind a stack of freight at the end of the wharf.

As Serenity placed the bonnet on her head and tied the ribbons beneath her chin, she glanced in the direction of the laughing men. They'd all returned to work, except for the foot-stomping frontiersman. He was coming straight for her. Turning her back to the man, she marched directly to the riverboat station. She ordered a lemonade for herself and asked for the tankard to be filled for Fay and Becca. Sitting in the shade, Serenity lifted a chipped porcelain mug to her lips. *Obviously the wealth of the riverboat doesn't extend to the concessions on shore,* she thought. She closed her eyes and sipped the cold refreshing liquid. "Mmm, delicious," she muttered under her breath before taking a second drink.

"Yes it is, isn't it?"

Serenity glanced over her shoulder in the direction of the unfamiliar voice and found herself face to face with a rawhide-covered chest. Taken aback, her gaze shifted upward to a clean-shaven face. The man chuckled, removed his animal-skin hat, and dipped his head toward Serenity. "Let me introduce myself—Luther Kane, wilderness guide for the United States Army."

Serenity whirled to face the lemonade stand.

"And you are?" the guide asked.

Refusing to reply, she drank the rest of her cool drink as quickly as possible. She could feel a headache coming on from drinking the cold lemonade so quickly, but nevertheless she grabbed the metal tankard and headed back across the clearing to where Fay and Becca waited. The laughter of Mr. Luther Kane followed her.

"You're right, Aunt Fay. We need to be careful." Serenity handed the tankard to the older woman. "There are many dangerous critters in these parts, and most of them walk on two legs!"

A few minutes later, Aaron strolled up to where the three sat. Fay, irked with her younger son, dragged him out of hearing distance. Words like *irresponsible, undependable,* and *unreliable* drifted to where Serenity and Becca sat. Serenity tried not to look in their direction, but Becca wasn't so discreet. "Mama's really peeling his ears back this time."

"Suppose so," Serenity nodded, her attention resting on the cluster of men standing by the riverboat station. With her face shadowed by her bonnet, she could watch the intrepid Mr. Kane without his knowing. For once she appreciated her "blinders" as she called fashionable women's bonnets.

A man sporting a gray beard and mustache approached Serenity and Becca. In his right hand he carried a Sharp's rifle. "You folks looking for a place to rest tonight?"

Serenity turned toward him in surprise. "Sir?"

He touched the brim of his wide-brimmed black felt hat. "The name is Fred Prior. I'm John Law around these parts."

Serenity continued to stare. Becca cocked her head to one side. "So which are you, Mr. Prior or Mr. Law?"

The man tipped back his head and laughed. "Mr. Prior, little lady. On the frontier, John Law is a nickname for an officer of the law. I'm sheriff of this fine county."

Serenity held out her gloved hand. "Nice to meet you, Mr. Prior. My name is Serenity Pownell and this is Becca Cunard. Over there is Mrs. Cunard and her younger son, Aaron."

Mr. Prior pushed his hat back from his forehead. "Been watching you for some time and it seems to me you might need help finding a spot for the night."

"Reverend Cunard and his elder son, Caleb, headed into town to find us a place to bed down. I'm sure they'll return soon," Serenity assured him.

"Reverend? A Bible-totin', Scripture-quotin' preacher of the gospel?" The sheriff frowned.

"Yes, sir. Papa knows God's Word inside and out," Becca volunteered.

The lawman laughed. "I'm sure he does, little lady. I'm sure he does." He paused a moment to stroke his beard. "If your menfolk don't return soon enough, I'll be glad to take you over to the Doran Mission for the night."

"The Doran Mission? Thank you, Mr. Prior, but we're looking for a boarding house."

"The Dorans have rooms to rent." The lawman sucked air through his teeth. "Good Christian women like you and Mrs. Cunard, you might find your sensibilities offended in one of the town's . . . er . . . rooming houses."

Serenity graciously tipped her head to one side. "Thank you so much, sir, for your offer, but I'm sure our men will return from town soon."

The words barely escaped her lips when Serenity spotted a team of horses and a wagon coming down the road toward them. "I think that's them now." She heaved a sigh of relief as the sheriff touched the rim of his hat respectfully and ambled toward the riverboat station.

"Who was that man?" Fay asked when she and Aaron returned to where Serenity and Becca sat waiting.

"County sheriff, or something like that," Serenity replied. "He told me about a place where we can sleep tonight if the men haven't found anything."

"Don't worry. The good Reverend and the magnificent Caleb will have our futures all worked out, I assure you." Aaron—his face darkened with anger and embarrassment from his recent bawling out—strode toward the approaching wagon.

"Aaron!" Fay's eyes flashed with anger as her call went unheeded. She shot an irritated glance toward Serenity and Becca. "I don't know what to do with that boy. Frankly, I'm afraid it's too late to do much of anything." She wrung her hands in frustration. "Poor Eli is beside himself with concern." The woman returned a wave to her husband as he leaped from the wagon and hurried toward her.

The family gathered around Eli. Before he could speak, Becca shared her news. "Guess what? We met the county sheriff."

"You did?" Eli glanced toward his wife.

"Yep," Becca continued. "Do you know what his name is?"

Eli shook his head. "Not until you tell me."

"Daddy!" the girl moaned. "His name is Fred Prior. He's the John Law in these parts."

"The John Law?" Caleb interrupted.

"Yep!" Becca nodded. "That's what they call frontier lawmen. Mr. Prior says we should get rooms at the Doran Mission. He says we might not like the rooming houses in town too much. He says they would offend our sensibilities."

Eli chortled at the five-syllable word his young daughter used. "Do you even know what that word means?" he asked, tousling her bonnet.

"No, but it's something we ladies have and you don't."

"Oh, really?" He laughed again. "Well, as it happens, your sheriff is right. Caleb rode out to the Doran place and made the arrangements for our stay." He glanced at his wife. "The Dorans need your help, Fay. They run a mission for the Indians, where they come for food, shelter, and medical attention. I'll tell you all about it on the ride to their place."

Caleb hopped down from the wagon. "Fortunately, the mission is north of town, so it won't take long to get there. There's a huge kettle of hot vegetable stew waiting for us and freshly made Southern biscuits."

"Yum!" Becca licked her lips. "I'm hungry enough to eat the entire stew, pot and all!"

"Homemade biscuits?" Serenity closed her eyes and sighed. Nothing sounded sweeter to her empty stomach.

~11~

Life at the Mission

As Caleb helped her down from the loaded wagon, Serenity grimaced at the appearance of the drab little Indian mission—three gray-brown buildings of sod and stone planted in the middle of the prairie. *Hardly an advertisement for frontier living,* she thought. The lingering shadows of daylight glistened off the panes of glass in the windows. Beside each window was a sturdy wooden shutter to block out winter's cold.

Serenity scanned the western horizon, land and sky far as her eye could see. "So this is our new home."

"For the time being." Caleb followed her gaze. "Empty, isn't it? Not like Cayuga Lake. Are you sorry you chose to leave Buffalo?"

She shook her head slowly. "Mama always said, 'Home is where the heart is.' And my heart's definitely here."

Caleb placed a gloved hand on her shoulder. "I hope so. I hope you never come to regret your decision to leave your uncle's place."

"I probably will, at times, knowing me." Serenity chuckled and planted her hands on her hips. "Guess it's time to unload the wagon."

Caleb hopped onto the wagon and found a small valise. "Here, you take this. I think it's my mother's."

Serenity accepted the bag from him. Lifting a large crate to his shoulder, Caleb carried it into the barn where Mr. Doran stood directing traffic. Serenity picked up her portmanteau and turned toward the mission house.

"Serenity, do you want all your trunks carried into yours and Becca's room?" Aaron asked.

Serenity thought for a moment. "I'm too tired to do anything with them tonight. Just put them in the barn with the rest of the things. I'll sort through it all in the morning."

As she stepped inside the humble sod house, Serenity's first impressions shifted from disdain to pleasure. The aroma of hot vegetable stew and freshly made biscuits accosted her senses. She closed her eyes and took a deep breath. Opening her eyes, she saw the light from a fire in the large fireplace along the back wall dancing on the surface of a long, well-oiled oak trestle table and its benches, and off a plank floor of heavy pine. Not what she'd expected to find inside a sod house. Silhouette portraits decorated the white-washed wall behind the upholstered sofa, while two rockers were clustered around the flickering hearth on the right.

Serenity's gaze took in the neat, well-equipped kitchen on the left side of the room, where a blond woman barely older than she stood in front of a wood stove stirring the contents in an iron kettle. The chrome on the stove sparkled with care.

"Hello. Welcome," the woman called, wiping her brow with her sleeve. "You must be Miss Pownell. I'm Analee Doran."

"Nice to meet you, Mrs. Doran," Serenity smiled warmly. "Something smells delicious."

"Please, call me Analee. When I hear Mrs. Doran, I look around for my mother-in-law." Analee giggled and blushed. "Supper will be ready in two shakes of a horse's tail."

Serenity laughed. "I'll be glad to call you Analee, if you'll call me Serenity."

"Serenity, what an interesting name."

"My mother was Quaker. Her family was big on the virtues of the Bible."

Analee laughed. "Go ahead through that doorway and into the hall. Mrs. Cunard is arranging the sleeping accommodations. She can tell you where to put those cases." Mrs. Doran brushed a strand of flaxen blond hair from her forehead and smiled. Serenity noted the dark circles around the woman's eyes and thought she looked exhausted. *Well, maybe I can be of some help to lift the woman's load,* she thought.

"You have a lovely place here."

The woman smiled. "Thank you. I do the best I can with what I have."

Serenity ran her hand over the red-and-yellow scrap quilt on the back of the upholstered sofa. She traced one index finger over the finely stitched petit point flowers on the two throw pillows.

"Did you do these pillows?" Serenity asked.

"Yes. The winters on the prairie are long. Petit point makes the time pass more quickly."

"You did a lovely job. They're beautiful. My mother used to do petit point as well as crewel work."

"She doesn't do it anymore?" the woman asked.

"No, she died last spring."

"Oh, I'm sorry—"

"It's all right. Accidents happen." For the first time,

Serenity realized she was finally healing from the hurt of her losses and smiled.

"Do you have any samples of her work with you?" her hostess asked.

Serenity shook her head sadly, removing her bonnet from her head. "No, everything was lost in a fire."

"A fire? I'm so sorry."

Before Serenity could reply, the men thundered into the cabin. Mr. Doran seemed to be in the midst of a coughing fit. Analee hurried over, a worried look on her face; but the coughing subsided as Mr. Doran took his seat at the table.

Serenity hurried to her assigned room, poured cold water into the washbasin, then washed her face before returning to the great room to help finish the meal preparation.

"Looks like I'm too late to help," the young woman said, seeing Analee placing the last bowl of soup on the table.

Entering the room, Fay called down the hall to Caleb, "Will you please carry Becca to the table?"

"Sure, Ma." Caleb lifted Becca from one of the rocking chairs and carried her to the table. "Come on, ragamuffin. It's time to eat."

After Mr. Doran blessed the food, Serenity dipped her spoon into her bowl of vegetable stew and lifted it to her lips. "Mmm, this tastes even better than it looks."

"I'm glad you like it," Analee replied. "There's plenty more where that came from. Here, help yourself to the biscuits."

After all the fancy foods onboard the riverboat, Analee's home cooking satisfied the travelers' appetites.

At the end of the meal, Mr. Doran invited Eli to conduct an informal worship service. Eli took out his Bible and related the story of Abram leaving his home in Ur to travel to only God knew where. "And everywhere Abram stopped, he built an altar of gratitude to God. Tonight, around this table, we, like faithful Abram, need to build an altar of thanksgiving to our Keeper and our God." Eli reached for his wife's hand on one side and Aaron's on the other. The rest of the group, including the Dorans, followed his example as he offered a prayer of praise and gratitude for safe travel.

Serenity thought to herself, *Yes, Lord, it has been safe, except for the snake bite. Were You in control of that too?*

As if he heard Serenity's thoughts, Eli continued, "And Lord, my precious Becca's leg has been so slow to heal after that snake sank its fangs into her ankle. Glorify Your name through my child's pain."

Morning and evening since the fateful event, the reverend's prayer was the same. Good days when the swelling seemed to subside and bad days when the ankle and lower calf flamed fiery red, it didn't matter. "Glorify Your name, Lord." That was his prayer.

Does Uncle Eli have all the answers, Serenity wondered. *Does he know something the rest of us don't? Does he have a secret access to God's kingdom?* Serenity had been watching and listening to the reverend for a long time. And instead of understanding him better, she only succeeded in uncovering a new mystery to his faith. *How can Your name be glorified through a snake bite, Lord?*

After dinner, the men went out to the barn to bed down with the animals for the night while Serenity and the Cunard women helped Analee clean the kitchen. Analee's eyes sparkled as Fay answered her numerous questions about life aboard the riverboats. She cooed with pleasure at Becca's description of the perfectly appointed tables, the gleaming silver, and the glittering chandeliers.

When asked about her life in Independence, Analee sighed. "I was born on a plantation in Louisiana. And while we were a large family, we had servants to care for our needs."

"Serenity's parents were rich too," Becca added.

"Sh!" Fay touched her fingers to her lips with a scowl. "That was not polite."

Serenity smiled wistfully as she dried a bowl with the cotton tea towel and placed the bowl on the shelf with the others. "She's right. I grew up surrounded by more comforts than most."

"Yeah, she had—"

"Becca! Shush! Analee, you were telling us about your home?"

"I don't mean to complain, but life is hard out here. It seems like I can't keep up with everything there is to do, especially getting ready for winter."

"And your mission to the Indians?" Fay asked. "Tell me about that."

"Hmm, not much to tell. We've been here for four years now, or is it five? I can't remember. Anyway, the Wyandoth and the Shawnee people listen when Cyril preaches about God; and they appreciate the grain and supplies we give them to tide them through the winter months, but they don't trust us. We're still the invading enemy, I fear." Analee glanced quickly at Fay. "I believe in my husband, Mrs. Cunard. I wouldn't have left Louisiana if I didn't."

Fay put her arm around the slight woman's shoulders. "I'm sure you do, dear, as do I. And, from what I see, you are an excellent helpmate."

Without warning, the woman buried her face in her apron and cried. When she lifted her head, she wiped her eyes with her sleeve. "I feel so foolish." The young woman's face reddened. "I don't even know you and here I am baring my soul to you."

Fay smiled and patted the woman's shoulder. "Don't feel embarrassed. It happens to me everywhere I go."

Analee gulped and sniffed. "Thank you. It's nice having another woman around. I don't want to complain, but sometimes life is so hard and unfair."

"You're right," Fay comforted. "Life isn't fair, but God is still good. I'm sure it's by His design that we're here with you now."

Analee lifted her chin and stiffened. "Good? What is so good about burying my infant son on this God-forsaken prairie?"

"There, there." Fay drew the young woman into her arms. "No place is God-forsaken in God's holy universe. But, looking out at the vastness of the prairie, I imagine there have been many times that it felt God-forsaken."

The door swung open to a gush of cold air. Mr. Doran entered the house, followed by the Cunard men. "Temperature's dropping tonight. Gonna be a snappy one."

Serenity hung the last of the copper-bottomed kettles from the iron rack near the fireplace as Fay helped Analee dry her eyes. When the two women turned to face the men, Analee had replaced her tears with a broad smile.

As the men shed their heavy coats by the door, Mr. Doran talked about the needs of the Plains Indians and the purpose of his mission. "When God called me to start this mission, He never promised it would be easy. Nope, He didn't do that." The man stomped his feet emphatically on the rag rug by the door. His enthusiasm was captivating, Serenity thought. No wonder Analee followed him to what appeared to her a wasteland. "And if this isn't the end of the earth," she muttered, "I'm sure you can see it from here."

The warmth of the winter fire drew the two families deep into conversation. As the hour grew late, Becca's eyes began to close. "Looks like we have a sleepy girl." Fay pointed to her daughter.

Eli scooped the child into his arms and carried her to the room assigned to Becca and Serenity. Serenity and Fay said their goodnights and followed Eli from the room so they could help Becca dress for bed.

As Fay unwrapped the girl's leg, her eyes widened. The infection with its swelling had crept further up Becca's leg. Fay avoided glancing in Serenity's direction, but both women were thinking similar thoughts. *Would Becca lose her leg? How would being an amputee glorify God, especially in this harsh land?* Serenity wondered.

Becca moaned as her mother tenderly washed the girl's leg with cooling water. "Serenity, do you know where we might have packed the extra bandage strips before we left the boat this morning?"

Serenity leaped to her feet and grabbed her shawl. "I stuck a few rolls into my steamer trunk before we left the riverboat. I'll go get them."

"No, let one of the men get them for you."

Serenity laughed. "They'll never be able to find them in that mess!" The young woman whipped out of the room, down the short hallway, and into the great room. "Excuse me. Gotta get something out of my trunk."

Aaron shot to his feet. "I'll get what you need."

She waved him away. "Thanks for offering, but don't bother. It's easier for me to get it than to explain how to find it."

"Take a lantern." Mr. Doran sprang to his feet and lit one of the small lanterns stored on a shelf near the cabin door.

"Is it safe for her to be out there alone at night?" Caleb asked, already heading for his jacket on a peg by the door.

"I'll be fine," Serenity laughed over all the fuss. "I'll be back in no time. Besides, Onyx is out there, remember?"

"She'll be safe," Mr. Doran assured the Cunard men. "Especially with the dog by her side."

Reluctantly, Caleb returned to the rocker where he'd been sitting. "Just call if you need me."

Serenity opened the door and stepped out into the cool night air. Onyx, asleep on the stone doorstep, snapped awake and barked. Together, they made their way to the barn by the light of the lantern, though the myriad of stars overhead would have lighted the pathway. Hugging herself against the chill, Serenity paused before entering the barn. "This is the strangest place, Lord. One minute I think I hate it here, and the next, You scatter a thousand diamonds across the sky and I think I could live here forever."

The sweet odor of new hay accosted her as she entered the barn, filling her with the warmth of life. In the dark, a horse whinnied. A second snorted. A cow mooed. Onyx trotted directly to the spot where the trunks had been deposited. The dog sniffed the stack of containers and whined.

"Stop it, Onyx. That's irritating." Setting the lantern on a nearby stall post, she located the steamer trunk and found the rolls of bandages as expected, next to a pair of her ruffled bloomers. She'd forgotten about the bloomers. The young woman giggled to herself. "How embarrassing! I wouldn't have wanted either Aaron or Caleb to find these."

Clutching the rolls of bandages to her chest, Serenity closed the trunk. "You should sleep in here tonight, Onyx. You'd be a whole lot warmer, you know." She reached to retrieve the lantern and frowned at the sight of a trunk she'd never seen before. "That's not one of our trunks. Onyx stop whining."

The dog continued sniffing the unfamiliar trunk, then whining and pacing in agitation. "What is the matter, boy? What's wrong?"

Picking up the lantern, she studied the trunk in question while the dog continued his strange behavior. "No, I can't open it," she told the dog. But examining it more closely, she noticed that the clasps hung open. "Probably it belongs to our host. It would be rude to—"

Serenity's eyes popped open when suddenly she heard a gasp come from the trunk. Onyx barked and leaped about in a frenzy. Placing the lantern on the lid of her own trunk and setting the bandages beside it, the young woman glanced about the darkened barn to be certain no one was around. She took a deep breath and lifted the lid. From within, two large round dark eyes stared up at her. Serenity inhaled sharply, as did the small black child curled up in the bottom of the trunk.

The frightened child popped out of the trunk and dashed through the barn door and into the night. Serenity's mouth dropped open in surprise. It was the same person she'd collided with onboard the riverboat. She stared at the worn quilt in the bottom of the trunk and mumbled, "How did she get here?"

"So you found her." Aaron stepped out of the shadows. "I was afraid you would."

Serenity whirled about to face him, her eyes wide with fear.

"Old O'Gilvie's runaway girl. Felicity and I have been protecting her since we boarded the Mississippi riverboat."

Serenity shook her head; her jaw hung open in confusion. "You helped a runaway slave girl?"

"Five actually." Aaron's face beamed in the lamplight.

"Five? And Mrs. Rose helped you?"

A crooked grin filled his face.

Serenity's thoughts were ajumble. "So that's what you were doing associating with that woman?"

He grinned. "You could say that."

"Do your folks know?"

He shook his head. "Naw, this was my project. Caleb and my father are always involved in heroic gestures. This one was all mine."

"Aren't you going to tell them? They think—" Color crept up Serenity's neck and face. "I did see you kissing her on the deck one night."

"I was afraid you had." Aaron closed the lid on the trunk and sat down. "Felicity is a beautiful woman, and, well, I made a mistake. But that doesn't diminish the good we did."

"I guess not. . . . But how did you get involved in this scheme?"

Aaron hoisted one leg onto the trunk. "In the course of conversation that first night, she learned why we left New York. That's when she told me she's a former slave, a quadroon from New Orleans." He picked up a piece of straw and chewed on it for several moments before continuing. "She ran away to Michigan and passed herself off as white. That's where she met Jim Rose, her husband."

"Speaking of which," Serenity asked, "what happens now that she's back with her husband?"

A shadow crossed the young man's face. "She's home with her husband; and I, well, I begin my new life, at least I will once I conduct this slave girl to Kansas."

"What then?" Serenity gently touched the man's arm.

He shrugged.

Serenity wrapped her shawl tightly about her body. "I'm sorry, but I think you should tell your parents what you've been doing."

"I will, in time. But, now, if you'll excuse me, I have to go searching for Regina." Aaron strode from the barn without looking back.

Remembering the gold bars in the bottom of her own trunks, Serenity checked to be certain they were still safely hidden. "Tomorrow I must bring them into the house," she told herself.

Onyx pressed against Serenity's skirts. "Good boy. You're a good boy, Onyx." She patted his head, gathered the bandages in her arms and the lantern in her hand, and returned to the house.

Caleb looked at her strangely when she entered, but asked no questions. Serenity was relieved. The last thing she wanted to do was cause additional conflicts between the two brothers.

Morning came much too early at the mission. Onboard the riverboat, Serenity had gotten accustomed to awakening late. This day she awakened to the clatter of pots and pans coming from the great room. Wanting to do her share to help Analee, Serenity leaped from the bed and threw on one of her cotton gingham dresses over her slips and brushed and pinned up her hair before hurrying to the kitchen. Fay stood at the table shredding potatoes while Analee diced an onion for hash browns.

"Good morning." Fay looked up from the pile of freshly shredded potatoes. "Did you sleep well?"

"Good morning, Aunt Fay, Analee." Serenity tied a kitchen towel around her waist. "I did when I finally adjusted to the stillness of the bed and the silence."

The women laughed. "Me too," Fay added. "Once I awoke and wondered why the paddle wheel had stopped. Is Becca awake?"

Serenity shook her head. "Sleeping like an angel, if angels sleep." She held out her hands. "Hmm, bread baking?"

"Fresh every morning." A note of pride crept into Analee's voice. "Cyril loves his bread."

"Serenity," Fay interrupted, "we could use some fresh milk from the barn."

The girl looked aghast. "I'm sorry, Aunt Fay, but I don't know how to milk a cow, I'm afraid."

Fay laughed. "The men are doing the morning chores, honey. All you need to do is bring us a full bucket."

"Oh." Relief flooded across Serenity's face. "Is the bucket out there or—?"

"Over by the wet sink, the large galvanized one." Analee pointed to the pantry beyond the kitchen. "Could you also bring back a couple squash from the root cellar?"

"OK." Serenity skipped over to the pantry and found the bucket.

"Behind the door, you'll find a gunnysack for carrying the squash," Analee called.

"Got it," Serenity called back, hurrying out the side door toward the barn.

Heavy, black clouds cast a gray pall on the countryside. She eyed them suspiciously. *Could the first snow fall this early in the season,* she wondered. A biting wind out of the west answered her question. Recalling the warmth she'd enjoyed in the barn the previous night, she broke into a run.

Aaron met her at the open barn door. "A little chilly," he said, taking the pail from her hands.

"Brr! I'll say." She shivered and rubbed her arms. "I'm here to get a bucket of milk for breakfast and a couple squash from the cellar."

"Where's the girl?" Serenity asked.

"Safe for now. We'll leave for Kansas tonight." Aaron strode over to a side door in the barn, where Serenity followed him down the six steps into a root cellar. "Mr. Doran tells me this is not only for food preservation, but is also a shelter when a tornado comes."

Serenity glanced around at the dirt walls with no windows. The walls were lined with shelves of preserved food as well as pickled eggs in large kettles, drying herbs suspended from the low rafters, barrels of apples, sacks of potatoes, and steamed fruit hanging in linen bags. A claustrophobic place to be sure, Serenity noticed.

"A tornado?" She'd read about tornadoes in her science book as a student at the ladies' academy outside of Boston. She didn't like what she remembered.

"Yep, guess they can be a problem around here in the spring and the fall."

Serenity loaded three good-sized squash into the bag.

"They pack quite a wallop too," Aaron chuckled, standing between her and the stairs.

"Excuse me—" Serenity tried to pass, but whichever way she went, he stepped into her path.

"Ya gotta give me a kiss first," the younger Cunard teased.

Serenity glared. "Aaron, please let me by. Analee needs these squash."

"Come on, you play little games with Caleb. Why not me?"

"Aaron! Let me by. Now!" The young woman pushed him to one side. Reluctantly, he let her pass.

"So that's how it is? Big brother gets the girl too?" Aaron's lips tightened, his eyes narrowed.

"I beg your pardon! If you're looking for a replacement for Felicity, I'm not it." She arched one disdainful eyebrow, remembering the words she'd heard her mother say: "There are some women who refuse to settle for a man who plays at romance."

Emerging from the root cellar, Serenity found herself face to face with Caleb's boots. He stood on the top step, his arms crossed and legs spread. "Is everything all right?"

"Actually, no." She smiled up into his irritated face. "I need a bucket of milk for breakfast. Could you help me, please?"

Caleb picked up the bucket Aaron had left beside the root cellar door and helped Serenity up the last step. "What was that all about? Was my little brother bothering you?" he hissed.

She lifted her nose confidently, though her knees shook like jelly. "Nothing I can't handle."

Caleb eyed her suspiciously. "If you ever need me, let me know."

Her eyes softened. "You really are a good man, Caleb Cunard. Thank you for caring." Her fingers rested on his bare forearm. A tremor passed between them. Their eyes met in surprise. Neither spoke for an instant. Then Serenity cleared her throat. "I'd better get that milk."

Caleb nodded, unable to speak. He strode across the barn to the stalls, poured the milk from his milking pail into the bucket, and returned to where Serenity waited. "I'll carry it inside for you. It's heavy. Here, let me take the sack as well."

Clutching the rough-textured gunnysack and swinging it gently from side to side like a school girl, she smiled up into his face. "Thank you, but I can manage it."

Caleb's dark eyes sparkled. "I'd forgotten how cute you look in the morning."

His words took her aback. She cast him a coy grin. "Why, Caleb Cunard, are you flirting with me?"

His smile broadened. "Maybe. Would you like it if I were?"

Her eyes twinkled. "Maybe." Casting one last grin toward Caleb, she skipped out of the barn and sashayed toward the house.

"Hey, wait for me," he called, breaking into long strides to catch up with her.

Serenity glanced over her shoulder to measure how far he was behind her when she spotted Aaron leaning against the barn door, his arms folded and his face hard.

~12~
A New Kind
of Love

THE SNOW DIDN'T COME AS EVERYONE EXPECTED. Instead, the weather took a turn for the better, as warmer temperatures during the day brought on a pleasant Indian summer. More often than not, Felix Bonner used whatever excuse he could find—or so it seemed to Serenity—to visit the Indian mission. One day he delivered a letter from back East to Eli. Another day he arrived in his fancy brougham with a crate of fresh apples from St. Louis. "I thought you folks would enjoy these pippins. They make great pies, so my housekeeper has discovered." He patted his stomach and licked his lips.

One morning Caleb was home when Felix arrived. Instinctively, Serenity sensed the tension between the two men. On the riverboat up the Mississippi and across the Missouri, the bounds of propriety kept the two men's behavior in tow. But out here on the prairie, Serenity wasn't sure what might happen. While she knew she was the spark, she had no idea what to do about it.

From the clothesline, Serenity waved and went to meet the young attorney as he climbed down from his carriage. "My, aren't you looking beautiful today." He grinned and took her hand.

Serenity blushed. "You always know what to say to make a girl feel good."

"It's true. The sun brings out red highlights in your hair." He reached his hand toward a wisp that had escaped the confines of her chignon, but froze at the sound of Caleb's voice calling from the barn.

"So, what are you doing way out here?" he called, wiping his soiled hands on a rag from his pocket.

"Caleb, just the man I came to see."

By the look in Caleb's eye, Serenity could see he doubted the lawyer's words. "Well, come on into the barn where we can talk while I repair Doran's tack. The harness straps are in mighty bad shape."

Serenity returned to hanging the weekly wash on Analee's clothesline. She picked up several clothespins and stuffed them in her mouth. Straightening out a bedsheet, she draped it over the line and pinned it in place. As she bent over to get a second sheet, she heard shouting in the barn.

Serenity cast a nervous glance toward the barn. "What in the world?" The voices grew louder.

". . . imperialism through and through!" Serenity heard Caleb shout.

Felix's reply was equally impassioned: "From coast to coast, that's America's destiny if we intend to survive as a united country!"

"But do we have to pillage and destroy everything in our way?" Caleb snapped.

"Look, maybe you'll understand more when you see your first pioneer wagon limping back to Independence after an Indian attack."

"They wouldn't attack if we weren't driving them from their land!" Caleb argued, full voice.

As Serenity secured the second sheet in place, she debated whether or not she should go to the barn and interrupt the two men.

"Now hold your horses, Caleb," she heard Felix shout. "When it's your father or your sister killed by Indian arrows, or Serenity, we'll see if you still feel—"

"Leave Serenity out of this!"

"That's the real issue here, isn't it? Not the Indians or the Mexicans, but Serenity."

"I don't know what you're talking about," Caleb growled.

"I think you do," the lawyer argued. "Do the two of you have an agreement I don't know about?"

The wind whipped a wet sheet against Serenity's face. She pawed herself free of the soggy cotton. *What in the world is going on in there?* She dropped the wooden clothespins atop the wet clothes still in the basket and headed for the open barn door. She stepped inside the barn. The two men were standing toe to toe, fists clenched and teeth set on edge.

"Hello there, what's going on? I can hear the two of you all the way over by the clothesline."

The men's faces reddened. Caleb rubbed the back of his neck while Felix wiped his face with a handkerchief. Felix recovered first. "Everything's just fine, Miss Serenity. We're just discussing politics—you know, male things."

Serenity arched her eyebrows. "Male things, Mr. Bonner? The only real politics I heard was two roosters scratching around in a hen yard."

Caleb chuckled nervously and eyed Felix. "She's got ya there, Bonner."

Serenity watched as Felix stretched out a hand toward Caleb. "Friends?"

Caleb eyed the outstretched hand for a second, then

slowly grasped it. "Sorry. I sort of lost my composure for a while there."

"Hmmph! Me too, and I'm a lawyer." His face reddened a second time. "I'm trained not to do that."

"And what about me?" Serenity asked, her hands firmly planted on her hips.

Caleb scratched his head. "I wouldn't exactly call you—"

"Of course you're a friend, Serenity," Felix interrupted, taking one of her hands into his. "And a dear one at that."

The young woman eyed him curiously. "You're treating me like a child who needs to be appeased. Why?"

"It's not that. It's just that friendships are different between two men than they are between a man and a woman." When Felix touched the back of her hand to his lips, Caleb growled and snatched Serenity's hand from the lawyer's grasp.

"Don't you have wet clothes to hang or something?" Caleb snarled at the young woman.

"I beg your pardon?" Serenity glared and snatched her hand away from Caleb's.

Caleb reddened, then glanced down. "I'm sorry. That was inappropriate of me."

"You can say that again!" she hissed.

Felix cleared his throat and mumbled something about heading back to town. Caleb and Serenity walked him to his carriage and waved good-bye until it disappeared from view.

"Now, what was that all about?" she asked.

"I don't want to talk about it right now." He turned and walked into the barn.

"Fine!" Serenity swung her skirts about and headed toward the clothesline.

A strained silence passed between the two during the

rest of the day and into the evening. Occasionally during the evening meal, Serenity intercepted questioning glances passing between the other members of the family; but she chose to ignore them.

The next morning Serenity sat on an upside-down bucket in front of the sod house, churning the day's supply of milk into butter. Of all the morning chores, Serenity enjoyed churning butter the most. She used it as a special time when she could discuss her concerns with God. This particular morning, Caleb was on her mind. Caleb and Felix.

A cry came from inside the house, and Serenity knew Fay must be changing the dressings on Becca's leg. It had been a rough week for Becca and her parents, as the child's leg refused to heal from the snakebite. They had been unable to locate a doctor at any stop along the river and Becca's leg had not improved since they reached the Doran's mission. Dr. Gates had driven out from town twice to see Becca. Each time, before he left, he shook his head and mumbled his regrets to Fay. Every morning and every night the Cunard family and the Dorans gathered about Becca and prayed for her healing. But when Fay changed the girl's bandages, the leg appeared more fiery and swollen than before.

This morning, Serenity scolded God for taking so long healing Becca. "The little girl has suffered so much, Father. Can't You do something?" She paused after her frustrated outburst. "Forgive me, Lord. You are God. You know what is best. I know that."

The young woman turned her face to the sun's rays and closed her eyes, basking in its warmth. She didn't see two Shawnee Indians, a man and a woman, approach where she sat until their shadows fell upon her. With a woolen blanket wrapped about her shoulders, the woman clutched a leather pouch in her hands. By their weathered faces, Serenity imagined them to be in their late forties. She'd heard several tall tales about the Plains Indians since arriving in Independence, but so far she had only seen a few Shawnees from a distance. Now her heart leapt in fear.

Cyril and Eli had gone into town on business. Caleb had gone with them. And who knew where Aaron might be! Ever since he'd returned from Kansas, he'd been scarce. Onyx? The two had arrived so silently that Onyx remained stretched out asleep on the grass several feet away. Serenity shot a quick glance toward the front door of the mission house, then toward the barn. *Where is Analee? Wait a minute, dummy,* she scolded, *this is a mission, an Indian mission. What should I expect to see here?* Taking a deep breath, Serenity smiled and rose to her feet.

"Hello, may I help you?" She spoke slowly and distinctly.

The man removed his hat from his head, and in correct English he said, "I am Joseph Blackwing. This is my wife, Gray Sparrow. We are here to see the sick child."

"Sick child?"

The man nodded once.

"Uh, she's in the house. Becca's in the house." Serenity gestured toward the sod building behind her.

The couple waited, their hands by their sides. *What am I supposed to do next?* Serenity wondered. She smiled back at the visitors. "I think Mrs. Doran is in the house. Would you like to see her?"

The Indian man tipped his head toward the young woman. "We are here to see the child."

"I'll find Aunt Fay." Serenity ran to the house and burst through the front door. "Aunt Fay, Analee, there are two

Indians here who want to—" The young woman stopped midsentence and slowly glanced over her shoulder. Her face reddened. The couple stood directly behind her.

Fay stood in the doorway to the bedroom wing of the house while Analee looked up from her spinning. The Doran woman rose to her feet. The bobbin fell to the floor, but the wheel kept spinning. "Joseph and Gray Sparrow, I've been hoping you'd come by." Analee hurried to greet her visitors, taking their hands in hers. "How are you? I haven't seen you for a very long time."

"We are back from the high country," the Shawnee man explained. "The young bucks report that a child is sick from a snakebite. She is a guest of yours, Mrs. Doran?"

"Yes," the woman sighed. "We're doing all we can. Dr. Gates has been here twice and he can do nothing. We are leaving the child in God's hands."

A tight grin formed on the Indian man's face. "Perhaps Gray Sparrow will be the hands of your God."

Serenity bristled, but stood silently awaiting Analee's reply.

"Perhaps God sent you to the child, Gray Sparrow." She turned and gestured toward Fay. "This is the child's mother, Fay Cunard. And you already met my other guest, Serenity Pownell."

The Shawnee man nodded toward me. "Serenity, what a pretty name. Are you serene?"

Serenity gulped. "I try to be."

He smiled. "Perhaps, not yet. You are young. You will become your name as you grow in wisdom, daughter."

A look of irritation flashed across her face, but the visitor appeared not to notice. Instead, Analee started toward the pantry. "Joseph, may I get a drink of fresh cider for you and Gray Sparrow?"

The man shook his head. "We are not here to take, but to give. Is that not what the Good Book says, 'It is better to give than to receive?' Where is the little girl?"

Analee started in surprise. "Yes, it certainly does." She pivoted toward the bedroom, gesturing for both Fay and the Indians to follow.

"No." He lifted his hand. "I will stay here while Gray Sparrow cares for the child."

"Does she understand English?" Analee asked.

"She understands, but does not speak. She lost her tongue as a child when trappers pillaged her village."

Serenity gasped aloud. Fay and Serenity exchanged concerned glances, then followed Analee and the Shawnee woman to the bedroom where Becca lay resting. The previous night had been especially difficult for the little girl. Neither Becca nor Serenity had slept much. Serenity tried to comfort the child, but nothing eased her pain. The girl thrashed about so much that Serenity took one of the quilts from the shelf behind the bed and curled up with a pillow on the floor at the foot of the bed.

Fay hurried ahead of the Indian woman to prepare Becca for their arrival while Serenity followed behind Analee and Gray Sparrow. Entering the room, they saw Becca braced up with pillows so she could greet her unexpected guest.

The child grimaced in pain when Fay threw back the covers and removed the bandages. The Shawnee woman examined the girl's leg from one side, then the other. Opening the leather pouch she carried, she extracted several smaller animal skin pouches, a small gray stone bowl, and a pestle. She hummed an eerie, monotone tune as she tore several leaves into small pieces and placed them in the bowl. The oils from the herbs filled the room with a pungent aroma. Becca and the women watched as Gray Sparrow added a few drops of what appeared to be oil from a leather flask, then pulverized the mixture in the stone bowl.

Gray Sparrow paused to glance about the room. Spotting the clean bandages Fay had laid on the oak dresser in the corner of the room, she placed a handful of them on the bed. Dipping her fingers into the herbal poultice, Gray Sparrow slathered the concoction on the injury, then wrapped the leg with the fresh bandages.

After securing the bandage, the Shawnee woman gathered her herbs and equipment together and gently touched Becca's frightened face. The woman's lips moved as she bowed her head for a moment. Opening her eyes, she turned and walked to the great room. Joseph Blackwing waited by the door, his arms folded and his face unreadable.

Fay took the woman's hands in hers. "Thank you so much, Gray Sparrow. Thank you. How did your young men learn about my daughter's infection?" she said, facing Joseph Blackwing.

"We know what we need to know, Mrs. Cunard."

"Well, I am so thankful for your help today. Thank you once again."

Analee rushed through the great room to her kitchen pantry. She returned with a small willow basket filled with pickled eggs. "Here, please, enjoy. I know how much you like my pickled eggs."

The Shawnee man shook his head slowly. "Gray Sparrow will be back in two days to change the dressing. The girl will be walking before the Sunday services." He bowed slightly to each of the women, opened the door, then departed, his wife following closely on his heels.

Fay ran to her daughter's room. "How do you feel, honey? Do you want me to remove those bandages?"

"No." The girl shook her tangled curls. "It feels kind of good."

"Well, whatever it is"—Aunt Fay sniffed the herbal mixture again—"I guess it can't make the infection much worse than it already is."

When the men came home from town that evening and learned of the Shawnees' visit, Mr. Doran exploded with joy. "They're listening. The Shawnees are listening! I preach God's love and feel like they never hear a thing, but they are listening and this proves it."

"What is the story with Joseph Blackwing?" Fay asked. "He speaks excellent English."

Cyril nodded. "Joseph speaks fluent French as well. He was raised in the East by a merchant and his French-speaking wife." The man cast his gaze heavenward. "It hasn't been all in vain. Thank You, Lord."

By bedtime, Becca's fever had subsided. Eli carried her out to the great room to participate in worship. Mr. Doran read the love chapter, 1 Corinthians 13.

Two days later, Gray Sparrow returned and applied a sour-smelling poultice to the greatly improved leg. By Sunday, Becca rode in the wagon when the family went to the Shawnee village for the church service.

Her first visit to an Indian village, Serenity eagerly took in everything—the teepees draped in animal skins, the chanting, the children, the beautiful beadwork on the women's moccasins. She eyed the strange meat rotating over a fire as well. When offered a piece, she knew better than to ask of its origin. *Whatever it is,* she thought as she bit into the sizzling meat, *it certainly tastes good.*

On the drive home, Serenity fell asleep. When she awoke, she was embarrassed to find her head resting on

Caleb's shoulder. She mumbled an apology and scurried into the house.

Later, as Serenity took a stroll under the stars before retiring for the night, she thought about the beautiful example of love she'd witnessed. A woman, maimed for life by white men, shared her healing love with a white child she'd never met before. *Truly Gray Sparrow's gift spoke of God's love,* she thought.

Scooping her skirts in her hands, Serenity hiked up a small incline to the highest spot on the mission property. From there, it seemed like forever was at her fingertips. The light from the mission house glowed in the darkness of the moonless night. She sat down on a large boulder, gathered her knees to her chest, and gazed westward.

Her mind wandered back to her home in New York. She thought about the love her parents showed for runaway slaves, risking their personal comfort and their fortune for people they'd never met. She thought about the quiet witness the Cunards demonstrated aboard the riverboat. "That's what Your love is all about, Lord, isn't it?"

And now, the Dorans. *Life should be more than just eking out an existence, even here on the prairie,* she mused. *Even the wealthy Josephine lives her life giving to others,* she thought with a smile. "Lord, I'm not a healer like Gray Sparrow, nor a preacher like Uncle Eli. Whatever I am, Lord, please use me somehow. Show me where You need me and what You need me to do."

Serenity rose to her feet and turned slowly toward the mission house. For a moment, she watched the light from a lantern bob along the pathway from the house to the barn.

She yawned and stretched. *Tomorrow will begin earlier than I wish,* she thought, turning her feet toward the mission house. As she entered the barnyard, the words from a hymn she'd heard Fay sing to Becca came to her mind: "Softly now the light of day . . . "

Walking past the barn, she heard someone harmonizing with her. "Free from care, from labor free . . . " Recognizing Caleb's deep baritone voice, she turned and smiled at him as he came toward her. He fell into step beside her and together they sang the last line to the old hymn: "Lord, we would commune with Thee."

"Hi." A silly grin filled her face.

"Hi," he replied. "I thought you got lost out here."

"You were worried about me?"

"I always worry about you," he admitted.

"That's nice," she cooed, stumbling over a rock in her pathway. His strong hands caught her. He held her a second or two longer than necessary, his dark eyes gazing into hers. "You need to be more careful." His voice was husky.

"Yes, I guess I do." She smiled up at him. "Thank you for being here to catch me from falling."

"My pleasure." Releasing her arms, he touched the brim of his hat. "I plan to always be here to catch you." He grinned. Grasping her hand in his, they strode toward the house together. "You come out here every night."

"I try. The night air clears my mind so I can sleep."

"You should take a lantern with you."

She chuckled gently. "I come out to see the stars. A lantern would ruin the effect." The warmth of his hand cradling hers brought a glow to her cheeks.

"I see what you mean." He set their arms to swinging. "It really is beautiful out here at night, isn't it?"

I could walk like this 'til morning, Serenity thought. All too soon, they reached the house. Caleb held the door as Serenity entered, only to discover that the Dorans had already retired for the night. The man's cough had worsened since the Cunards first arrived at the mission, and now it wracked his entire body.

Fay and Becca had also gone to bed. Only Eli sat in a rocker beside the fire reading. He looked up from his Bible.

"Well, hello, you two. I was about ready to send out the buffalo scouts." He laughed while Caleb and Serenity blushed. "Fay's settling Becca in for the night. It's wonderful to see Becca up and about again."

"Sure is, Pa. By the way, where's Aaron?" Caleb asked.

A frown coursed Eli's face as he glanced down at the open book before him.

Serenity moved closer to the fireplace as if to warm her hands over the dying coals. Caleb did the same.

Eli looked up and eyed them curiously. Then slapping his thigh, he stood up. "It's time for me to hit the hay—busy day tomorrow." He strode to the hallway, casting a glance over his shoulder. "Don't stay up too late, you two."

Serenity shot a look of surprise at Caleb. "What did he mean by that?"

A wry smile crossed the young man's face. "Who knows?"

Serenity sat down on the raised stone hearth and stroked Onyx's head. Smoothing her skirts over her knees, she hugged her knees to her chest. Without a word, Caleb dropped himself to the floor in front of her and took her hands in his. Onyx pushed his muzzle onto the young man's lap.

Serenity studied Caleb's face in the light of the open fire. She studied the contours of his cheekbones and his strong angular chin. Something had changed between them in the last few days, of that she was certain. And she thanked God for whatever caused it.

Caleb cleared his throat, but his words still came out

husky and filled with emotion. "Serenity, I've been thinking. You and me, we, uh . . . " Red crept up his neck and into his face. He dropped his head and flexed the muscles in his jaw for several seconds before speaking again. "Serenity, would you be favorable to my courtin' you? I've talked this over with my father and he agrees it's time."

"It's time? I don't understand."

"Well, it's been long enough after the loss of your parents, and you are now eighteen, and all . . . " His words trailed off. Finally he lifted his eyes to her, a frown deepening on his brow. "Of course, I won't interfere if Felix Bonner holds your affections."

She snatched her hands from his grasp. "Caleb Cunard. I don't believe you. I've told you before, Felix does not hold my affections. He's a friend, that's all."

A crooked grin lifted one side of Caleb's mouth. "Not in his mind, I assure you."

"That's ridiculous. You are imagining things."

"Believe me, it's not my imagination."

"Did he ever say anything of the sort to you?" she asked.

He shook his head. "He doesn't have to."

Serenity clicked her tongue. "Well, if you're so good at recognizing other people's feelings, why has it taken you so long to identify mine?"

Caleb blinked in surprise.

"I've done everything but accost you." Remembering the kiss she stole aboard the riverboat, she blushed. "Maybe I've done that too, come to think of it."

Caleb's face reddened as well. "Then you agree?"

Lovingly she caressed the side of his face, appreciating the roughness of his beard on the palm of her hand. "Definitely," she whispered hoarsely.

Caleb captured her hand in his and drew it to his lips. His eyes glistened with tears. Tenderly, he kissed each of her fingertips. "You are so beautiful, Serenity Pownell. It seems like I've loved you forever."

"Forever? I thought you saw me as a pesky sister."

He threw back his head and laughed. "Hardly. I assure you that I have never thought of you that way!"

"I'm glad." She studied his eyes for several seconds. "When did you first know that you loved me?"

"In Boston, in Mrs. Crookshank's office."

"No!"

"Oh, yes. I wanted to reach out and protect you from the awful news of your mother's death. I wanted to shelter you in my arms." He rose to his feet. Taking her hands in his, he drew her up to face him. "Serenity Pownell, I love you so very much. I will always be here for you, to protect you from all the hurts and dangers of life."

Security blinked a few times, trying to catch her breath.

"Say you love me too." His eyes pleaded with her.

"Oh, I do. I do love you. You've held me at arm's length for so long, I began to wonder if you'd ever love me in return."

He drew her to him. "No more." Focusing his gaze on her lips, he slowly dipped his head toward her. She closed her eyes. Her heart pounded in eager anticipation. Their lips met, tenderly at first, but deepening into a soul-satisfying kiss, one that sent shock waves all the way to Serenity's toes. She hoped it would never end.

When he released her, Caleb stepped back and stared at Serenity in surprise. "Whew!" He inhaled sharply, then exhaled a ragged breath. Surprised with the emotion the kiss unleashed in him, he stared at the young woman for several seconds, then crushed her against his chest. His heart beat erratically as he bent his head toward her lips once more.

Without warning, the cabin door flew open and crashed against the wall. Aaron staggered into the mission house, his hair disheveled, his clothes dirty and torn. "Well, well, well, sorry to interrupt your little party." His words slurred into one another. "Just continue doing whatever you were doing." He staggered across the room to the kitchen pantry. "Do you think old Cyril has anything around here to drink? Besides water, that is." He giggled and stumbled over a chair beside the door.

Caleb sauntered to his brother's side. "Looks to me like you've had enough to drink for one night, li'l brother." He took his arm. "Here, let me help you to bed."

"Always the big brother. Always the hero." Aaron giggled again and leaned on Caleb's shoulder.

Caleb shot a glance at Serenity. "Sorry. I'd better get him to bed before he injures himself. Good night, sweetheart." He pressed his index finger to his lips and blew it to her.

"Goodnight," the girl whispered. Alone, Serenity strolled over to one of the rockers and made herself comfortable. There was no way she'd be able to sleep after all that had transpired that evening. Noticing Eli's Bible laying beside the chair, she opened its well-worn cover. On the dedication page, it read: "June 15, 1826. To my precious husband Eli on our wedding day. 'Whither thou goest, I will go. Whither thou lodgest, I will lodge.' I will love you 'til death do us part. Lovingly yours, Fay."

Serenity mouthed the rest of the words to the vow made in the book of Ruth. "Thy people shall be my people, and thy God, my God." Pressing the book to her chest, Serenity whispered a prayer of her own: "If only Caleb's and my love can be as strong and as beautiful as Aunt Fay's and Uncle Eli's, Lord."

—13—

More Love
to Give

Independence, Missouri
October 19, 1850

Dear Josephine,

I never imagined I'd find myself west of the Mississippi River, but here I am living on the brink of a wild and untamed land. Sometimes I think I can see beyond the horizons—into eternity, in fact. And at night—the stars are incredible. Some nights they're so close, I think I can reach up and snag one for my own.

You wouldn't believe the people here. To call this place civilized would take a lot of imagination. Spanish vaqueros rub shoulders with genuine mountain men. Indians in full regalia buy tobacco and salt for the winter alongside Russian immigrant farmers. Ladies-of-the-evening shop for gingham and lace in the dry goods stores just as pastors' wives and Sunday school teachers. Barroom brawls erupt every Saturday night; yet, on Sunday morning, families and roustabouts alike fill the pews of the local churches.

Because of the loose morals associated with the rooming houses and hotels in town, the Cunards chose to seek shelter at a local Indian mission for the winter. Cyril and Analee Doran came here from Louisiana to build the sod and stone mission. It's the fulfillment of a longtime dream of Cyril's. From where I sit, I don't think either of the Dorans are well enough to run the establishment. She's recovering from the loss of a baby, and he's got some fierce lung disease that grows worse by the day.

Analee's father, Chesterfield Bancroft, arrived at the mission this morning. He seems very disgruntled and has been rude to Mr. Doran. I haven't figured out what this is all about yet, but time will tell. The pompous little cotton emperor (at least that's what I like to call him) can't wait too long or he'll be stuck here 'til spring. Eeeugh! What a thought!

In the meantime, Aunt Fay and I have taken over much of the housework Analee had been doing, including the food preservation for winter. Ugh! An incredibly horrid task! We work from morning 'til night boiling, chopping, pickling, salting. It never stops. There's always another gunnysack of food to be processed.

But our larder is getting full. The storm cellar looks like a meat market in downtown Boston. Slabs of corned beef hang from the rafters. Crates of apples are stacked in the corners along with gunnysacks of potatoes. My favorite is the barrel of pickles. At the rate I'm eating them, they won't last past Christmas! Yum!

Josephine, I never knew the average woman worked so hard! If I never see another slab of corned beef again, I will be happy. I can't help but ask myself why any intelligent woman would want to marry any man, have babies, and work herself into the grave just keeping her family fed! No wonder women die young.

Speaking of romance, Caleb and I are officially courting. He works at Ross Camp blacksmithing. We spend most evenings together chatting by the fire with the family. Sometimes he sits in the kitchen while Becca and I finish the dinner dishes. And believe it or not, he's been known to pick up a dish towel every now and then and dry a pot or a pan! I can't remember my dad ever doing such a thing.

The three of us take long walks together, Caleb, Onyx, and I. (Onyx is as sassy as ever.) And we talk. It seems like Caleb and I never run out of things to say. He tells me about his day at Ross Camp, and I tell him about my adventures learning how to operate a real kitchen—not one like I had back home with dozens of servants to do the hard part. And we talk about our dreams. You'd be surprised how similar my dreams are to his. I know, I'm talking out of both sides of my mouth. First I disparage marriage, then I tell you about Caleb. I don't know how to explain it.

Serenity's mind drifted from the sheets of parchment paper in front of her to the silent prairie beyond her bedroom window. A movement in the shadows by the barn caught her attention. She watched as a man, uncertain on his footing, weaved in and out of the shadows. Instead of coming toward the house, the man slid open the door to the hayloft and disappeared inside.

A shiver skittered up Serenity's spine. Something in his mannerisms told her it was Aaron. He came home intermittently of late; most of the time he stayed in town. When he did return to the mission, he and Eli inevitably had an argument in the barn—she could only imagine about what. One morning when she and Fay rode into town for canning supplies, Serenity had seen the younger Cunard son coming out of a questionable rooming house. If Fay saw him as well, she didn't say so, though there was a marked change in the older woman's countenance for the rest of the excursion.

"How can Aaron be so insensitive to his parents? How can he bring such shame on them?" she asked God during her evening prayer that night. "I don't understand him at all." She hurt for her Aunt Fay and Uncle Eli, and included them in her prayers.

Chesterfield Bancroft had been at the mission for less than two days when Serenity first encountered the true man beneath his well-groomed facade. It was wash day. The basket she carried towered over her as she juggled it through the mission house's back door into the great room. Not knowing anyone was about, Serenity plunked the basket on one of the shiny oak benches beside the table. She straightened, grasping her middle back. "Ooh!" she groaned.

"Young lady," Mr. Bancroft's sharp voice sounded from the sofa, "do not set that wicker basket on the table bench. It will scratch the wood. Carry it to your room to fold, if you please."

Serenity looked startled. "Sorry." She picked up the basket of clean bed linens. "If it bothers you, of course I'll fold the linens in my room."

"Thank you!" He pointedly lifted the book he'd been reading to his face. "Servants these days!"

Servant? The surprised girl dropped the basket to the floor. All her aristocratic upbringing flooded back to her as a wave of indignation. "Servant, sir?" She stood with her hands planted defiantly on her hips.

The plantation owner held the open book before his face. "Young lady, I will ignore you until you speak to me with respect, proper to a gentleman, an older gentleman, I might add."

Serenity could feel her nostrils flare with rage. One side of her brain realized that he, indeed, was her elder, and she must treat him as such. The other half wanted to give him a giant piece of her mind.

She strode around the basket, her arms folded across her chest. "Mr. Bancroft, perhaps you are not aware of my position in the Doran Mission. I am not a servant, and you, sir, are hardly a gentleman!"

The man rose to his feet to find himself a good three inches shorter than the young woman. His chest puffed out as he pressed the closed book to his chest. He lifted his nose. "Oh, yes, I'm sorry. It's not your fault that you're one of those Northern lassies who lack proper breeding."

Remembering her school friend, Eulilia, a cultivated flower of the South but hardly a spineless milksop, Serenity smiled the sweetest smile she could manage. "Sir, I discovered while traveling with my late parents that good breeding has more to do with common courtesy than with geography."

Chesterfield Bancroft's eyes flashed with anger. He took

a couple of steps in Serenity's direction, flexing and unflexing his fists as he walked. "If you were my daughter, I'd—"

She batted her eyelashes as she'd watched Eulilia do so often. "You would do what, Mr. Bancroft?"

Before he could answer, the cabin door opened. Serenity whirled about, delighted to find Caleb casting a giant shadow across the cabin floor.

"What was that you were saying?" Caleb asked, his eyes narrowing into two angry slits. Serenity could tell that he'd heard everything, and smiled.

If Mr. Bancroft had been angry before, he was now consumed with fury. The man had built a full head of steam and intended to use it on anyone in his way. "So you're one of those thieving Yankees. I heard why you left New York State."

"In case you weren't aware, Miss Pownell and I are paying guests in your daughter and son-in-law's establishment. We expect you and all others connected with the operation of this facility to treat us accordingly, sir." His gaze took in the basket of sheets. "Need help carrying that basket, Serenity?"

She nodded. "It is pretty heavy."

"Where would you like me to put it?" Caleb lifted the basket.

"On my bed would be fine," she said without thinking.

Caleb picked up on the direction the man's mind would go with that comment. "Perhaps I should put it in my mother's room. I'm sure she'll want to help you fold when she arrives from town."

"Good idea, thank you." Serenity blushed. "You're always such a gentleman."

Caleb beamed. "Glad to help."

Serenity followed him from the room without glancing back at Mr. Bancroft.

When Caleb left the cabin, Serenity recalled her surly attitude toward the older gentleman, wrestling with her guilt for almost an hour. Then, tired of the battle, the girl surrendered. She strolled slowly into the great room.

"Mr. Bancroft?" she asked timidly.

The man looked up from his book, his face rigid and cold.

"You were right before. I was being disrespectful to you, my elder. Please forgive me."

The man searched her face for any trace of sarcasm. When he found none, he frowned. "I, too, am sorry, Miss Serenity. I had no cause to treat you with disrespect. I think I was taking out on you my irritation at my daughter and her husband." The man's words sounded sincere, but his face did not change.

Serenity shrugged. "Thank you for understanding. Friends?" She extended her hand.

He stood and bowed from the waist. "Friends."

That evening both Felix and Aaron arrived in time for supper. Serenity was stirring the potato soup when she spotted Felix's fancy brougham bouncing along the dusty roadway. Her hands flew to her hair. "I'm a mess!" she announced to no one in particular. She glanced down at her apron in horror, then tried to brush the sweaty curls from her face. Flour coated her apron almost as well as it had the butcher-block breadboard upon which she'd rolled the dough into loaves for baking earlier that day.

Serenity dashed across the great room and down the hallway to her bedroom, removing her ivory combs as she ran. She raced to the bureau and snagged her brush through her tangled curls. As she replaced the combs in her hair, one of her hands brushed over her other hand and felt the roughness of her skin. Tears welled up in her eyes. Where had her soft delicate hands gone? She traced one long, tapered finger across the callouses on her other hand. "Once my hands were the envy of classmates and friends alike," she sniffed. "Now look at them!"

She could hear the men entering the mission house. Swiping away the tears in her eyes, she picked up her cut-glass perfume bottle and spritzed a few drops of her dwindling supply of French perfume on her neck.

By the time she returned to the great room, the Cunards, Felix Bonner, and the Dorans, along with Analee's father, were chatting together around the fireplace. While Becca set the table, Fay filled the soup bowls and Analee sliced a freshly baked loaf of bread to place on the table.

"Good evening." Serenity shot a coy grin toward Felix as she moved to help in the kitchen.

"We stopped to talk with Mr. Bonner while we were in town and invited him home for a good homemade meal," Fay volunteered, taking the flatware from Serenity's hands. "You've done enough today, dear. Go sit down. You must be exhausted. Where's Caleb?"

"Fetching some fresh milk," Serenity said, falling onto the sofa.

Analee fluttered about the kitchen, a nervous young hostess. "Cyril, why don't you introduce my father to Mr. Bonner?"

Awkwardly, Cyril swung around while Mr. Bancroft stood from his chair. "My father-in-law is visiting from Louisiana. He owns a large cotton plantation there." Addressing Mr. Bancroft, Cyril said, "Mr. Bonner is an attorney here in Independence."

"Pleased to meet you, Mr. Bonner." The two men shook hands, each respecting the other's station, yet it was clear there was a dislike between them.

"So, you are an attorney? How did you happen to set up shop here, of all places?" Mr. Bancroft asked, taking his seat again.

Felix smiled. "Actually, I was born here. I studied at Harvard, then returned home to practice law."

Mr. Bancroft smiled. "So you're part of what we easterners call, 'frontier justice'?"

A flash of anger crossed Felix's face, then disappeared as quickly as it had come. "Frontier justice is swifter and often more fair than the justice administered by law books."

Mr. Bancroft grunted. "What does your law say about the theft of one's personal property?"

The lawyer pursed his lips. "Why do you ask?"

"I've only been here for two days, counselor"—the plantation owner expanded his chest and hooked his thumbs around his suspenders—"but I've uncovered the identity of a family of felons on the run from the law."

"Really?" The attorney slipped one hand in his side pants pocket.

"Without a doubt. They are part of the Underground Railroad. You've heard of it, of course. It seems that the state of Missouri has unwittingly given asylum to these thieving vermin." The plantation owner shot a satisfied glance toward Eli, then Aaron. "Rumor is, they've resumed their criminal activities."

Felix gave a crooked grin. "Is that so? You know, Mr. Bancroft, in some places aiding and abetting runaway slaves is not a criminal offense."

"It is in the state of Missouri," Mr. Bancroft shot back.

The look on Cyril's face was one of bewilderment and confusion. Serenity watched as he sent a silent cry for help to his wife. Shaking herself alert, Analee invited her guests to the table. "I hope you all have good appetites tonight. Serenity made more than enough stew for everyone." Analee swept to her father's side and coaxed him to the table just as Caleb appeared with the milk. Once everyone was seated, Cyril offered a blessing for the food.

The conversation at the table was stilted, as if each diner waited for the atmosphere to explode with violence. Once the guests congratulated their hostess and Serenity for the good food they were enjoying, everyone reverted to their private thoughts. Everyone but Aaron.

Aaron looked like he was "loaded for bear," as he often called it. He slathered his bread with freshly made butter, then took a bite. "Tell me, Mr. Bancroft, why do you believe you have the right to own another human being?"

Color rushed to the plantation owner's face. "I never dreamed I would break bread with Northern abolitionists at my own daughter's table," he muttered loud enough for everyone to hear.

"Papa," Analee placed her hand on his. "Please, for me?"

Felix speared a chunk of potato with his fork. "Actually, a better question to ask might be why does America need slavery? Other countries are beginning to realize their economy can survive without slave labor. Why not the United States?"

"Sir," Cyril interrupted, "certainly you realize that the South's entire economy is based on slave labor, unlike the North who espouses the use of young children in their factories. Their indentured servants are hardly more than slaves, I think."

"You're right, of course, Mr. Doran." Eli patted his mouth with his cotton napkin. "There are many injustices in this world. And I believe the good Lord put us here to right our brothers' wrongs."

"Speaking from my own upbringing," Cyril expounded, "my parents' slaves are treated like family. Their backs have never been striped with the whip. They live comfortable lives on my father's estate, growing old with their children and grandchildren by their sides."

"Comfortable lives! I think there's more to freedom than comfort!" Aaron leaned forward into the table. "My folks are following a dream to move to California. But if we were colored, we wouldn't be allowed—no matter how kind our owner was!"

"Aaron," Felix addressed the young Cunard like an accomplished mediator, "there's more to the slavery issue than setting people free."

"I agree," Mr. Bancroft nodded wisely. "We're talking about a state's right to determine its own laws. Our country's in serious trouble should the federal government take that right from us."

"You're right. It's not a simple issue with simple solutions, Mr. Bancroft." The young lawyer took another slice of pumpkin bread from the bread tray and buttered it. "Everyone will need to compromise a little to gain a lot."

"I might not understand states' rights," Serenity added timidly, "but I've seen the stripes on a small girl's back made from the overseer's stinging whip, and my mother was a Quaker. So I learned about human rights from the cradle."

Caleb, sitting beside Serenity, smiled and patted her hand that was folded on her lap.

"More lawbreakers!" Mr. Bancroft muttered.

Serenity arched one eyebrow and gazed at the older gentleman. "God's law or man's, Mr. Bancroft?"

Felix, sensing a new wave of tension brewing, interrupted.

"That, we as responsible voting citizens, gentlemen, will be called to decide."

A frown knitted Serenity's brow. An argument she'd overheard between her parents regarding women's right to vote flashed through her memory. It was the only evening she ever remembered seeing her father grab his pillow and storm to the guest room to sleep. Her mother threw a bottle of expensive French perfume at the closed guest room door. Serenity bit her lower lip.

Fay shook her head sadly. "Well, I would hate to see our country turn into a battlefield over this issue—"

"That is coming, Mrs. Cunard." Mr. Bancroft leaned back and placed the palms of his hands on the table. "The Northern factories can't live without our cotton and our molasses."

"And the South can't live without the Northern economic structure for very long either," Eli waxed eloquent. "We need one another, like a family. We are the only country in the world joined together, not by customs or creed, but by God-given principles. If no one on either side loses his head, we'll get through this, a stronger and wiser nation."

"Sometimes Americans forget that our country is no longer thirteen tiny colonies clinging to the shoreline of the Atlantic," Felix reminded. "The way people pour through here each spring heading west, it won't be long before the western territories will be states too."

"You know, I am encouraged." Caleb leaned forward, his gaze scanning the faces at the table. "If we, of such diverse opinion, can sit down and break bread together out here on the edge of civilization, maybe there is hope after all."

Mr. Bancroft frowned. "All we plantation owners want is our property back. Do you know how much it costs these days to replace a healthy young buck on a New Orleans slave block?" He whistled out of the corner of his mouth. "And the upkeep—" He clicked his tongue. "I'm willing to operate under the law if the Negro-lovers are held to the same standard. If you, Mr. Cunard," he said staring at Aaron, "came across one of my cotton wagons, being an honest man, you would return it to me, right? Why should the most expensive of my farming equipment be any different?"

"Because, sir," Serenity interrupted, "a human being is infinitely more than a farm wagon or a thoroughbred animal."

"That, my dear Serenity," the lawyer reminded, "is fundamental to our discussion this evening. That is where beliefs differ. Mr. Bancroft feels just as strongly about his position as does the young Mr. Cunard." He glanced at Aaron. "Before it's settled, this debate will need to make its way from dinner tables and drawing rooms to finally be decided in Congress and the Supreme Court." Felix's smiled faded. "On this point I happen to agree with Mr. Bancroft. I'm afraid it will include a military action, perhaps even a civil war."

"Oh, dear Lord, no," Fay gasped. "America's sons killing one another? European governments might resort to violence that easily, but Americans? God forbid!"

"Ma'am," Felix Bonner tipped his head toward Fay, "I do hope you're right. May I say, Miss Serenity, this is the most delicious pumpkin bread I have ever eaten. And, I'll have you know, my mama made great pumpkin bread."

Serenity smiled and blushed.

"Here, Mr. Bonner, have some more." Analee passed the bread plate to the young attorney.

"Don't mind if I do. How about the rest of you gentlemen?" Several hands reached for the last few slices.

Serenity started to her feet. "I'll be happy to slice some more bread."

When she returned, Caleb rose to his feet, took the plate from Serenity, and handed it to Felix. He remained standing. "Serenity and I have an announcement to make this evening. May I tell them, Serenity?"

The young woman looked stunned. "I-I-I guess so." She wasn't totally sure what he had in mind.

Wrapping his arm possessively about her waist, Caleb drew her close to his side. Serenity blushed at the familiarity he displayed in front of the others. He'd held her in his arms when they walked alone in the moonlight, but never in front of others. Becca giggled behind her table napkin.

"Serenity and I have been officially courting these last few weeks," Caleb began. A kindly chuckle circled the table. Felix gazed down at the napkin on his lap.

"Big news there, big brother," Aaron laughed sarcastically.

Caleb ignored his younger brother's comments. "Last night we talked about having a Christmas wedding."

"Christmas! Oh, how romantic," Analee swooned. "Isn't that beautiful, Cyril?" Cyril beamed a smile at his wife as her face glowed.

Felix rose to his feet, took his half-filled glass of milk, and held it out toward the couple. "Let me be the first to congratulate the two of you. I hope you realize what a gem of a wife you're getting, Cunard. Beautiful, witty, and makes great pumpkin bread as well. For what more could you ask?"

Cyril and the others stood and toasted the young couple.

"May I be your bridesmaid?" Becca asked. "I've always wanted to be a bridesmaid."

"You'd better. There's no one I want but you."

"Can I wear pink?" the child asked.

Fay hugged her young daughter. "These are things for Serenity and Caleb to work out, sweetheart." She leaned across Becca and hugged Serenity. "Now, you'll not only be my daughter of the heart but also my legal child as well."

Something happened at the table that night. The strong animosities and prejudices were suspended for a short time in the joy of the young couple's announcement. Only Felix seemed troubled with the news. When the evening drew to a close, Caleb and Serenity walked Felix to his waiting carriage. The lawyer shook Caleb's hand and kissed Serenity's cheek. "The better man won," he said, then laughed at his own remarks. But in the darkness of night, Serenity could tell that his laughter didn't quite reach the sadness she'd detected in his eyes.

"Can I hitch a ride with you back into town?" Aaron asked striding up to the carriage. In a lower voice so his parents couldn't hear, he added, "I need a good stiff drink."

Caleb rested his hand on his brother's arm. "No, Aaron—"

"Hey, I don't belong here any longer, big brother. My life slaps Mama and Papa's principles in the face. And, believe it or not, I still care. It hurts me to see them hurt."

Caleb refused to let go. "Aaron, you belong with us. We're family, remember?"

"Yeah . . ." Aaron studied his brother's eyes for a moment. "I hope you always feel that way."

Caleb's hand dropped to his side. He drew Serenity close as Aaron climbed into the carriage beside Felix. They watched in silence as the carriage with Aaron's horse tied behind disappeared into the darkness.

Caleb lifted his eyes to the skies overhead. Dark ponderous clouds blotted out the moon and the stars. "Looks like bad weather brewing."

Gently caressing his arm with her hand, Serenity cooed, "Don't worry about Aaron. Everything's going to be fine."

Caleb ran the back of his fingers down the side of her face. "Serenity, I love you. Do you know that?"

Before she could respond, he kissed her. When he released her, she touched her fingers to her lips. His kiss had shaken her once again. She gazed into Caleb's deep brown eyes. "The right man definitely won. Do we have to wait 'til Christmas to marry?"

Caleb threw back his head and laughed. "You are a delightful surprise, Miss Serenity Pownell, soon-to-be Cunard." He swept her off her feet. With her arms pinned to her sides, he swung her around in wide circles. "I love you! I love you! I love you!"

Their joyous laughter floated into the sod-and-stone mission house, bringing a mixture of happiness and bitter-sweet memories to the inhabitants.

—14—
Unforetold Happenings

THE NEXT MORNING, WHILE SERENITY AND the other women prepared breakfast, Mr. Bancroft strode into the great room and greeted everyone with a cheery good morning. After planting a kiss on his daughter's cheek, he tossed a few pieces of kindling on the coals in the fireplace. "A mighty homey place you've made for yourself, Analee."

The young woman blushed with happiness. "Thank you, Papa. I try."

Seconds later Cyril returned from the woodpile with additional logs for the fire. "Nippy out there." Cyril placed the logs on the hearth. "Not snow weather yet, but nippy."

Mr. Bancroft leveled his gaze at his son-in-law. "Good morning, Cyril. You and I need to talk." The two men sat at the table.

While Serenity and Fay tried not to listen, they couldn't help but overhear the conversation between Mr. Bancroft and his son-in-law while busying themselves around the kitchen. In the process, Serenity discovered a different side to the pompous Mr. Bancroft.

"My offer is still open, Cyril. We need a good school teacher in town. The two of you could live in the summer house on the plantation until you get on your feet."

"But the mission—" Cyril argued.

"True, but our need for a good teacher is equally great. And I know you'd be a good teacher."

"Thank you, sir, but—"

"Cyril, you're a sick man. This prairie dust is going to run you into the ground. And surely you can see that my little girl is not well either. She's fatigued and overworked. You both need some southern sunshine to perk you up— and some of Grandmama's famous cooking too."

Cyril shook his head. "I appreciate your offer, sir, but I'm just beginning to break through to the Shawnee Indians. They're on the verge of trusting me. I can't turn my back on them now. Can't you understand?"

Mr. Bancroft's voice hardened. "What I understand, son, is that you are risking your life and that of my daughter's out of stubbornness." He reached for Analee's hand. "Sweet Analee, I hate having to say this, but I would be a negligent father if I encouraged you and Cyril in this experiment at the risk of your lives." He paused and swallowed hard, tracing the veins in his daughter's hand with his index finger. He took a deep breath. "I can no longer, in good conscience, financially support your mission here in Missouri." With his decree spoken, the older man's narrow shoulders drooped. "Maybe if your life gets a little more difficult, you'll listen to reason."

He glanced over his shoulder to where Serenity and Fay stood slicing potatoes. "Your money will run out about the time your guests leave, I presume." Seeing his daughter's tears, his voice softened. "You're always talking about this God of yours,

Analee. Well, maybe this is His way of telling you it's time to come home." The man turned and walked out the front door.

Later, when Serenity was in the cold-cellar choosing apples for a pie for supper, she overheard Cyril talking with Eli.

"How do you know when God is leading in your life?" Cyril asked.

"That's a difficult question to answer. Fay and I usually talk over the situation, then we pray about it individually, asking God to direct us to the same conclusion."

"And if you're still divided after you've prayed?"

"Then we wait on the Lord. Sooner or later, God makes His will known."

"Analee wants to go home. But I can't believe God wants us to abandon everything we've worked so hard to build out here in the prairie."

"Son, always listen to your wife's counsel. Sometimes I think the Holy Spirit can touch a woman's mind easier than He can a man's. Perhaps it's because women are accustomed to submitting, while men are designed to lead, hence confusing leadership with behaving like a dictator." The man chuckled. "Of course, I'd never tell Fay that."

Serenity frowned. *No,* she thought, *surely Uncle Eli wouldn't suggest that Cyril retreat from the Lord's work.* Yet, even she could see the slow deterioration in the man's health, something Cyril refused to admit. His bouts of coughing and wheezing disturbed everyone and came more frequently.

That evening, as she sat in the darkness of her room, Serenity thought about God and obedience. *How does God guide His children? Is it as simple as Uncle Eli makes it sound? Does God sometimes change His mind and send people back home? If I were Analee, what would I do if my father insisted I leave Caleb's side to return home? Who would I obey? What does a wife do if her husband is wrong?* Lighting a lantern, Serenity sought for answers in her mother's Bible. For the next two hours she read about Abraham, Ruth, and Jonah.

Becca awakened and sat up in bed. "Serenity? Are you all right?"

"Yes, sweetheart. Go back to sleep." So as not to keep the girl awake, Serenity tiptoed to the great room. The coals in the fireplace still glowed from the evening flames. Padding over to the stove in her stocking feet, she heated a pot of water and made herself a cup of chamomile tea.

Sitting by the smoldering embers wrapped in a quilt, the question of God's leading continued to haunt her. She skimmed through the Old Testament and into the New, reading where Jesus sent His disciples out two by two. She also read the story of Philip, and of Paul's determination to go to Rome, where history proved he would meet his death.

Another hour passed. Knowing that the next day would be as busy as the last, Serenity forced herself to blow out the flame of the lantern and go to bed.

Before climbing onto the husk-filled mattress to sleep, Serenity prayed: "Dear Father, I'm so confused about everything. Yet I can see that the one constant in all the stories I read is the person's willingness to follow You. I don't know the future, but You know my heart. There's nothing I want more in this world than to follow You, to love You, and to serve You. I give You my everything, Lord, including my future . . . " She paused. "And Lord, that includes Caleb. Amen."

On Friday morning, Serenity and the Cunards gathered around Analee as Cyril drove Mr. Bancroft into town. From there, the plantation owner would take the stage to St. Louis, then a steamboat home.

"It will be refreshing once the rains come," Analee sighed. "Excuse me please, but I think I'll take a walk to the cemetery."

Serenity and Fay watched the grieving mother trudge up the hill toward the western horizon. She approached a small plot of earth surrounded by a fence made of twigs and branches, then knelt beside the newest wooden headstone.

"How lonely she must have been before we got here," Serenity mused out loud, "with Cyril visiting the Indian camps so much of the time."

"I'm going to start the bread," Fay said.

"Sounds good. Do you have any clothing you need repaired? I need to get my sewing kit from my trunk," Serenity explained. "I must repair the sleeve on my pink calico. Caleb likes that dress." Her words drifted off into embarrassed silence. Fay gave her a hug and a kiss on the cheek.

"Yes, I do, as a matter of fact. Eli tore the pocket of his best britches. Would you mind?"

"Love to. I can sew while you bake. We can keep each other company. Tomorrow, Caleb and I plan to drive to the Indian village with Cyril and Analee, if she's feeling up to it. Becca said she'd like to go too, if it's all right with you. Cyril wants Analee and me to tell Bible stories to the children while he and Caleb assess the tribe's most critical needs for winter."

"Then I'll make three batches of bread. That way you can take two with you. Eli and I thought we'd drive into Independence for the day. With Becca going with you folks—" Aunt Fay's eyes twinkled with mischief.

Serenity chuckled to herself as she sauntered toward the barn. Uncle Eli and Aunt Fay? Courting? She shook her head in disbelief. She couldn't imagine those two level-headed people behaving like she and Caleb, holding hands and stealing kisses in the moonlight. She giggled and shook her head at the idea.

Because of the size of the bedroom she shared with Becca, Serenity left most of her possessions in the trunks in the barn, including the gold bars. Every few days, she found an excuse to wander out to examine her silken finery and her gold. Whenever she held one of the shiny bars in her hands, she felt safe, close to her father.

Opening the first trunk, she gazed down at the red velvet-lined interior. Her rose silk gown lay carefully folded on top. She lifted it out. Holding it up to her body, she shook the skirts free of wrinkles. "It's so beautiful." The temptation to slip into the gown for a few minutes overcame her better judgment. Once she'd removed her cotton work dress, she dropped the silken gown over her head. While still lost in the ruffles and skirts, Serenity heard the sound of male voices coming from the hayloft above her head.

Oh, no! She tugged quickly at the skirts and fumbled with the tiny satin-covered buttons, wondering if the men had seen her. Finally dressed, she scooted into a corner.

"I won't help you set up a station here at the mission!" Eli's voice rose with emotion. "I'm sorry, Aaron, but the mission is not ours to use."

"But, Pa, you supported Caleb when he and the assemblyman transported runaway slaves north," Aaron whined.

"The assemblyman and his wife believed in what they were doing. The Dorans feel differently. As their guest and as a man of God, I must respect their rights."

"But, they're wrong, Pa! You yourself preach against slavery," Aaron argued.

"Yes, and if I owned this land, I would be as eager as you to establish an Underground Railroad station. I'm sorry, son, and I apologize to you as well, Mr. Ward, for coming all the way out here for nothing."

When Serenity fastened the last button on her bodice, she silently gathered her skirts in her hands and tiptoed toward the open barn door. Peering around the edge of the hayloft, she spotted the two Cunards and immediately identified the third man. It was Ned Ward from the docks. She'd met him the day she arrived in Independence.

"But we're so close to the Kansas border, Pa." Aaron couldn't let go of his plan. "Once across the state line, the slaves would be free."

"Is there anyone to help them then?" the preacher asked.

"We're working on that side of the problem," Mr. Ward admitted.

"Have you considered establishing a safe haven at Fort Atkinson?" Eli asked. "Before you can establish the escape routes, you need a terminal and caring people to help the runaways fend for themselves. That's why the railways to Canada and Rochester, New York, are so successful." The reverend paused. "You need to establish a secure base before risking your lives on this project. I know your heart is in this, son, but get your head involved as well."

Serenity realized she'd never be able to escape from the barn without being seen. Stepping back into the shadows, her silk crinolines rustled.

"What was that?" Aaron leaned over the edge of the loft. Serenity ducked behind a stack of crates.

The men listened for a few seconds, then resumed their discussion. "Mr. Cunard," Mr. Ward said, "the only way we can establish a safe terminal is to send someone to the fort. It needs to be someone who can command the respect of the military."

Eli chuckled. "I know where you're going with this. You're very good with words, Mr. Ward. Are you a minister of the gospel?"

The colored man laughed. "Not me—my daddy. I preached my first and only sermon to a pen of calves at the age of five, or so the story goes."

The older man laughed again. "The day may come when the good Lord calls you to a higher cause."

"Higher than freeing my people?"

"Mr. Ward," Eli began, "freeing enslaved bodies is temporal. Freeing their souls is eternal."

"So will you, Reverend Cunard?" Ned Ward asked. "Will you go to Fort Atkinson and establish a terminal there while Aaron and I set up the necessary stations on this side?"

Aaron's eager voice broke in. "It shouldn't take more than a couple of weeks. You could be back before snow flies."

"By spring," Mr. Ward added, "everything should be in place for the first runaways."

Serenity froze. *Would Uncle Eli agree to such a plan,* she wondered. *What would Caleb think?* Her mind reeled with questions as she waited for the three men to leave the hayloft.

The next morning, Fay entered the kitchen with red eyes. Her usual smile had been replaced by a determined frown. Becca and Serenity looked at one another.

"What's wrong, Aunt Fay?" Serenity asked after Analee went to the chicken house to gather eggs.

The older woman closed her eyes for a moment. She heaved a resigned sigh. "You'll find out sooner or later, I suppose. Eli is taking a trip to Kansas, of all places. I don't know why, but I have bad feelings about this."

"Why does Daddy want to go to Kansas?" Becca looked confused.

"I don't know exactly, but you can be sure it doesn't involve preaching!" Fay shook her head. "He and Aaron are up to something."

Serenity started to say she knew why he was going, but Analee opened the door, her basket full of freshly laid eggs.

"Those hens don't seem to know winter's coming," she said. "We'll need to pickle some of these eggs before they spoil."

Serenity wrinkled her nose. Pickled eggs! One of her least favorite foods.

That evening, Caleb seemed distracted when they took their evening stroll to their favorite spot on the knoll. Serenity tried to coax him out of his mood, but nothing seemed to work, though he did grasp her hand tighter than ever.

When they reached the highest point, she slipped her arm around his waist. "Honey, I know what's going on with Aaron and your father. I was in the barn when they talked with Mr. Ward about it."

Caleb shot a startled glance at Serenity. "You do? Don't you say a word to anyone, you hear? Not even to my mother."

A pout formed on Serenity's lips. She removed her arm from his waist and folded them in front of her. "Why not your mother? She deserves to know what's going on. It affects her life too."

"It's Dad's place to tell her, not yours."

"But—"

"Please, Serenity, promise me you won't say anything to anyone." He took her two hands in his and stared deep into her eyes. "The pro-slavery sentiment in these parts is powerful. People have been tarred and feathered for making public their anti-slavery opinions."

"Is that why you're not involved this time?" She looked up at him, awaiting his reply.

His eyes darkened. "Do you think that?"

"That's what Aaron implied yesterday in the barn."

He drew her to him. She pressed her ear against his chest and listened to the steady beat of his heart. When he began to speak, she snuggled closer. She loved feeling the deep resonance of his voice as he spoke.

"I am not involved because I have responsibilities, a job, a soon-to-be wife to support. Your father didn't get directly involved in the day-by-day operation of the system in New York for the same reason. But I assure you, I will do my part when the time is right." He caressed her back and neck. "I'm not going to be a kept husband, my dear. When we settle into our own home, I want it to be one I purchased with money I earned."

Serenity looked up at him. "But Caleb, once we marry, all that I have is yours, remember?"

"Not now, Serenity." He pressed her head against his chest once more. "I'm still having trouble accepting that."

Serenity pulled away from him. "That's ridiculous! Sometimes I hate those gold bars! Look what my inheritance did to Uncle Joel and Aunt Eunice. I lost the only family I had because of money!"

Caleb took her hands in his and lifted them to his lips. "Honey, give me time. God and I are wrestling this one out."

"Well, you don't have very long. Christmas will be here before you know it."

Again he drew her into his arms. "And it can't come too soon for me." This time she rested in his arms, content in the security they represented.

Two days later Eli kissed his family good-bye and

headed south for Fort Atkinson, a fort entirely constructed of sod. One of its nicknames, Fort Sod, came from that fact. The other nickname, Fort Sodom, sprang from an entirely different source. Serenity wondered what the reverend would find and if his quest would be successful. She'd lost so much due to her parents' involvement in aiding and abetting Southern slaves. A part of her wanted to help the slaves; another part of her yearned for the peace and security she'd known before ever hearing of the Underground Railroad, conductors, stations, and terminals.

"That's selfish of me, Lord," she whispered. "I'm sorry I feel this way, but I do."

The rest of the week Cyril loaded feed sacks onto his farm wagon while the women baked bread and sorted foodstuff and clothing Analee had collected from the people of Independence for the Indians. Becca and Serenity spent their days carting sacked food to the wagon.

"Sunday, we're going out to the Wyandoth village. It will probably be our last visit until spring," Cyril predicted. "Each morning, I smell snow in the air."

Serenity could hardly wait. One of the highlights of her week was going to either the Wyandoth or the Shawnee village to tell stories to the children while Cyril and Analee conducted church services for the adults. Each time she and Becca visited, the children begged to hear the story about David and the giant. As she related the incident, one of the children would pretend to be David while Becca pretended to be the giant. Even though the Wyandoth children understood little English, they always laughed when Becca toppled to the ground.

And inevitably, one of the Indian children would strut up to her and say, "Me David, chief of the Wyandoth tribe, greatest warrior of the Indian nations." This would open the way for her to follow the David and Goliath story with the story of Jesus. The crucifixion brought tears to the children's eyes, but they cheered each time she told them about the resurrection morning. "And someday this same Jesus will come through the clouds"—she would point up at the billowing cloud bank—"and take us to live in a beautiful land called heaven."

"This heaven," one child liked to ask, "it will have thousands of deer roaming for food, and plenty of running water to drink?"

"The most beautiful meadow you've ever seen can't compare to what heaven will be like." Serenity would then wax eloquent describing a heaven that a Wyandoth Indian child could picture and enjoy.

Another reason she enjoyed the ride to the Indian village was Caleb's presence. She and Caleb would sit in the back of the wagon, their feet dangling over the edge of the floorboards. Becca sat with them, while Aunt Fay and the Dorans rode on the buckboard. On the way home, Becca would curl up in a thick horse blanket and sleep while Serenity and Caleb sat in the back, sharing another blanket. Sometimes they'd sing or tell stories about their childhoods, but most of the time they'd talk about their dreams and expectations. As she snuggled in the crook of Caleb's arm, her head pressed against his chest, she listened to the steady beat of his heart and felt safe and protected.

This Sunday at the Indian village proved to be more of an adventure than she imagined. She'd finished telling the David and Goliath story and was telling about Jesus feeding the five thousand, when one of the older Indian girls ran to her.

"Come, White Mother needs you." The girl seemed agitated.

"Me too?" Becca asked.

"No, just—" The young woman tried to say Serenity's name, but couldn't.

Serenity rose to her feet. "Becca, you finish the story today while I see what your mother wants." Serenity scooped her skirts in her hands and ran to keep up with the teenage girl. They crossed the compound in record time to find the women of the tribe standing around a bearskin-covered teepee, crying to the spirits.

Serenity lifted the rabbitskin robe that covered the doorway to find Fay and Analee kneeling on each side of a moaning, pregnant girl who was about to deliver what Serenity assumed would be her first baby. Serenity recognized her as the chief's daughter. *She's younger than I,* she thought.

An old woman sat by the young woman's head, rocking and massaging her forehead. All the while she chanted an eerie melody, a haunting obbligato to the girl's moans.

"It's all right, White Feather. We'll help you," Fay assured her patient. "Serenity, please go to the wagon and get my valise. This baby is breech. We must do something or both the mother and the newborn may die."

~15~
Facts of Life

DIE? SUCH A THOUGHT HAD NEVER ENTERED Serenity's mind. Giving birth was supposed to be a beautiful thing; that's what her mother told her. Of course, Serenity knew babies died on occasion. The mound on the hill at the mission attested to that. But the mother too?

Serenity ran as quickly as possible, her skirts lifted to her knees. She realized she'd been protected from knowing much about the details of childbirth. Living on her parents' estate in Cayuga, she'd never been allowed to visit the barn during a birthing of a calf or colt. Birthing was something no one ever talked about, except for the whispered and cloaked remarks made by the ladies of her mother's quilting circle.

When Serenity became a woman, her mother explained what to expect as a female, but death wasn't part of the picture drawn for her. Actually, Serenity had felt quite knowledgeable compared to some of her friends at the ladies academy, who could only fantasize about the relationship between a husband and a wife.

Serenity reached the wagon and climbed aboard. She located Fay's valise beneath the seat. She didn't hear Caleb until he called to her. "Is something wrong?" he asked.

"Your mother needs this right away." Serenity spat out the words as fast as she could. "Here, take it to her! She's over there." She pointed in the direction of the teepee.

Caleb took the bag from her hands and charged across the camp to where the Wyandoth women held their vigil. Serenity did her best to keep up, but she kept stumbling over her long skirts. He handed the bag to one of the women outside the tent. His mission accomplished, Caleb ran back to Serenity. "Are you all right? You don't look so good."

"I-I-I'm fine."

"Are you sure?"

"Yes," she nodded. She could feel a wave of panic sweeping through her stomach. "Go, go back to what you were doing."

"All right, if you're sure you're OK." Reluctantly he backed away from her.

"I'm sure." Serenity took a deep, cleansing breath. She watched until Caleb returned to Cyril.

Determined, she pulled her thoughts together. Approaching the teepee, Serenity took another breath before entering, then pulled back the animal-pelt door and stepped inside. That's when she heard a baby's squall. The women clustered about the tent cheered. Serenity watched the drama unfold as Aunt Fay handed the healthy baby boy to his grandmother.

However, horror filled Serenity as she looked down at the new mother, awash in blood. Blood! So much blood! She'd helped dress beef for preservation and clean chickens for dinner, but this was different. Her head swirled; her stomach lurched. She turned and dashed from the tent, gripping her stomach. "I'm going to be sick! I know I'm going to be sick."

She ran to the creek and collapsed on a rock beside the slow-moving water. *My mother went through that for me? Aunt Fay birthed three children like that?* Her mind swirled in confusion. *I don't understand why any woman would—* The scene inside the tent flashed through her mind a second time. She gagged.

The news of the newborn spread across the encampment like prairie fire. The men shouted, patting one another on the shoulders as if returning from a successful buffalo hunt. All thought regarding the winter supplies was abandoned. The chief's new grandson was cause for a celebration.

Serenity clutched her stomach and curled into a tight ball, trying to shut out the noise. When Becca came looking for her, she'd fallen asleep.

"Mama sent me to get you, Serenity. She says you need to come and see the new baby."

"No. No, I can't."

"But you must. The chief will be insulted," the girl hissed.

Serenity shook her head. "I can't. Please don't make me."

Becca looked down at her soon-to-be sister-in-law and huffed in frustration. Serenity burrowed back into her ball, so Becca returned to the festivities. A short time later, she heard footsteps approach.

"Hi, sweetheart." Aunt Fay bent down and caressed Serenity's shoulder. "What's wrong?"

"Nothing. Nothing's wrong."

The older woman eyed the girl skeptically. "I don't believe that for a minute. Now tell me what's going on."

Serenity sat up and stared at the woman who'd become a second mother to her. "I can't marry Caleb!"

"What? What brought that on? What did he do?"

"Nothing. I just can't marry him." The girl folded her arms across her chest.

Aunt Fay dropped down beside Serenity. "I don't understand."

"I've changed my mind, that's all. I don't want to marry him. I don't want to marry any man!"

A tiny rift of a smile gathered at the corners of Aunt Fay's lips. "Is it because of what you saw today? Have you never before seen a birthing?"

Serenity turned her face away from the older woman. Her chin quivered. "It was awful, just awful. I can't believe any woman would agree to suffer such indignities and pain. To think—Analee went through all that for nothing!"

Fay gathered the young woman into her arms. "Oh, honey, you may not understand now, but, trust me, you will. You will."

"But, it's so . . . so disgusting."

Aunt Fay kissed her forehead. "You're right—without love, it would be a pretty disgusting event. Love's the ingredient that turns birth into a beautiful moment. First, the love of a man and woman, then the mother's love for her newborn."

Serenity buried her face in Fay's chest.

"Honey, I have something to show you. Come." Fay rose to her feet, then helped Serenity stand. Serenity stared in horror at Fay's blood-soaked skirt and bodice.

"No, I can't." The girl resisted, but Fay took her hand and led her to the tent. They wove their way through the celebrating Wyandoths. She caught Caleb's questioning glance as she passed. Catching the unspoken exchange between the couple, Fay shook her head at her son, then asked permission of the new grandfather for them to enter the teepee. Proudly, he held the animal-skin door for them.

Serenity tried to pull back when Fay ducked to enter the tent, but the woman refused to let go of her hand. "Come on. This is something you must see."

Once inside the teepee, it took several seconds for Serenity's eyes to adjust to the darkness. When they did, she was surprised to see the chief's daughter reclining on a buffalo skin and covered with a blanket made of rabbit skins. A sleeping baby lay in her arms. Her husband sat by her side.

The Wyandoth princess smiled up at her. "Isn't he beautiful?" she whispered. "Isn't my son beautiful? He will be a great warrior."

Serenity couldn't speak. Could this be the same woman who less than an hour ago was writhing on the floor in pain?

"Would you like to hold my son?" the young mother asked.

"I-I-I—"

The baby's father took the child out of his wife's arms and placed him in Serenity's. "My firstborn son," he said proudly.

Reluctantly, Serenity accepted the infant from his father. Looking down at the tiny red face and the shock of thick, ebony hair, Serenity stared in wonder. She could feel the child kick his tiny legs. For no reason, the tiny body stopped wriggling. He stared at her intently, as if trying to memorize her face.

The nervous young woman felt the child's warmth through the small woolen blanket. She marveled at the contented grunts the baby made as he stuffed one of his tiny fists into his mouth and sucked on it. "I think he's hungry." She returned the baby to his mother's eager arms.

Serenity watched as the mother helped the baby begin to nurse. Feeling self-conscious at seeing the woman's bare breast, Serenity glanced at the baby's father. By the way he watched his wife give nourishment to their child, he'd forgotten the white women were present. Slowly Serenity backed out of the teepee.

Fay put her arms around the younger woman and walked with her toward the wagon. "As a mother, I can tell you that once you hold your precious child in your arms, the pain you endured minutes previous fades into a distant memory."

"But you said she almost died."

"That's true. Laughing Dove could have died if we hadn't been here to help her." Fay continued, "'There is a time to be born and a time to die.' Today wasn't Laughing Dove's time to die, but it was the child's time to be born. The real one hurting today is Analee."

The two women approached the wagon as Cyril held his sobbing wife in his arms. "We'd better be going," he called over his shoulder. "It will be dark before we reach the mission."

Caleb helped his sister board the wagon, then lifted the silent Serenity onto the back of the vehicle. He leaped up beside her. "Are you all right? I'm worried about you."

Serenity reddened and glanced away. *How foolish I must look, acting as I did. After all, having babies is part of living, though I'm still not sure I want it to be a part of my life.*

"Are you cold?" Caleb asked.

She shook her head. Ignoring her reply, Caleb wrapped a blanket about her shoulders. "Just in case," he said.

Except for Cyril's sporadic coughing, they rode in silence. As they continued, the moist night air set off the man's spasms. They'd not traveled far before his coughing forced him to halt the horses. He asked Caleb to drive, then coughed continually the rest of the way home. At the house, Caleb and Analee had to help him in.

For the next few days, Serenity avoided Caleb. He eyed her curiously, but didn't approach. She needed to think about the events she'd seen. The birthing had shaken her more than she could have imagined. Serenity knew she had to explain her behavior to him eventually, but first she had to come to terms with it herself.

Cyril's coughing kept the household awake most nights. Each morning, when he staggered out of the Doran bedroom, he looked paler and weaker than ever.

Fay forced the man to drink cups full of chamomile tea mixed with peppermint. "It's good for the throat and chest," she explained. She administered hot packs to his chest and back to ease his congestion and wheezing.

At breakfast on the following Friday, Fay announced that she was going to make a trip into town. "I need to purchase the ingredients for an elixir I used at home in New York," she explained.

When Cyril offered to drive the horses and wagon for her, she insisted she knew how to handle a team alone. "My father taught each of us girls how to work with horses. I can run a team as well as any man."

"Take her word for it, Mr. Doran. She's good." Caleb laughed, then turned to his mother. "I'll hitch up the team before I leave for work. You ladies have a good time together." He smiled at Serenity. She gave a tentative smile in return.

Aunt Fay picked up her dirty dishes and carried them to the dry sink. "Would you like to go with us, Analee? A day on the town might be nice before the snows come."

"No, I think I should stay with Cyril," Analee replied.

"Do I get to go?" Becca asked.

"Of course," Aunt Fay laughed. "You're one of the girls, right?"

Becca leaped to her feet. "I can hardly wait. This means I won't have to do my school work today."

Fay laughed again. Despite the lack of a school close enough for Becca to attend, she made certain that the girl continued her studies. The older woman commented one day as Becca sat at the kitchen table struggling with her math, "If I were going to stay here for any time at all, I think I'd conduct a school for the Indian children. They're so hungry to learn."

Cyril had overheard her remark. "Really, Mrs. Cunard? That's what I've been wanting to do since we first arrived. But I just haven't had the energy." He then broke into another coughing fit.

Excited about the visit to town, Serenity could barely wait until the morning chores were completed in order to leave. It had been over a month since they arrived at the mission and she'd only been in town once or twice.

As the wagon bounced over the ruts in the road, Serenity thought of Josephine. *She would be aghast if she had to refrain from shopping for any length of time. The woman lives to shop!*

Thinking about the illustrious Mrs. Van der Mere, Serenity realized that although she'd written several times, she hadn't heard from the woman since receiving the letter telling of her father's death. Serenity wished the telegraph wires were strung as far west as Independence; then she could send a message to Josephine. She relaxed against the seat. If Felix Bonner was right, the lines would be in the following summer. *Of course, by then,* she reasoned, *we'll be on our way to California.*

She felt a tug on her sleeve. She looked over to find Becca grinning up at her.

"Let's sing."

"What?" Serenity asked.

"Let's sing," the child insisted.

Fay cast a smile at her daughter. "What do you want to sing?"

"How about 'Go Tell Aunt Rhody'?" Becca's eyes sparkled with happiness.

"I don't like that song," Serenity said. "How about 'Oh Susannah'?"

"OK." Becca began: "O, I came from Alabama with a banjo on my knee . . ."

Serenity and Aunt Fay joined in, breaking into three-part harmony on the chorus.

"Hey, we sound pretty good," Serenity admitted by the time they finished the tenth verse.

Fay laughed. "Good enough to call the hogs out of the corn."

The wagon hit a bump. Serenity reached for her bonnet. "Let's do 'Clementine.'"

They made it into town in record time, and except for eating a lot of dust, in reasonably good condition. As they walked along the quiet boardwalks in front of the businesses, Fay commented that come spring the place would be alive with hundreds of Easterners heading west.

Serenity's skirts swished about her ankles as she walked. "Caleb says the forges at Ross Camp are running night and day, building wagons to sell come spring." Serenity pointed at a mercantile. "Could we go in there?" she asked.

"By all means." Fay led the way. The older woman ran her fingers over a stack with brightly dyed woolen yarns. "Inferior quality," she said. "My grandmother used to make the softest woolen shawls. Of course, she spun her own wool. I used to spin, but I don't seem to have the time anymore."

"I've always wanted to learn how to knit," Serenity admitted. "Could you teach me?"

Fay nodded, her attention already shifted to spindles of

thread lined neatly in rows on a shelf. "Knitting's a good pastime for a woman. Keeps her from developing cabin fever in the winter, so they say."

Serenity spotted a glass case filled with satin ribbons of all widths and colors. She peered into the case like a child peering into a candy store. "Aren't they beautiful?"

Becca joined her. "Imagine having ribbons to match every outfit!"

Serenity looked at the child in surprise. "I always did."

"Really?" Becca stared at the array of colors once more. "You were lucky."

"You know, Becca," Serenity began, "if I restyle my rose silk gown for you to wear for my wedding, you'll need matching ribbons to tie back your curls."

"Really?" The child turned to her mother. "Mama, did you hear? Serenity's going to let me wear one of her special gowns for the wedding. And I'll get to wear matching ribbons too!"

Fay raised her eyebrows in surprise. "Is the wedding still on for Christmas?"

Serenity looked surprised. "Certainly."

The older woman scowled. "I wasn't sure. You and Caleb have been acting strange lately."

After Serenity bought several yards of petal pink satin ribbons for Becca, they left the mercantile and crossed the street to the general store. There, Fay made her purchase, the ingredients for the elixir she would concoct for Cyril. She placed the items in her purse. "I certainly hope this will help Cyril regain his strength. It's suppose to enrich the blood."

The three females walked around town for several hours. Then, tired and happy, Serenity and Becca waited in front of the mercantile while Fay turned the horses around. Once onboard the wagon, the women headed for home. They hadn't ridden for more than a half hour when Caleb came riding up from behind them. He pulled alongside of the buckboard as Fay halted the team.

"What are you doing here?" she asked. "Why aren't you at work?"

"Mama, something's happened to Daddy. He's been seriously hurt, an arrow wound by some rogue braves."

"What?" she gasped. "How did you—"

"The sheriff brought the message to me at Ross Camp. I need to go to him."

"Of course you do, son, and so do I." She flicked the reigns and shouted at the team of horses. The whip cracked above the horses' heads. The wagon leaped forward. Serenity and Becca held onto their bonnets and the iron railing on the back of the buckboard.

"Mama, stop!" Caleb shouted after her.

Fay ignored her son's shouts.

Arriving at the mission, Fay stormed toward the house. "I'm going to my husband! He needs me and I intend to be there for him!"

Caleb strode beside her, trying to reason with the woman. "But Mama, the trip will take at least a week. And who knows when the snows will come?"

"Son, I am going and that's final. You may stay here if you wish, or lead the way." Aunt Fay charged into the house. The door slammed behind her.

Serenity looked at Becca. Becca rolled her eyes toward her brother. "Caleb," the child reasoned, "if Mama says she's going to Fort Atkinson, she's going."

"I know!" He stormed into the house after his mother.

Serenity and Becca busied themselves helping Analee prepare the supper meal while from the next room they could hear the loud voices of mother and son.

At the supper table that evening, Aunt Fay announced she would be leaving for Fort Atkinson in the morning. She asked Cyril if she could borrow one of his riding horses to get into town where they would rent a team and wagon.

"Of course," Cyril replied. "We don't mind having Serenity and Becca stay here with us while the two of you are gone," he added.

"That will give me time to work on my wedding dress and on Becca's gown as well," offered Serenity.

Caleb sent a surprised look at Serenity. She smiled her sweetest smile.

"I'd feel better if Aaron were here," Fay sighed. "There's no telling where he might be."

Serenity glanced across the table at the older woman. "If he shows up, we'll tell him what happened. In the meantime, Cyril and Analee will take good care of us."

Fay's eyes misted. She dropped her head, concentrating on the last vestiges of stew in her bowl.

When all had finished eating, Cyril read a Bible text, then led them in prayer. He prayed for Eli's recovery and for Fay and Caleb's safety.

Fay's eyes scanned the faces of each one present, then took a deep breath. "We leave at sunup; guess I'd better get packing."

Caleb carried his dishes to the dry sink. "Mama, it's late and you have a lot of packing to do, and Becca looks as if she's going to fall asleep at the table. Mrs. Doran, you prepared the meal, so why not let Serenity and me clean up?"

Analee blinked in surprise. "I couldn't do that."

"Of course you can. Cyril, take your wife for a walk in the moonlight."

Aunt Fay laughed. "If you want to be alone with Serenity, just say so."

"I want to be alone with Serenity before I leave tomorrow." Caleb turned to Serenity and grinned sheepishly. "I hope I didn't presume on you," he said. "But I think we have some things to discuss."

Serenity nodded, gathering her bowl and flatware and carrying them to the dry sink where Caleb stood. Caleb grabbed a bucket from beneath the sink and headed out the door. "I'll get the water," he called.

Recognizing their dismissal, the remaining Cunards and the Dorans took their leave. Caleb returned and poured part of the water into the iron kettle on the stove. Since they needed to wait for the water to heat, he walked over to the sofa and sat down. "Come here, darling. Let's talk."

Serenity swallowed hard. "I should wash off the table."

"Later. Please come here?"

Feeling like a six-year-old about to be scolded, she did as instructed. When she sat down beside him, he wrapped his arm around her shoulders and drew her close to him. "Over the last few days, you've been so distant. I tried to give you opportunity to talk about what's bothering you, but you've remained silent and aloof. Being honest and forthcoming with one another is important if we want to build a happy marriage."

Serenity nodded. "I know. I've been meaning to—"

"I'm relieved to know that you are still planning to marry me, that you still love me."

Serenity stared up at him in surprise. "Of course I still love you. I will always love you, Caleb."

"Then help me understand what's going on in that beautiful head of yours."

Tears welled up in the young woman's eyes. She sniffed them back and took a deep breath. "It was the baby, at the Wyandoth camp."

"What about the baby?"

"It was so horrible, the blood and all. I can't go through childbirth. As much as I love you, I just can't."

He tilted his head to one side. "You never mentioned that you don't want children."

"I do, or I mean, I did until I saw the chief's daughter." She tried to sniff back her tears.

They sat in silence for several minutes, holding one another. "I don't know what to say. I feel that our love would be incomplete without children. Children are a gift from God," Caleb said.

Serenity reached into the pocket of her apron and removed a cotton handkerchief. She blew her nose. "I do too."

He chuckled. "Honey, you can't have it both ways. Either you want children or you don't."

"I want them, but I don't want to have them. I know it doesn't make sense . . . That's why I've been so upset. If I didn't love you as much as I do, I wouldn't think twice about staying single for the rest of my life!"

Caleb scratched the side of his head in wonderment. "I guess I can take that as a compliment."

"Oh, yes!" Serenity burrowed as close to his side as she could.

"As much as I'd be willing, I can't birth our children for you." A frown settled on Caleb's face. He rubbed her arm for several seconds. When he spoke next, she could hear the pain in his voice.

"It sounds to me like you need to do a lot of praying

about this before we take our vows. Maybe this trip to Fort Atkinson is the best thing that can happen for us right now."

Serenity whimpered and slipped her arms around his chest. "I'm going to miss you so much."

"Oh, honey." Caleb held her tightly to him. "You have no idea how much I'll miss you."

~16~

The Long Wait

SERENITY'S LONG WAIT BEGAN THE MOMENT the wagon carrying Caleb and Fay disappeared down the road. Caleb having been a daily part of her life for so many months, she hadn't realized just how much she'd miss him. She'd never been in love before, not even "in like," she reminded herself. There'd been times she wondered if perhaps her love for him was nothing more than a strong friendship. *Is our love enough to maintain a lifelong commitment?* she asked herself.

She wandered to their special spot on the top of the knoll and sat cross-legged on their rock, the folds of her gray-and-yellow calico dress wrapped around her legs. Her heart heavy with sadness, she hugged her knees to her and stared across the plains. She barely noticed when her lavender woolen shawl slid from her shoulders. Onyx stretched out on the grass beside her. Idly, Serenity scratched the dog's head.

What I need is a good cry, she told herself. *I hate saying good-bye. Why am I always saying good-bye?* She took a piece of dried grass and broke it into tiny pieces. *I wonder if it ever gets easier?*

She remembered her mother's tearstained face as she kissed her daughter good-bye at the ladies' academy in Massachusetts. The girl didn't know she'd never see her mother's lovely face again. Then she thought about the hurried good-bye she said to her father as he ran one step ahead of the bounty hunters. And now he's dead too!

She cried when Eli left for Fort Atkinson. And now, Fay and Caleb. A strange lethargy settled into her body. She remembered Fay's ending words whenever she prayed, and repeated them now: "Thy will be done." It sounded like giving up to the petulant young woman. Lost in her thoughts, she didn't hear Becca climb the knoll until she sat down by Serenity's feet.

The girl crumbled into tears. "I'm scared, Serenity. For my daddy, I'm scared."

With her fingers, Serenity combed the child's hair away from her tearstained face, as her own mother had done for her whenever Serenity was lonely. "It's all right, honey. Everything is going to be all right."

The girl lifted her head. Anger flared in her eyes. "You don't know that! You can't be sure."

"You're right." Serenity bit her lower lip. "All we can do is trust those we love to God's care and let Him do the rest."

"It's easy for you to say, it's not your parents and your brother—" Suddenly Becca stopped, realizing what she was saying. Serenity did understand, all too well. Shame filled the little girl's face. "I'm sorry."

Serenity's eyes watered. *All right, Serenity Louise Pownell, enough feeling sorry for yourself,* she told herself. *You think too much about your own problems. Becca needs you now.*

Serenity untangled her legs and rose to her feet. Wrapping her shawl about her shoulders, she asked, "Want to take a walk?"

Becca smiled, stood up, and dusted off the back of her skirts. Onyx opened one eye, yawned, and stretched.

"Come on, lazy." Serenity scratched the dog's head. "You could use the exercise too."

The two girls ignored the billowing storm clouds forming at the western horizon. They ignored the slight nip in the autumn air as well. They followed the ruts of the wagon wheels leading to the Wyandoth Indian encampment.

They'd not gone far when Becca broke into song.

"Onward Christian soldiers, marching off to war . . ."

Surprised, Serenity glanced at her, laughed, then joined her. Becca sang four verses word for word. After the first verse, Serenity resorted to "la-la-la-la."

The girls danced along the road as they sang. Even Onyx caught the spirit. Before long he was running ahead of the two girls, chasing jackrabbits and other rodents. The girls started when the dog frightened a family of quail, who sprang from their nest and filled the sky with their beating wings.

"This is fun!" Serenity laughed and removed the tortoiseshell combs from her hair. The wind caught her curls and swirled them about her shoulders. Becca twirled in circles, her skirts whirling about her ankles. Their laughter spooked a red fox, sending it bounding across the prairie with Onyx after it.

When Becca exhausted all verses of "Onward Christian Soldiers," she began, "When I Survey the Wondrous Cross," singing it in the same tempo and with the same gusto as the first song. Never having sung the quiet, melancholic hymn with quite so much life, Serenity was soon out of breath.

Finally Becca broke into "My Maker and My King." Not knowing the words, Serenity only listened. Hymns continued to pour out of the little girl as they walked. She had an unending supply. *How lucky she is,* Serenity thought, *to possess such a rich treasure of music. I wonder if she appreciates her inheritance?*

The sky grew dark. Storm clouds rolled across the sky, bringing with it gentle flakes that tickled the tips of Serenity's and Becca's noses.

"We'd better head back to the mission," Serenity said, interrupting the girl's song.

No lights shone from the windows as they approached the house. No one greeted them at the door. Serenity sniffed the air as Onyx yapped and paced back and forth. Serenity was accustomed to being welcomed by the aroma of bread baking and Analee stirring a pot of stew over the stove, but this time the only aroma as she stepped inside the cabin was from the logs burning in the fireplace.

Bewildered, the girls exchanged questioning glances. "Where are the Dorans?" Serenity whispered. Why she was whispering, the young woman didn't know. "Analee?" she timidly called, peeking down the hallway toward the master bedroom. She called again, louder this time. No answer.

Becca wandered over to the oak dinner table. "Look, a note. It's addressed to you."

Serenity picked up the sheet of paper and read it aloud.

"Dear Serenity, There's been an emergency. Cyril has taken a turn for the worse. I tried to find you to tell you I'm driving him to the doctor's office in Independence. We'll stay the night there and return tomorrow. Myrtle has been milked. There's leftover stew in the icebox pantry. Help yourself to whatever you need. See you tomorrow. Love, Analee."

"Oh no, Cyril's much worse. Poor Analee. What will be next? First your folks, then this." Serenity scanned the note a second time. "All we need now is for one of us to fall and break a leg or something!"

"Serenity! Don't say that!" Becca blanched at the thought.

Serenity tried to laugh off her remark, but her insides trembled with fear. She'd never before been totally alone. Through all the tragedies of the last year, there was always someone to lean on, to talk to, to care for her. By the look in Becca's troubled eyes, Serenity realized that she alone was available to care for Becca.

Serenity folded her hands together as if about to pray. She touched her fingertips to her chin in thought. "So, would you like to make some cinnamon rolls?"

"Really? With walnuts on top?"

"We can look—" Serenity whirled about, looking for one of Analee's aprons usually left hanging on a hook in the kitchen. She tied it to her waist and announced, "Let's go!"

Before long the two girls had flour from one end of the oak table to the other. Their chatter filled the room. The fire in the fireplace crackled, and lanterns provided enough light for the girls' baking project. While the rolls baked, Serenity and Becca sat in front of the fire, spinning their dreams.

"I'd like to go to a school like you did," Becca admitted.

"You would? I never knew that."

"I'd like to learn how to be a proper lady." The girl hugged herself. "The way I figure it, one must be a real lady to attract a proper gentleman. And I'd like to marry a man like your father."

"My father?"

"Hmm. I used to have a crush on him when I was little," the girl admitted.

Serenity smiled at the words coming out of the mouth of a ten-year-old.

"And what about you?" Becca asked.

"I used to think I'd marry a rich man and we'd sail away to Europe or China or somewhere. But now, I think I'll be happy being married to"—she blushed when Caleb's face surfaced in her mind—"a kind and loving man."

"He doesn't need to be rich?"

"No, not really. Having riches can be more of a burden than a blessing sometimes."

After gorging themselves on freshly baked cinnamon rolls and steamy hot chocolate, the girls cleaned up the kitchen. Serenity banked the fire in the fireplace while Becca dressed for bed. The girls read from Serenity's Bible, then prayed together before Becca hopped into bed.

"I'm not sleepy. I think I'll read awhile," Serenity said, placing a kiss on Becca's forehead.

"OK, good night." The girl snuggled down beneath the heavy quilts and closed her eyes.

A strange silence filled the sod house as Serenity returned to the great room. No gentle snoring came from the bedrooms down the hall. No bed springs creaked. No friendly house noises. Even the wind had died down with the coming of the snow.

She wandered over to the window and peered out between the gingham curtains into the darkness. It was snowing harder now. She'd always enjoyed the first snowfall of the season. Wrapping her shawl about her shoulders, Serenity opened the door. She paused before stepping onto the hardened ground in front of the door. She watched as snowflakes drifted to the ground and melted. The snow turned the world into a landscape of blacks and whites.

Glancing toward the barn, she said aloud, "I should check the animals."

Onyx, who'd been laying beside the fire, brushed past her legs and into the snow. Serenity gazed down at her feet. "Doesn't look like it will stick. I wonder where Fay and Caleb are right now? I hope they're safe."

Serenity wrapped her arms about herself. "I'm sure they're safe. Didn't we pray before they left that God would take care of them?" she reminded herself.

She lifted her face to the snowflakes, letting them pelt her cheeks and eyelids. She sighed, then ran to the barn, giving the animals a quick look, then ran back to the house. Finally she swung the heavy wooden bar across the inside of the door and tested it with a jiggle.

Serenity walked over to Analee's bookcase and found a copy of Nathaniel Hawthorne's book, *Twice Told Tales*. Removing it from the shelf, she settled down for an evening of adventure. At some point, she fell asleep.

The next morning she awoke to Myrtle's plaintiff moos. Serenity sat up and rubbed her eyes. The sun was already high above the eastern horizon. She gazed about the room, her eyes resting on Becca asleep on the sofa.

"Becca? What are you doing out here?"

The child stretched and smiled. "I was lonely."

Serenity laughed. "Right now it sounds like Myrtle is lonely, or at least, uncomfortable. We'd better milk her."

The ten-year-old sat up and stretched. "Probably so."

"I don't know how to milk a cow. Do you?"

Becca laughed. "Of course, it was one of my chores during haying time."

"Good. Will you teach me?"

The girl leaped over the back of the sofa and ran to her

bedroom to dress. Serenity followed.

"Put on some old clothes," Becca warned, "in case Myrtle gets feisty."

"Feisty?"

"Yup."

Feisty didn't sound good to Serenity, but she was determined to master this new skill. She dressed and followed Becca to the barn.

Once inside, Serenity grabbed the red milking stool next to Myrtle's stall and walked around to the cow's right side. "What do I do first?"

"Switch sides," Becca laughed. "You're on the wrong side of her. She won't like it."

Serenity laughed and approached the cow from the left. "Now I know where the phrase 'getting on someone's wrong side' came from!"

Becca giggled. "Some cows don't seem to have a correct side. They're ornery no matter what. Myrtle's not like that."

"I'm glad for that."

Becca began instructing Serenity on the technique of milking a cow. She watched as Serenity squeezed and worried poor Myrtle. Whenever a squirt or two hit the bucket, the bovine swished her tail in Serenity's face. "Can't we do anything with that tail? Tie it somewhere?"

"Where?" Becca giggled. "She's just testing you."

"Testing me?"

"Yup. She's trying to decide if she likes you." Becca picked up a handful of hay and fed it to the cow. The animal nuzzled the little girl. "Cows aren't very bright animals, but they can be loving."

"Come on, Myrtle, you like me," Serenity coaxed. "You know you do."

The coaxing helped. Within a short time, Myrtle's milk dropped. Soon the pail was full. The girls lugged the pail into the house without spilling any. While Serenity stirred the batter for griddle cakes, Becca skimmed the cream off the top of the milk and set it aside.

"I'll churn the butter today," Becca volunteered. "You know, this is kind of fun, just the two of us here. It's like playing house."

Serenity groaned, flexing the tired muscles in her hands. "Except this is real, not play. I wonder what time Cyril and Analee will return?"

Becca ran her index fingers across the top of the foamy cream and slurped it in her mouth. "Mmm, this cream is yummy. Myrtle's a fine cow."

"I don't know about being fine." Serenity spooned a dollop of batter onto the hot skillet. The oil sizzled. She jumped back to avoid the splatter. "Tsk! Grease on my yellow gingham! It's bound to leave a spot."

After breakfast, the two divvied up the chores, completing them in no time. Several times during the day, Serenity caught herself gazing down the empty road toward town. She suspected that Becca did as well.

When evening milking time arrived, Becca offered to do the chore if Serenity would make her famous corn bread for supper.

"Won't hot johnnycake taste just as good with your freshly churned butter?"

Becca looked at her.

"OK, corn bread," she sighed.

The snow began to stick soon after dark. The girls watched for the Dorans to return, but they still weren't in sight at bedtime.

The Dorans didn't make it home that night, the next night, or the next. Another storm blew across the prairie a few days later. By then the girls had stopped talking about the Dorans' imminent return. *We have everything we need,* Serenity reminded herself.

Late one afternoon, Serenity was in the cold cellar choosing potatoes for their supper when Becca thundered into the barn. "Someone's coming!" she shouted. "A carriage is coming up the road."

"Who is it?"

The girl shook her head. "Should I get Cyril's shotgun?"

Serenity dropped the potatoes in the gunnysack she carried under her arm and dusted off her hands on her apron. "Run to the house and stay out of sight unless I call for you. We don't want just anyone knowing we're here alone. Now, go!"

Both had heard stories about renegade Indians or drunken cowboys robbing the homes of settlers, especially when they knew the male family members were away.

Becca darted out of the barn, across the clearing, and into the house. Onyx bounded after her. Serenity took a deep breath, then strolled out of the barn just as a cutter, drawn by matching sorrels, pulled to a stop in the yard. Felix Bonner leaped from the sleigh.

"Miss Serenity!"

"Mr. Bonner, what a pleasant surprise!" Serenity sighed in relief. "What are you doing here?"

"I'm here to take you and Miss Becca into town."

"Why?"

Felix removed his hat and fiddled with the brim. "Mr. Doran passed on last night. Bad lungs, I understand. Heavy blood loss."

"Oh, no!" The woman's hand flew to her mouth. "That's terrible. How is Analee doing?"

"Mrs. Doran was the one who sent me out here. She's worried about you two."

Serenity shook her head sadly. "I figured something must be wrong when they didn't return."

Felix reached in his breast pocket and took out a small sheet of paper. "Here's a note she wanted me to give to you."

Without warning, Onyx bounded out of the house and up to Felix, barking a familiar hello. Serenity took the sheet of parchment paper from Felix's gloved hand.

"Well, how ya' doing, old boy? Taking good care of your pretty mistress?" He scratched the dog's head behind each ear. Onyx slobbered with pleasure.

Serenity read the letter.

> Dear Serenity, I don't know how to say this except to say it. Cyril died last night. I can't stay here in this God-forsaken place any longer. I'm leaving for Louisiana on tomorrow's stage. I'm hoping to sell the mission before I go as I need the money to cover my travel expenses.
>
> I've asked Mr. Bonner to see that Cyril is buried in the plot next to our baby. At the end of this letter, I've listed the items I wish to take with me. If you could send these things to Independence with Mr. Bonner, I would be grateful. I'm sorry to leave you in the lurch like this, but I never want to see that ugly sod house again! It killed my husband and my son, but I won't let it kill me! Sincerely, Analee Bancroft Doran

Unable to speak, Serenity stared at the letter. The short list of personal belongings at the bottom of the sheet of parchment would barely fill a small trunk: a change of clothing, a scrapbook, a stack of letters, and the baby clothes she'd embroidered. Serenity turned suddenly and called to Becca. The girl came running from the house.

Serenity faced Felix again. "What do I do now? I must care for Becca until the Cunards return." Her lower lip trembled. "Should we move into one of the boarding houses in town?"

The lawyer scowled. "I don't think that's a good idea. I'd invite you to stay in my home, but that would set all the righteous tongues in the county to wagging." He gazed about the barnyard. "Well, one thing is certain, you can't stay alone here."

"First things first. I need to pack up the things Mrs. Doran requested. I think she has a small metal trunk in her bedroom." Serenity headed toward the house.

Becca ran to catch up with them. "What are we going to do, Serenity?"

"I don't know yet." She pursed her lips as she walked. "Caleb and your folks will be back from Fort Atkinson by next week, I should think." Serenity strode into the mission house and down the hall to the Doran's bedroom. "If Analee sells the place, we'll have to move," she called over her shoulder.

Serenity opened the top bureau drawer as the letter instructed and began sorting through Analee's personal items. "Becca, perhaps we should pack a few things for the next couple of days as well."

Becca hurried from the room. Serenity glanced over her shoulder. "I don't know what to do about poor Myrtle. She needs to be milked twice a day."

"Don't worry about Myrtle; I'll hire someone to come

out and care for her until the place sells. There's always a cowboy around town who can use some money."

Serenity had no trouble finding the items on the list; Analee had been precise as to their location. When Serenity opened the large wooden travel trunk at the foot of the Doran's bed, she inhaled sharply. On top, wrapped in soft flannel, was a stack of delicately-embroidered infant saques—the first items on Analee's list. Tears filled Serenity's eyes as she recalled the infant grave on the grassy hillside. "And now her husband. Lord, it isn't fair."

Serenity placed the tiny clothing into the small metal trunk with the other items and hauled it to the great room, then hurried to pack her own things. Trying to decide what she'd need for the next few days didn't take long. When she removed the velvet pouch containing her mother's jewelry and the leather pouch that held the coins she had left from St. Louis, she remembered her gold bars in the barn. *Should I leave them or take them with me?* she wondered. Before closing her valise, she placed her mother's journals and Bible on top of her clothing, then clasped the latch and placed the case with the other luggage.

After dousing the fire in the fireplace and in the iron stove, Serenity boarded the shutters and closed the cabin door. For a moment she gazed at the knoll, wondering where Analee's husband would be buried, then followed the trail to the rock where she and Caleb talked and kissed in the moonlight. *Here I am saying good-bye again,* she thought, then shook herself. "I shouldn't be thinking of me at a time like this! It's Analee that needs my prayers."

Abruptly, Serenity came to a decision. Turning her back on the grassy hillside, she strode purposely toward the barn, passing the sleigh where Becca and Felix waited. "Be back in a minute," she called. She threw open the first trunk and dug to the bottom. Lifting the false bottom, she eyed the gold bars. "I think you'll be safe enough until I get back." She pushed the two trunks under the eaves of the barn and kicked loose hay around them. She heaved a satisfied sigh. "There! That should take care of everything."

Learning
to Live

FELIX BONNER SLAMMED HIS FIST ON THE TOP of his massive black walnut desk. "Serenity, you can't do this. I will not allow it!"

"I beg your pardon. It is my money. I can do with it as I please," Serenity argued.

"If Caleb were here, he wouldn't allow you to make such a horrid mistake. As his friend, and more importantly as your friend, I feel I must stop you from making this terrible mistake."

"Felix, I asked for your help because you are a friend. But I did not ask for your permission." Serenity searched for the right words to say. "Analee needs my help. If she's going to make it back to her father's place in Louisiana before spring, she must leave on the next stage."

A wry smile tilted one side of Felix's mouth. "There is another option, you know. I could buy the mission as an investment."

"And how will that solve Becca's and my housing situation?"

His eyes grew serious. "You could marry me. I'd take good care of you. I'd never leave you alone and go gallivanting to Kansas."

"Felix, be serious. You know full well Caleb didn't

gallivant anywhere. His parents needed his help. He couldn't predict a snowstorm."

The young lawyer inched closer, gently running his hands along the woman's upper arms, his eyes searching hers. "You're right about Caleb, of course. But I am serious about the marrying idea. I would treat you like a princess."

Serenity stepped back, her calves bumping against the wooden chair seat. "Felix, please . . . You know Caleb and I are engaged to be married."

"I had to try, Serenity." Felix ran his fingers through his thick brown hair and took a deep breath. After a second, he straightened, rounded the desk, and gazed out the window onto the muddy street.

Serenity touched his arm. "I'm sorry, Felix. If it weren't for Caleb—" Horses drawing wagons and carriages passed by. A light scatter of snowflakes drifted past the dusty window.

Resignation filled Felix's face as he turned toward the young woman. "You are being foolhardy choosing to spend even a few days alone out at that mission. And, not only are you risking your life, but Becca's as well."

"Wives much younger than I have been stranded alone on the prairie for months at a time and lived to tell about it. Besides, Becca and I won't be totally alone, you know. The God who guided us west in the first place promises never to leave us, never to forsake us." Serenity smiled, then turned toward the attorney's desk where a highly polished wooden tube sat. She picked up the tube and put one end to her eye as she spoke. "Felix, you should know that the money I am paying Analee for the mission does not deplete my reserves, only my cash in hand." She had no intention of telling him about her gold bars. Aiming the tube toward the window light, she exclaimed, "O-o-o, how beautiful!"

"It's a kaleidoscope," he explained. "Turn the brass ring."

She did so and squealed once more with delight. "I've never seen something so lovely. How does it work?"

"Inside, bits of colored glass reflect off small mirrors. Serenity, back to the problem. You're spending a lot of money for almost worthless acreage."

"The way I see it, the Cunards and I will need a place to stay until spring. My purchasing the place meets everyone's needs." She gestured with her hands. "We've already settled in at the mission. And you have yet to suggest an alternative."

Felix tapped the edge of an envelope on the inkpad in front of him. "I would agree with you if they were here, but they're not. In the meantime, you and Becca shouldn't be at the mission alone without a man close by to protect you."

Serenity turned the brass ring at the top of the kaleidoscope and exclaimed with delight. "Like a thousand precious jewels . . ." Then, as an afterthought, she added, "I'm sure Caleb and his parents will be back before the end of the week. That means we'll be alone at the mission for three days at the most."

Felix ran his fingers through his hair. He cast a distraught look at the determined young woman. "This is foolish. I should just assume guardianship of the both of you and refuse to allow you to do this. That's what I should do!"

Serenity's jaw hardened. She set the kaleidoscope on the desk. "I wouldn't do that if I were you, Mr. Bonner." She spoke his name with as much authority as she could muster.

The impact of the fire in her eyes forced him to soften. "I don't want to do anything so extreme, I assure you."

She sat in the office chair and closed her eyes for a moment. "Felix, if you truly are my friend, you won't oppose my decision. I prayed about this all night, and I am certain it is what God wants me to do."

"Hmmph! Cyril thought God led him to build the mission, if I remember right. And look what happened to him."

A tremor of fear passed through Serenity. Felix had touched the very nerve that disturbed her the most. She glanced down at her gloved hands to hide her momentary disquiet. "Felix, are you going to help me?"

"What will you do with the mission when the Cunards leave for California come spring?" he asked.

She shrugged her shoulders. "Sell it, I suppose."

"And if it doesn't sell?"

"It doesn't sell." She gazed into the attorney's eyes and lifted one provocative eyebrow. "Forgive me, Felix, but I thought the issue was Becca's and my safety, not my wise or unwise investment in this property."

"What will you do if Indians show up at your door?"

Serenity giggled at the idea. "It is an Indian mission, remember?"

"What about a band of cutthroats? Will you laugh then?"

She heaved a deep sigh. "I'll deal with the problem when it comes, like any other homesteader would do."

Felix pinched the bridge of his nose and shook his head. "All right. I know I'll be sorry for this, but I will help you. Be back here at my office at three this afternoon, along with Analee, and I'll have a deed drawn up." The lawyer left his office without another word.

"Felix," Serenity called after him. "The stage leaves at three."

"Two-thirty then!" He threw open another office door and let it slam behind him.

Serenity had no trouble talking Analee into the proposition. Real estate in Western Missouri in late autumn ranked in sales as high as spring bonnets. As the two women waited in Felix's office, Serenity studied the other woman's grief-ridden face.

Analee's one thought was to leave the area as soon as possible. In her grief, she blamed Missouri, the Indians, and anyone else remotely connected for the loss of her husband. "When I get home to Louisiana," she said, "I will never again step across the state line!" She gazed down at her gloved hand. "Do you know how rough and chapped my hands have become? I used to be the belle of the county. My hands were as soft as a magnolia blossom, my face as smooth as a rose petal." She burst into tears. "Look at me. I'm an old woman at twenty-one!"

Serenity tried to think of how to comfort her. All she could do was pray.

"Get out, Serenity. Get out while you can. You weren't meant for the harsh life on the frontier. No woman was," Analee wailed.

For a moment Serenity was taken aback as doubts that had lingered after leaving Buffalo resurfaced. She'd given up the style of living to which Analee would return. Analee's skin would once again grow soft. Color would return to her cheeks. She'd be laughing and dancing again by spring.

Analee grew silent, leaving Serenity alone with her thoughts. *Lord, what have I done?* Serenity's heart cried out in anguish. *How can I pretend to know Your will for me?*

At two-thirty, Felix Bonner entered the office where the two women waited. He looked at Analee, then at Serenity. "One last time, Serenity. Are you sure you want to do this?"

Serenity studied the fluttering gestures of the grieving widow as she attempted to hold back a flood of tears. *Lord, will Analee ever let go of the bitterness she now feels? Will she learn to trust You once more?* Serenity's heart filled with peace as she looked up at the lawyer. "I've thought of little else since we spoke this morning, Felix. I'm ready to sign the papers."

After reading through the contract, Serenity wrote her name on the line indicated and handed the papers to Analee, who didn't bother reading, but scribbled her signature as quickly as possible.

"Bless you, Serenity, bless you." Analee wept and kissed Serenity's hands. "I will always be grateful for your kindness. I would pray for you, if I thought it would make a difference."

Serenity's eyes glistened with tears. Nothing seemed sadder to her than to see this young woman, stripped of her faith, returning home in defeat. "I'll be praying for you as well, Analee. Maybe someday you'll be able to see and understand the blessing in all of this."

"Blessing? From a spiteful and vindictive God?" She rose to her feet, looped her purse strings about her wrist, and strode out of the office.

Serenity hurried after the young woman. As she passed through Felix's outer office, Serenity called to Becca. "Hurry. We need to catch up with Analee."

They followed the grieving widow to where the east-bound stage was loading. Without looking back, Analee climbed onto the stage and drew down the window shade on their faces and on her life in Independence.

Serenity and Becca waited until the stage departed for St. Louis. "She's so unhappy. Do you think she'll ever be happy again?" Becca asked.

"That will be up to her, I'm afraid."

The child drew closer to Serenity's side. "I don't know what I'd do if any of my family died."

"After my mother died, I thought I'd never smile again,

but God sent your mother and Mrs. Van der Mere to help me. I'm sure He has someone who will be available to reach Analee's heart as well."

"You think so?"

Serenity squeezed the girl about the shoulders. "I know so."

While Felix went to get his team and sleigh, Serenity and Becca strolled along the wooden walkway past a barbershop and a hotel to the local post office. "Since we're here in town, we might as well check to see if we have any mail. Maybe there's a message from your folks," Serenity suggested.

The girl's eyes lit up. "You think?"

"I don't know, but it's possible."

They stepped inside the drab one-room building. Serenity walked over to the caged area and asked for any mail addressed to either the Cunards or Serenity Pownell. The short, rounded man behind the bars grinned at the two girls, then wriggled his skinny mustache as if trying to dislodge a fly. "Hmm, let me see . . . "

He pawed through a wooden box marked A–H. "Nothing for Cunard. What was the other name?"

"Pownell, Serenity."

The mail clerk dug through a second box labeled J–Q. "Pownell . . . Pownell . . . Pownell! Serenity Pownell. Here! Came in yesterday from Fort Atkinson." He grinned, pleased with his success.

She thanked him and tore open the seal.

"Serenity! Mr. Bonner is out front," Becca warned. Wanting to read the letter in private, Serenity stuffed it into her valise.

"Come on. We don't want to keep him waiting."

"Aren't you going to read it?" Becca asked.

"I will, but not in front of Mr. Bonner. Come on."

The ride back to the mission was made in silence. Serenity knew that Felix was wrestling with what he'd just done. When they arrived, he helped them carry the luggage into the mission house.

"I'll arrange for my man to bring your wagon and horses out here tomorrow, if that's all right with you." The concern in Felix's eyes disarmed Serenity.

"I'd appreciate that. I was wondering how I'd get the horses home."

Felix took her hand and touched his lips to her gloved fingers. "Is there anything else I can do for you before I leave?"

"Sort of." Serenity squirmed under his gaze.

"Sort of?"

"Could this man of yours teach me how to saddle up a horse and hitch up a wagon?"

Felix shook his head and laughed. "How are you going to manage alone out here, even for a day?"

Serenity straightened and tilted her nose defiantly. "If I can learn to milk a cow, I can saddle a horse as well."

"I'm sure you can." He cast her a bemused smile. "I doubt there are many things you couldn't do if you set your mind to it. You're a remarkable woman, Serenity Pownell. And if you weren't affianced to Cunard, I'd—" He stopped abruptly. "Well, it's getting late. I'd best be on my way."

Serenity walked with him to his waiting carriage. "Thank you again, for everything. And don't worry. We will be fine."

He climbed aboard the carriage and picked up the reigns and buggy whip. "I wish I were so sure of that."

"Trust me," Serenity laughed.

"Trust or no, I will be out to check on you if Caleb isn't back by Sunday."

"I'll save you the trip. If Caleb and his folks aren't home by then and if the roads are clear, Becca and I will hitch up the wagon and attend the morning services at the Baptist church. A little religion wouldn't hurt you either, you know."

His face brightened, despite his concern. "It's a date, and so is dinner following. Tell the Cunards they're invited as well."

"All right. I look forward to it."

"We'll sacrifice the fatted calf," he teased.

Serenity stepped away from the carriage. "Country fried chicken will do!"

Flicking the whip over the horse's head, he shook the reigns. The horse snorted and lifted her front feet proudly.

Serenity waved and hurried back to the mission house. She had no intention of watching the carriage disappear down the road. Once inside, she snatched the letter from her purse.

Becca ran to Serenity's side, peering over her shoulder. "What does it say?"

Serenity's smile faded as she scanned the letter. Finished, she clutched it to her chest. "I will not cry; I will not!"

Becca frowned. "What does it say? When are they coming home?"

"Your father's injuries require them to stay a while to let him heal before transporting him in the wagon." Serenity bit her lower lip. "Caleb says they hope to make it home by Christmas, if there are no heavy snowstorms to block the roadways."

"Anything else? Did he say anything else?"

"Your mother and father send their love and assure you that they are praying for our safety." *If they only knew*, she thought.

Thankful she hadn't shared the letter with Felix, Serenity busied herself and Becca with the evening chores.

The enormity of what Serenity had done hit her as she milked Myrtle. She pressed the side of her head against the cow's warm belly to block out the latest wave of worries that the letter implied.

Gathering her wits about her, Serenity forced herself to dwell on Caleb's closing message: "I love you, Serenity. I can hardly wait to make you my wife. When I see you again, I'm going to give you the biggest kiss you've ever received. It will make your boots clatter."

When the milk stopped flowing, Myrtle nudged the distracted young woman. "Oh!" Serenity laughed and patted the animal on the side. "Sorry, old girl." She carried the pail of milk into the house where Becca had begun making bread pudding from the day-old bread.

That evening, after Becca went to bed, Serenity rocked in the rocking chair beside the fire. She watched the flames gyrate—weaving, touching one another, then separating again. "I can't do this, Father. I'm not strong enough. I can't look after Becca. Why, I need someone to look after me. I'm so scared."

Nothing in her life had prepared Serenity for the loneliness she felt that night. A cloak of fear engulfed her, causing her to shake uncontrollably. She wrapped the quilt about her shoulders and stared into the fire until the embers turned to ashes. Even the familiar passages of Psalm 91 and Hebrews 13:5 failed to touch her heart. Whatever peace she'd felt in Felix's office had long since vanished.

Over and over, she repeated the words of Psalm 23— "Though I walk through the valley of the shadow of death, I will fear no evil, for Thou art with me . . . "—only to find them reverberating against the lonely walls of the house.

Much to Serenity's surprise, the sun came up the next morning. The illogical side of her mind had doubted it would. And with the new day, there were animals to tend, butter to churn, and bread to knead. Water needed to be fetched from the well and the floors swept. *Work will be my salvation,* she thought as she bundled herself up in one of Cyril's jackets and trudged to the barn to milk Myrtle. *All I have to do is live one day at a time,* she reminded herself. *Just for today.*

By the time she returned to the house, Becca was awake, dressed, and mixing the ingredients for flapjacks.

"Hi." The girl greeted Serenity with a bouncy smile. "Snowing again?"

"Yeah. I think we're in for a big one this time."

"I thought the last storm was mighty big."

Serenity laughed as she carried the bucket into the pantry. "I strung a guide rope between the barn and the house in case the storm turns into a blizzard. Felix said the blizzards can be so bad on the prairie that farmers have frozen to death less than ten feet from their kitchen doors." She gazed at the stock of food supplies on the shelf. "How about molasses on our flapjacks this morning?"

"Sounds good," Becca replied, humming as she worked. "Which do you want to make today? The bread or the butter?"

"I don't care." Serenity took off Cyril's heavy coat and exchanged it for one of Analee's aprons. She tied the apron around her waist and returned to the great room. "Whatever we do, let's do it together, OK?"

Becca smiled, her eyes dancing with innocence. "Sure. It's more fun that way."

Serenity forced herself to return the smile as she set the table for their breakfast. "Is the water hot for tea?"

"Yes ma'am, it sure is."

"You were a busy little beaver while I was doing the chores this morning," Serenity admitted.

"Well, as Mama always says, 'Working together cuts the work in half,' or something like that anyway."

Serenity chuckled to herself. "Did you gather the eggs too?"

"Oops, I forgot." Becca sent her a sheepish grin.

"I'll do that while you finish fixing breakfast. It won't take long." She put on the jacket once again, grabbed the bowl of scraps sitting on the dry sink, and opened the front door.

When she unlatched the heavy wooden front door, the wind whipped it out of her hands and slammed it against the wall. Tiny flakes pelted her face as she hunkered beneath the coat and bucked the wind to the chicken coop. She collected the eggs, fed the hens, and trudged back to the house. Her last outdoor chore for the morning was to haul enough logs to keep the fire going in the fireplace and the stove.

The snow continued falling throughout the day, although *falling* was hardly the correct term. It was more like driving at a forty-five-degree angle. They could hear the icy pellets hitting the window glass. Becca opened the front door around midday to find several inches of newly fallen snow covering the doorstep. It covered all but the tallest clumps of golden prairie grasses. From what the girl could tell, there seemed to be no break in the clouds.

The aroma of fresh, hot bread lifted Serenity's spirits. Midafternoon, the two took a break from their chores and took turns reading from Hawthorne's *Twice Told Tales*. When it was time to milk Myrtle again, Becca volunteered to take her turn, but Serenity insisted the girl wait in the house. "I think I saw a container of chocolate in the pantry. A cup of hot cocoa would taste good when I get back. Use some of the cream I set in the snow outside the pantry door. And we can warm up the leftover stew for supper."

"That sounds good. You know what else would be good? Mama always made snow candy from the first good snow."

Serenity continued buttoning the jacket. "Snow candy?"

"Yeah, you boil down syrup, then pour it on a pan full of snow. It's yummy!"

Serenity laughed. "Sure, why not? Just be careful near the stove."

Becca's face grew serious. "Hurry back."

Serenity kissed the girl's forehead. "I will, sweetie."

The storm was on the verge of becoming a blizzard. Serenity slid her gloved hand along the guide rope even though she could still make out the outline of the barn. It gave her a sense of security. As she trudged through the foot-deep snow, she repeated in her mind, *"I will never leave thee nor forsake thee. Lo, I am with you always, even to the ends of the earth." Alone in a world of white,* she thought, *Missouri definitely qualifies, Lord.*

The cow mooed the moment the young woman stepped into the barn. Myrtle and Serenity were becoming fast friends. Before milking the impatient animal, Serenity checked the gold bars in the bottom of her trunks. The cold gleaming surface reassured her once more.

She finished the milking and fed the animals, bedding them down for the night. Taking the heavy milk pail in one hand and her lantern in the other, she strode across the barn, eager to return to the warmth of the house. Intent on her destination, Serenity didn't see the four Shawnee braves standing inside the barn door until she was about to pull it shut.

"E-e-i-i-i!" she screamed, dropping the milk and the lantern onto the barn floor. Somehow the lantern remained lit, but the milk splashed on her skirt and boots. Her first inclination was to run. But where could she go? They stood between her and the house and gun. "What are you doing here?" she gasped.

"Eat." One of the men said. "Food."

"Hunting deer," another man explained. "Lost in snow."

Serenity gathered her wits. *This is an Indian mission, or at least, it was. You can't turn these men out cold and hungry in this weather.* Realizing there was little she could do to defend herself anyway, she whispered a prayer heavenward and gestured for them to follow her.

When she walked into the mission house with four Shawnee braves following her, Becca screamed and cowered behind the sofa. All thoughts of snow candy fled her mind.

"Becca, remain calm," Serenity spoke in a low, controlled voice. "We have guests. These men are hungry. Is the stew hot yet?"

Becca nodded, her eyes luminous with fear.

"Fine, then let's serve them." Serenity turned to the men and gestured toward the table. "Please, sit. Eat." The men obeyed.

She removed her heavy jacket and hung it on the nail by the door. She strode to the pantry for a loaf of freshly baked bread. "We'll need the butter, Becca. And bring one of Analee's berry jams as well."

"Yes, ma'am." The girl scooted from the room. They passed one another in the pantry. "What's going on?" the younger girl hissed.

"Supper, I hope," Serenity replied.

The woman filled the bowls with hot stew and set one bowl before each man. Immediately, the hungry braves grabbed the hot bowls and lifted them to their lips.

"Wait!" she shouted. "Wait. We must ask God's blessing first. Becca?"

The men froze with their bowls in midair. They looked at the woman in surprise. Meanwhile, Becca slinked into the room carrying the bread and the toppings. She placed them on the table and darted behind the sofa once again.

"Becca, please sit down at the table so we can say the blessing."

"Yes, ma'am," the girl mumbled. She chose to sit at the farthest end of the table.

"Now, we will bow our heads and pray." Serenity closed her eyes and folded her hands. She thanked God for their food and for giving them a warm place in the storm. Opening her eyes after the amen, she noticed the men and Becca were staring at her. She suspected they'd done so throughout the blessing. Then, with the grace of Mrs. Josephine Van der Mere, she picked up her soup spoon, dipped it into the stew, and took a sip.

The leader of the Shawnees watched her for a moment, then imitated his hostess's actions. When the hot flavorful liquid touched his tongue, he smiled at Serenity, then grunted instructions to his friends. They too set their bowls down on the table and used their spoons.

"Becca, please pass the bread and the butter to our guests." Serenity smiled at the terrified little girl sitting opposite her, then turned to the leader of the four. "You must try some of Analee's jam. It is scrumptious."

She slathered a slice of bread with jam and handed it to the leader of the group. He studied it for a moment, then timidly tasted it. A wide grin filled his face. He said something to his companions and laughed heartily. They laughed with him. Serenity prepared a slice of bread with jam for each of the men and smiled at their reaction to the sweet preserves.

Serenity carried on her own conversation throughout the meal. When the men held up their bowls, requesting seconds, she graciously refilled their bowls. "Fighting a snowstorm builds quite an appetite."

Becca cowered in fear, barely touching her stew. She looked like a bird ready to take flight at any moment. "It's all right, honey." Serenity's smile broadened. "If you want to do something, you can pray."

The girl nodded, blinking back her tears.

The men finished off the stew, the evening's supply of milk, two loaves of bread, and two bottles of jam. The leader of the group leaned back, rubbed his stomach, and grinned. He said something to his men. They laughed.

Serenity tensed as the men rose to their feet and wrapped their animal skin jackets about their bodies. The leader said something to Serenity and bowed. Taking it as a thank-you, she smiled and returned his bow.

"You are welcome to bed down in the barn for the night," she said.

The leader appeared to understand English even though he did not speak it. As each of the men repeated their leader's ritual, they headed out the door.

"Wait!" Serenity called. "Wait one second." She ran to the pantry, returned, and handed the men another loaf of bread and a jar of jam. "Here. You may get hungry on your journey home."

The men glanced at one another in surprise. The leader thanked her in his own peculiar way, then led the men from the house. Serenity watched as the men trudged through the snow toward the barn. "We'll have to shovel a path to the barn in the morning," she told Becca. "We don't have any snowshoes, do we?"

The girl remained at the table, frozen with fear. "Snowshoes? Shoveling paths? We might not be alive in the morning to worry about any of that."

Serenity laughed. "Don't worry. It's going to take more than an Indian attack to get you out of helping with the shoveling tomorrow morning."

"That's not funny!" The girl's lip protruded into a tremendous pout. "They could come back and kill us in our sleep!"

"Yes, I suppose they could," Serenity admitted.

"And you let them into the house?"

"Yes, I did."

The child eyed Serenity curiously. "Aren't you the least bit afraid?"

"Yes, I am."

"I could load the gun," Becca volunteered. "Caleb taught me how to load and shoot last spring."

Serenity shook her head. "You might kill one, but you'd never get the thing loaded a second time before the other three would be upon you. No, we did the only sensible thing under the circumstances. Besides, isn't feeding the hungry what the entire gospel of Jesus Christ is about?"

Becca hung her head. "I guess you're right. Sorry I didn't help much."

Serenity laughed as she gathered the bowls from the tabletop. "You looked like a cornered possum."

"I felt like one."

~18~
Learning to Love

SOMETIME DURING THE NIGHT, THE SNOW stopped falling. Serenity and Becca awakened to blue skies and blinding sunlight sparkling off the new-fallen snow.

While Becca fixed a pot of porridge for breakfast, Serenity put on a pair of Cyril's boots, gloves, and his coat, then clomped into the great room. "Gotta go milk Myrtle."

Becca laughed. "Those skirts are going to trip you up in the snow."

"You're right, but I don't know what else to do."

"One time after a big snowstorm back home when the men were gone, Mama and I dressed in my brothers' trousers and shirts to play in the snow."

"Your mother?" The idea of Aunt Fay wearing men's clothing scandalized the young woman.

"We had the greatest time. Sometimes I wish I were a boy so I could wear trousers as well."

"Becca, don't use that word."

"What word?"

"Trousers."

"What do you call them? Pants?"

"No! That's worse." Serenity looked horrified. "In

polite society, such clothing is called inexpressibles, unmentionables, nether garments, and sit-down-upons."

Becca giggled. "That's funny."

"But proper etiquette, nonetheless."

Becca looked at the cornmeal she'd measured into the mixing bowl. "If I help shovel a path to the barn, we could be done twice as fast. Maybe we could make a snow fort or something. We could eat later."

Serenity glanced toward the door, then back at Becca. "Do you really think we should?"

"I'll race you getting changed." Becca charged from the room with Serenity at her heels.

The two girls shrieked with laughter seeing one another dressed in Cyril's woolen pants and flannel shirts. Serenity examined herself in front of the mirror in the Doran's bedroom. She twisted first one way, then another. "I can't believe I'm doing this!"

Having been a small-framed man, Cyril wore pants that didn't allow much wriggle room in the hips for either Serenity or Becca. Becca put on a second pair of boots and a heavy Indian mackinaw. She searched in the Doran's bureau until she found another pair of leather gloves as well. With mufflers wrapped about their necks and heads until only their eyes were visible, they ventured out into the snow.

"Last one to the snow, shovels first," Becca shouted and dashed for the door. As her hand touched the latch, she halted and turned to face Serenity.

"What's the matter?"

"The Shawnees. What if they're still in the barn?"

Serenity thought a moment. "I guess we'll ask them to breakfast."

Becca rolled her eyes heavenward and hauled open the door. A gust of cold air accosted her face as she stepped out into the blinding sunshine. Serenity followed and closed the door behind them. "Where do you think we'll find a shovel?"

The girls looked at one another. In unison, they said, "In the barn."

Serenity turned toward the barn and gasped in surprise. "Look." She pointed at a perfectly shoveled path stretching between the house and the barn.

"What if they're still asleep inside the barn?" Becca whispered.

"No, they're gone. The pathway is too clear. They must have just shoveled it. The wind hasn't had time to create drifts." When the two girls reached the barn, Serenity opened the barn door and peered inside, half expecting to come face to face with a war party. Instead, she spotted a bucket of milk and a covered basket sitting in the middle of the floor.

She wandered into the barn looking for traces of their night visitors. There were none. Serenity bent down and lifted the cover off the wicker basket. "Look, Becca, look! Our guests even gathered the eggs for us. What do you bet they fed the chickens as well?"

"Fed them what?" the child asked.

"Who knows?" Serenity handed the basket to Becca and picked up the bucket of milk. "Let's take these back to the house, then we can play."

They romped in the snow most of the morning. Too fine for building snow forts or snowmen, it was perfect for making snow angels. They ran to the top of the hill.

"I wish I had my sled. Daddy wouldn't let me bring it along," Becca lamented. A world of white stretched to each horizon.

"We can lay down and roll," Serenity suggested. "Race you to the bottom!"

Shrieking with laughter, the girls rolled down the hill, then ran to the top to do it again. It wasn't until the sun was high overhead that Becca stopped and rubbed her stomach. "I'm getting hungry."

"Me too." Serenity stood and brushed as much snow from her clothing as possible.

"Mama uses a broom." Becca tromped to the front door.

"Good idea. The broom is in the pantry. Let's go around to the back door. Race you!" Serenity charged through the deep snow, her height an advantage over the ten-year-old's stride. After brushing the snow from each other's clothing, they shed their heavy outerwear, including the pants and shirts, and ran to their bedroom to put on their slips, stockings, and dresses.

Serenity tightened the laces to her camisole. *Feels good to be a female again,* she thought.

"Do you think we can do that again tomorrow?" Becca said, eyes sparkling.

"Maybe so. Tonight, let's make some of your mother's snow candy. You'll have to teach me how."

"OK." The child's eyes glistened with happiness, her earlier fears tucked away for awhile.

Serenity tied an apron about her waist and hurried to the kitchen. Instead of making the porridge Becca had started mixing, Serenity added the necessary milk, grease, and salt to the cornmeal for cornbread. "And for dessert," she added, "we'll have applesauce!"

There was one thing Serenity was especially thankful for: There would not be a shortage of food. While she had hated doing the work at the time, Serenity now appreciated each jar of corn on the pantry shelves and each slab of corned beef hanging in the cold cellar. With enough food preserved to feed the entire Cunard family as well as the Dorans until spring, there was plenty for just the two of them.

That evening, Serenity boiled down the syrup as Becca instructed. Becca filled a dishpan full of snow and set it by the pantry door. "Is the syrup ready? Is it boiled to the ball stage yet?"

"The ball stage?" Serenity let the syrup run off the spoon into the boiling pot. "What do you mean?"

"Here." The girl brought a cup of ice water to Serenity. "Drip a couple of drops of the syrup into the water." She ran her tongue over her lips as she watched Serenity follow her instructions. "Good! See? When it's ready, the syrup forms balls in ice water. Now, we pour the syrup onto the snow."

"You're a bright little gal." Carefully, Serenity carried the boiling pot of syrup through the pantry and outside. Becca watched as she poured the hot sticky liquid over the packed snow. The snow hissed and sizzled as the syrup coated the snow's surface.

"Be sure to soak the pot in water right away. This stuff makes great glue," Becca giggled.

Serenity filled the pot with water and left it to soak on the back of the stove. By the time she returned to Becca, the girl was breaking the sticky substance from the snow and eating it. "Isn't it delicious?"

Serenity broke off a piece of the taffy, stringing it from the pan to her lips. "Mmm! This was a good idea, Becca."

The girl beamed with pleasure. "It is good, huh?"

"Very."

Suddenly, shouting from the front of the house caught

both girls' attention. "Last night's guests have come back for seconds!" Becca cried, looking frightened.

With a long wooden spoon in hand, Serenity started for the front door. "I fully doubt it." A heavy fist pounded on the door. Onyx barked and growled menacingly. Someone called out.

Becca brightened. "That's Aaron!" She ran past Serenity and flung open the door. "Aaron, you're home!"

Instantly Serenity sensed something was wrong with the younger Cunard son. Pale and bleary-eyed, he staggered into the house. "Say, where is everybody?" he slurred. His feet tangled with a braided throw rug near the door. He stumbled, caught himself before he fell, and giggled at his feet.

Serenity had barely recovered from Aaron's unexpected arrival when two tough-looking men pushed past Becca into the house. "So, this is the place that harbors redskins!" one of the men snarled.

Serenity's blood ran cold. "I beg your pardon! Aaron, who are these men? And why are you bringing them into my house?"

Caleb's younger brother giggled and stretched out on the sofa, his snow-covered boots resting on the quilt. Serenity marched over to the sofa and snatched the quilt from beneath his feet. "Aaron, take off your boots! You'll ruin the sofa."

"Why should you care?" he giggled and threw back his greasy head against one of Analee's needlepoint pillows.

"Because this is my home. I own the place."

"Sure you do."

"I'm serious. Take your feet off my sofa."

His head wobbled as he struggled to focus on her face. "You what?"

"I bought the place when Mr. Doran died. Now get your boots off my sofa!"

She turned to see one of the men behind her lift the cover on a kettle of water heating on the stove and sniff. "What's to eat?" he growled. "I'm hungry. You said they'd feed us here!"

Aaron waved an absent hand in the air. "They will. They will. Tell Ma I'm home."

"You are dripping melting snow on my clean floor." Serenity grabbed the pot cover from the man's hands and rapped him on the knuckles with her wooden spoon. "Tell me, Aaron, who are your friends?"

He laughed and pointed a finger at Serenity. "That, boys, is Serenity Pownell, the daughter of an illustrious New York state assemblyman. She's about to marry my equally magnificent older brother, Caleb. Serenity, say hello to my friends." His head weaved back and forth, then thumped onto the pillow once more. "Where's Ma?"

"You still haven't told me who these men are!" Serenity walked over to the sofa and stared down at him, her hands planted firmly on her hips. Becca, still standing by the open door, stared at the drama playing out before her.

"Becca, slice up the potatoes I brought in the house for tomorrow's breakfast and the onion as well." Serenity took a deep ragged breath. She'd done well hiding her fears thus far. She didn't want to lose it now.

"And you, whoever you are," she pointed to the nearest man. "If you're hungry, introduce yourself and clean up the mess you've made on my floor. The mop is in the pantry."

"I h'ain't gonn—"

"You will if you want to eat!"

The man sputtered at his buddy, "I h'ain't gonna swing a mop, boss. That's women's work!"

Serenity glared at the man. "Around here, it becomes men's work when a man made the mess!"

Aaron sat up, leaning on one arm. "Hee hee! Serves my brother right, getting a shrew of a wife. What happened, sweetheart?" He leered at Serenity. "When did the little peach change into a lemon?"

"When you showed up at my door, drunk, dragging along two strangers, that's when. Will you gentlemen introduce yourselves, or shall I send Becca for the rifle?"

The second man grinned at the little girl and snorted. "Yeah, right. I'm quivering in my boots."

Serenity sauntered over to him, staring at his insolent face. She narrowed her gaze threateningly. "Names! I want names!"

The man's eyes shot open in surprise. "Uh, Bricker's the name."

"Is that your sur name or your given name."

The man chuckled. "I h'ain't never been called Sir before. Bricker's the only name I got."

Serenity extended her hand to the surprised man. "Then, good evening, Mr. Bricker, welcome to my home. Please make yourself comfortable. By the way, there's a mop in the pantry to get up the puddle of water you're standing in." She smiled sweetly and turned toward the other man, the one who appeared to be the leader of the three. "And you, sir, are?"

The man's gaze swept her from the hem of her skirts to the flyaway curls haloing her face. He ruminated for a moment, then lifted one eyebrow. "Savage, Tom Savage. Mighty purty filly, Aaron. Your brother must be daft leaving her alone for one minute."

Serenity answered the man's insolence with an arched eyebrow.

"Where are my parents anyway?" Aaron asked.

Serenity hesitated. "In town. I'm sure they'll be back any time."

"No, they're not, Serenity," Becca frowned at the woman. "Daddy and Mama are at Fort Atkinson—oh!"

Becca's voice faded into a whimper when she realized what she'd done. She and Serenity had talked about keeping their situation secret. Becca whirled around toward Serenity. "But this is Aaron, Serenity, not some stranger." Glancing at the strangers, Becca's resolve melted. "I'm sorry," she whimpered.

"It's all right, honey." Serenity took a deep breath. "Go start the potatoes. Our guests are hungry."

"Yes, ma'am."

"So," the man who called himself Savage, stepped up behind Serenity. She could smell the alcohol on his breath, which was hot on her neck. "So, you're here all alone?" He ran his hands lightly over her arms. "You smell pretty."

She whirled on him, her eyes fiery. "No, you don't, Mr. Savage. Aaron, tell your friend to keep his hands off of me! Aaron!" She glanced over her shoulder to find the youngest Cunard son passed out cold on the sofa.

"Can't hold his liquor," Bricker explained.

"Why don't you and I go in one of those bedrooms back there and play while little sister is frying up the potatoes?" Savage tugged at one of her curls.

Serenity lifted the wooden spoon as if to strike. "The only playing you will be doing, Mr. Savage, will be twiddle-de-dee with your fingers. If you lay your filthy hands on either me or Becca again I will clobber you."

"Ho-ho," Savage laughed. "Tough little filly. I like women with spunk."

"Ho, boss, she's not why we're here remember?" Bricker stood by the door, mop in hand.

Savage's eyes narrowed into a look of disgust. "You're right. I can wait 'til later. Can you, sweet plum? Hey, Blondie," he called to Becca, "those potatoes ready? They're sure smellin' mighty good."

A sudden knock at the door alarmed the two men. "The sheriff," Bricker hissed.

Savage sent a warning look to his partner, then grabbed Serenity's arm and thrust her toward the door. "Answer it."

Serenity stumbled, then caught her balance before reaching the door. Straightening her apron and collar, she reached for the door latch just as the knock sounded again.

Oh, Dear Father, what's next? You said You'd protect us from the snare of the fowler. Do Savage and Bricker qualify? She opened the door and stopped short. Her jaw dropped. "Mr. Blackwing! Gray Sparrow! What are you doing here?"

"We come in."

She couldn't read the solemn expression on the man's face. He and his wife stepped over the threshold. Uncertain as to what to say, Serenity backed up and waved them into the house.

Resenting the interlopers, Savage swaggered over to the Shawnee couple. "Get out of here, old man. Go back to your teepee."

Bricker snickered at Savage's bravado.

Savage turned to Gray Sparrow. "What's the matter, old woman? Cat got your tongue?"

Before Savage could laugh at his own joke, the woman opened her mouth to reveal an ugly stub where her tongue should have been.

Savage stared in horror, as did Bricker. Serenity glanced away.

"We stay." Joseph stood eye to eye with Savage.

"I told you to get out of here!" Savage looped his thumbs in his gun belt.

"We stay!" the Shawnee repeated. With hardly a movement, Gray Sparrow stepped aside to reveal a knife resting lightly at Joseph's right hand. Lantern light glinted off the eight-inch blade.

Savage stepped back, his gaze still fixed on the Shawnee. Bricker stepped around the door and spied the knife. "Whoa! This Injun means business!"

Serenity stepped forward and led Gray Sparrow toward the dinner table. "Mr. and Mrs. Blackwing are always welcome in this house. Please, won't you come in? We are just about to eat supper."

The Shawnee and the gunslinger circled one another like two roosters in a henhouse, never taking their eyes off the other. Savage was the first to look away. The uneasy truce remained throughout the evening meal. Only the unconscious Aaron remained oblivious to it.

Once he finished eating, Joseph Blackwing stood motionless beside the fireplace. Sheathing his knife, he picked up the fireplace poker. Gray Sparrow helped clear the table and start the dishes.

Wanting to get rid of Aaron and his friends as quickly as possible, Serenity suggested the three intruders bed down in the barn.

"Looks like you have several beds in here not being used." Savage craned his neck down the narrow hallway.

A chill skittered up Serenity's spine. "I don't think so. The barn will serve you well. It's plenty warm and there are blankets stored in the hay loft. And please, take Aaron with you."

Savage eyed Serenity with malice and desire. "You gonna

let these savages stay in your home while your brother-in-law-
to-be and his very best friends sleep in the barn?"

"Excuse me, sir. This is Mr. and Mrs. Blackwing. The
only savage in here is you, I believe."

The man bared his teeth in frustration. "Pick him up,
Bricker!"

"Why me?" Bricker started in surprise.

"Because I said so!"

The man strode out the door, leaving his companion to
wrestle Aaron to his feet and to the barn.

The moment the door closed behind them, Becca
rushed to Serenity's arms. Serenity turned toward the
Blackwings. "How can I ever thank you for coming to our
rescue? You will stay the night, won't you?" Serenity's voice
broke. "How did you know we needed help?"

"Trouble travels fast."

"You will stay the night?"

Joseph nodded solemnly. "We will stay until they leave."

"Thank you. Let me make up the Doran's bed for you—"
Serenity started toward the hallway.

"No bed," Joseph said. "We sleep on floor."

"Are you sure?" Serenity gazed first at Joseph, then at
Gray Sparrow. "It would be no trouble."

"We sleep on floor." Joseph bowed his head respectfully.

As Serenity and Becca washed and dried the dinner dishes, Gray Sparrow inspected the pantry, grunting her
approval every few minutes. The Shawnee woman fingered
the gingham curtains tenderly. Her eyes sparkled as she ran
her hand along the smooth oiled surface of the trestle table.

Serenity found several blankets stored in the large trunk
at the foot of the Doran's bed and gave them to the woman.

"Thank you again, for staying here tonight." Serenity

kissed the Shawnee woman's cheek. Gray Sparrow's eyes shone with happiness. The wrinkles in her cheeks broadened into a smile.

"You and Joseph can spread the blankets on the floor of the Doran's bedroom."

The Shawnee woman nodded and left the great room.

Serenity heaved a sigh of relief. She rubbed her neck with one hand. It had been a long day.

Becca kissed Serenity on the cheek. "I've never seen Aaron like that before. I'm sorry he brought those bad men here."

"Me too," Serenity confessed. "Alcohol does that sometimes. When I was little and my parents took me to parties in Albany, I often saw normally respectable and thoughtful men become abusive or silly after a few drinks of whiskey."

Becca hugged Serenity about the waist. "If that Savage man really tried to do something bad to either of us, I'm sure Aaron would have stopped him."

"I'm sure he would, dear. Now, how about going to bed? You're almost asleep on your feet."

Becca kissed her again, then headed for bed. "Are you staying up very long?"

Serenity shook her head. "Not too."

"I hope not. I don't think I want to be alone tonight."

"I'll be in in a few minutes." Alone in the great room, Serenity wandered to the rocker by the fireplace and sat down. She picked up her Bible and turned to Psalm 91. Halfway through the chapter, she paused and smiled. "You did send help when I needed it, didn't You, Father? You are so faithful. All along You've made sure someone was there to help me through. My father, Caleb, Cyril, Uncle Eli, Mr. Blackwing, Mr. Bonner . . . You're so good to me."

Serenity closed her eyes and pictured Caleb's laughing face. She relived strolling with him to the grassy knoll, doing dishes together, the taste of his tender kisses on her lips. The thoughts produced a deep ache within her. *Having Caleb gone feels like a piece of me is missing,* she mused. "Please come home soon, my precious one. Come home soon."

~19~

Sweet Rendezvous

THE MORNING AFTER AARON AND HIS friends' unexpected visit, Serenity slept fitfully. The sound of a pan rattling in the kitchen raised her from her tossing and turning. Thinking Aaron and his friends had broken into the house, she leaped from bed, threw on her robe, and grabbed the long-handled warming pan from under the covers.

"What?" Becca sat up in bed and rubbed her eyes.

"You stay here!" Poising the pan over her head, Serenity opened the bedroom door and crept toward the great room, preparing her mind for the attack. She burst into the great room, then froze.

Across the room, the startled Shawnee woman gasped, throwing a handful of flatware into the air. The spoons and knives clattered on the wooden floor beside her. Becca screamed and ran to Serenity. Outside the front door, Onyx barked and violently lunged at the closed door.

Gray Sparrow's eyes darted back and forth in confusion. She waved her hands frantically in the air and shook her head. The front door burst open and Joseph Blackwing charged into the house, stumbling over Onyx on the way.

"They come back?" he shouted, waving his knife in one hand and the milk pail in the other.

Serenity took one look at the excited Shawnee and doubled over with laughter. Between bouts of hilarity, she tried to explain, "I heard a noise . . . Aaron . . . Gray Sparrow . . ." Tears ran down her cheeks.

Joseph and Gray Sparrow silently watched until Serenity regained control. "I'm sorry. Once I begin laughing, I can't always stop." The young woman tried to explain her surprising entrance.

Gray Sparrow grinned a toothless smile. As Serenity wiped the tears from her eyes, she was certain she saw the beginnings of a smile at one corner of Joseph's mouth.

After breakfast, the Shawnee couple said their goodbyes. Serenity thanked them again. "I don't know what we would have done without you last night." Serenity hugged Gray Sparrow. "And you, Mr. Blackwing, how *did* you know we needed your help last night?"

"Not much happens that the Shawnee do not know," the man said just as mysteriously as he had the night before.

"But why did you come to help us?"

"Mr. Doran and his wife were kind to my people. And you, Miss Serenity, have also shown kindness too. You treat us like people, not like dogs."

His words left the young woman speechless.

He continued, "There is a verse in your Book that I learned while living in the white man's world. It says, 'He shall give His angels charge over thee, to keep thee in all thy ways.' Miss Serenity, please consider the Shawnee your earthbound angels." With that, the couple turned and walked out the cabin door.

"Thank you," Serenity called and waved, but they never looked back.

Red-skinned angels? Serenity laughed aloud as she rolled out the bread dough. *Why not?* she mused, shaping the dough into loaves. *Brown-skinned angels? Black-skinned angels? Is it the skin that makes a difference, or the heart?* She mulled the idea for some time.

Angels or no, she decided that God had used her Shawnee friends to keep His promises to her. She had no doubt but that the braves told the rest of the tribe about her situation. A new thought surfaced in her mind.

What if I hadn't treated the four braves kindly? Would I have thwarted the carrying out of the very promise I was claiming? *Strange ideas,* she thought. *I wonder if they'd curl Uncle Eli's ears?* The notion humored her as she covered the perfectly formed loaves with a tea towel, then placed them on the warming board at the back of the stove top.

A week passed of heavy snowstorms. Whenever Serenity and Becca worked outside in the cold, they wore Mr. Doran's trousers, or as Serenity chose to call them, "sit-down-upons." Inside the house, Serenity insisted they don their crinolines and dresses.

"And if you ever tell your brother that I wore sit-down-upons," Serenity warned, "I will personally string you up by your thumbs!"

"Ooh, I'm scared," Becca giggled.

The good times grew fewer the longer the two were isolated at the mission. While Serenity grew introspective, the little girl slept a lot, more than Serenity would have liked. The child helped with the chores without complaining; but as soon as she finished what was expected of her, she would slip away to the bedroom for a nap.

Serenity recognized the symptoms of cabin fever, with a touch of homesickness added, and encouraged Becca to do her studies; but the girl would only pout and stare into space or burst into tears and run to the bedroom.

The only time Serenity could reach the child was in the evening after worship when they read together. When they began reading *Jane Eyre,* neither she nor Becca wanted to stop reading each night. Serenity decided she would use Charlotte Brontë's book as a lure.

One snowy afternoon while Serenity sat on the sofa repairing a sleeve on one of her dresses, she suggested that they read another chapter in the book. Becca, who was stretched out on the floor in front of the fireplace, came to life. "Really? I'll go get the book." The girl leaped to her feet.

"Of course, I'd feel better about reading ahead in the story if you did a page or two in your arithmetic book."

Becca glared at the young woman. Serenity smiled to herself as, out of the corner of her eye, she watched the child decide what to do. Reluctantly, Becca walked into her bedroom and returned to the table, arithmetic book, chalk, and slateboard. In less than an hour, she'd completed the problems on three pages. "May we read the book now?"

"Would you like to read today?" Serenity asked. She knew that Becca enjoyed reading aloud.

The following Sunday dawned sunny and cold. Serenity and Becca battled the biting winds while completing the outdoor chores. With the milking done, Serenity handed the bucket of warm milk to Becca. "Here, take the milk into the house. I want to bring in a slab of corned beef for dinner. Would you like carrots and potatoes with that?"

"Sounds good." Becca picked up the milk pail and headed for the house. Halfway across the barnyard, the girl screamed and ran back to the barn.

Serenity charged up the cold cellar steps. "What's the matter? What's wrong?"

"There's a sleigh coming! Do you think it's Mama and Daddy?" Tears glistened in the child's eyes. "Do you?"

Serenity's heart leaped. Caleb! Could it be Caleb? She glanced down at her clothing and screamed. "Oh! He can't find me dressed like this!" She dashed to the rear of the barn where her trunks were stored. "I must change. What can I wear?"

"They'll be here any minute!" The child danced and shouted. She and Onyx raced to the open door, then back again.

Ignoring the girl's warnings, Serenity pawed through her first trunk. "The blue satin?" She held it up in front of her. "Too wrinkled! The beige lace? That one's in the house waiting for the wedding."

Suddenly she noticed that a corner of the lid to the false bottom was raised. Pulling it up, she stared down into the empty compartment. "No!" Leaping to her feet, she threw open the lid to her second trunk and pawed through the clothing to discover that the second hidden compartment was also empty. "My gold bars. They're gone. They're gone!"

"Gone? What's gone?" a voice called.

Serenity stood up and spun around to see Felix standing in the open doorway.

The man stared in surprise. "Serenity, is that you?"

"Of course it's me. Who did you think it was?" She snapped. A second man, whom she recognized as the town sheriff, stood beside the attorney. Becca lingered in the shadows behind the men, her face downcast.

"What are you doing here!"

"Well . . ." The attorney blinked in surprise at the venom in her voice. "I thought I'd drop by for a visit. I was worried about you. So was Sheriff Prior."

Serenity grabbed up the blue satin dress and held it in front of her. "We're fine. Becca and I are fine."

"I can see that." The attorney grinned.

"Wipe that grin from your face, Felix Bonner!" she snapped.

Felix tried to hide the smile, but it kept creeping back at the corners of his mouth. "It seems like you've adapted well to farm life, Miss Serenity."

She glared at him, then turned toward the other man.

"Sheriff, you're just the man I need. How do I go about reporting a theft. It seems I've been robbed of three gold bars."

"Gold bars? How big are they?"

"Twenty-five pounds each."

"Whew!" Felix whistled.

The lawman asked, "Sure you didn't misplace them?"

"Twenty-five pound weights of solid gold? Hardly!"

"Probably not." He grinned and nodded. "Had any visitors?"

"Visitors? Have we had visitors!" Becca interrupted. "First, Joseph Blackwing and his wife, then four Indians, then Aaron and his friends, then Mr. and Mrs. Blackwing returned—"

Felix looked aghast at the child, then shot a confused look toward Serenity. "What are you operating here, Serenity's Inn or something?"

"I am not amused."

The sheriff stroked his mustache thoughtfully. "I thought so. Felix, didn't I tell you those varmints were up to no good?"

"You did, Abe," Felix replied.

"What varmints?" Serenity asked.

The sheriff glanced about the barn before answering. "Those renegade Indians. We believe they've been robbing and pillaging homesteads throughout the region."

"The Shawnees?"

"They're thieving polecats," the sheriff sniffed. "Can you tell me where your gold was stored?"

Serenity nodded and led them to the trunks.

Sheriff Prior's eyebrows shot up to his hairline. "You left your valuables in the barn, then allowed strangers to sleep in the vicinity?"

Serenity's face reddened. "I guess it wasn't too smart of me, was it? But they were so mannerly."

"Mannerly Indians? Never heard of such a creature," the sheriff snorted.

"Sheriff," Serenity began, "I don't think the Shawnees stole my gold. I would more likely suspect Aaron's friends. They showed up drunk, especially Aaron."

"Yeah, drunk as a skunk!" Becca added. "I didn't like that Mr. Savage or the man who called himself Bricker."

The thought of the two men sent chills up and down Serenity's spine. "Do you know these men, Sheriff?"

"Bricker and Savage were here?" Felix's eyes widened.

Serenity sent Felix a sarcastic glare. "Becca told you that—"

"She didn't mention their names!" The man glared in return.

The sheriff shook his index finger at the woman. "You, little lady, are lucky they only took your gold. They could have killed you." The sheriff paused a moment. "Hmm, those two have been spending money like water the last week or so."

Becca asked, "Can't you arrest them before they spend the rest of Serenity's inheritance?"

"It's not as easy as it sounds. I heard tell they headed south to Texas before the last snowstorm. Tracking them now would be impossible. Of course, I could arrest Aaron for his involvement."

"My brother? He didn't go with them?" Becca asked, her voice tight with emotion.

"No, he's still at Mary's Place, last I heard."

"Mary's Place?" Becca brightened.

The sheriff reddened, casting a hopeful glance toward Felix. He, too, blushed. "It's a boarding house in Independence," Felix gulped.

Becca folded her arms across her chest and eyed the attorney. "You mean a bordello!"

"Becca!" Serenity snapped. "Where did you hear a term like that?"

"That's what Daddy calls it. I heard him arguing with Mama one night. Daddy said Aaron was living in a bordello!"

Serenity placed her hand on the girl's shoulder and spoke gently. "Ladies don't use such terms."

"Why?"

"They just don't." Serenity cleared her throat, then straightened. "What do we do now, Sheriff?"

The man shrugged. "Not much we can do, I'm afraid, miss. I'm sorry."

Serenity frowned. Her brow knitted as she considered her loss. *My loss?* she thought *What loss? The gold has done nothing more than weigh down my trunk. And while it is the last tie to my father,* she mused, *it doesn't compensate for his absence.* A giggle gurgled up in Serenity's throat.

The men stared in surprise when the young woman giggled. Covering her mouth, she chuckled again, then broke into laughter, but only after she snorted in a most unladylike manner. Her laughter continued until she was gasping for breath. She doubled over with laughter, then flopped down into the closest mound of hay.

Stunned by Serenity's actions, Becca reached out to the laughing woman. When she did, Serenity grabbed Becca and the two of them rolled across the hay.

"She's gone berserk!" the sheriff said helplessly. "What do we do?"

"I don't know," Felix admitted. "I don't have much experience with hysterical women."

"And I do?" the lawman asked. "Why do you think I'm a forty-seven-year-old bachelor?"

Serenity's laughter subsided, with only occasional spurts breaking into her speech as she tried to explain what had prompted her bizarre behavior.

"Don't you see?" Serenity explained. "Caleb was all atwitter about my wealth. He was having a difficult time coming to terms with it. Now, I don't have any money and our problem is solved! And you know what else? I want to have a baby!"

The men stared at her in horror. Recognizing what she'd said and the shock on the men's faces, she tried to redeem herself. "Not just any baby, but Caleb's baby! Isn't that amazing?"

The sheriff approached her with caution. "Are you sure you're all right, Miss Serenity? Could Miss Becca fetch you a drink of water, perhaps?"

Serenity laughed at the uneasy concern on the man's face. Suddenly feeling devilishly free of society's inhibitions, she laughed again. "I'm all right, gentlemen. Honest. Please forgive me." She gasped, trying to catch her breath between bouts of hilarity. "It's a family thing. My mama says my quirky laughter came from her side of the family. It used to drive my Quaker grandfather wild when one of his daughters had what he called 'a laughing fit.'"

For a moment Serenity's thoughts drifted back to the big house overlooking Cayuga Lake. "As a child, I loved it whenever my mother 'let her hair down,' as Daddy called it, and started laughing. Sometimes she and I would giggle so hard we'd roll on the parlor floor, laughing with one another. We could never convince my father to join us."

Serenity giggled again. The men looked uncertain as to what, if anything, they should do.

"I'm all right now, I assure you," she chuckled. "No more histrionics, I promise."

"Histrionics?" The sheriff scowled.

"Laughter, Sheriff. I'll try not to laugh anymore." She giggled even as she said the words, then inhaled deeply. "Whew! I needed that. It's been a tense few weeks around here."

Felix offered her his hand. "Are you sure you're feeling well?"

Serenity smiled and allowed him to help her to her feet, then take her arm.

"I think we should go inside the house. Perhaps it might help if you rest a bit. Losing all your money must be traumatic."

"Not really. Losing my money solved more problems than it created; really it did." The young lawyer's face filled with doubt.

She allowed him to lead her into the house. "You know, Felix, you said something interesting out there in the barn."

"I did?" He led the woman to the sofa and insisted she sit. Felix sat down beside her and held her hand. "Becca, would you heat some water? I think Serenity needs a cup of chamomile tea."

"Don't you want to hear what it was?" Serenity leaned her head back against the sofa. "Make enough tea for everyone, Becca."

"If you want to tell me."

"You asked if I were running an inn. 'Serenity's Inn,' you called it." She didn't wait for him to respond. "That's a mighty good idea, don't you think? An inn for families traveling west with children? A place that is clean and set apart from the, uh, boarding houses in town."

Felix pursed his lips thoughtfully.

"Hmm, it really is a good idea," Serenity continued. "I mean, this little sod and rock structure has six bedrooms already. Even with the entire Cunard family living here we'd have at least one extra room. And Cyril had plans drawn for a schoolhouse. With a few modifications—"

Suddenly Serenity sat up with a start. "While the tea is steeping, I think I need to change my clothing. Will you gentlemen excuse me, please?"

Becca and the two men eyed one another, uncertain as to what to expect next. Serenity smiled sweetly at each of them, then retired to her room. Minutes later she appeared in a petal pink calico gown, her dark curly hair pinned atop her head. Tiny ringlets spiraled down the sides of her delicate face. A ruby brooch secured the lace collar about the neck of her dress.

"Gentlemen?" She stepped into the great room. Felix and Sheriff Prior's mouths dropped open in surprise. "Forgive me, but you must be hungry. It is past dinnertime." She strolled past the men and into the kitchen. "You will eat something, won't you?"

The men nodded slowly.

"Wonderful. Becca will get both of you that promised cup of tea while I set the table. Do you both like potato-onion soup?"

Felix and the sheriff silently nodded a second time.

"Good. It's one of my favorites as well." She busied herself placing small plates and bowls on the table. "You mentioned something about arresting Aaron, Sheriff?" Serenity glanced toward the silent lawman. "I'm not comfortable with that. True, he probably mentioned the gold to the other two men; but I don't believe he had anything to do with the theft. He may be young and foolish, but he's not a thief."

Becca shot a look of gratitude at Serenity.

The sheriff rolled his tongue in his cheek, then said, "That's very generous of you, Miss Serenity. Understandable though, being family and all."

Becca served the men their tea while Serenity completed setting the table.

"I didn't tell you, Serenity," Felix began. "After you bought the mission, I sent word to Caleb by way of a military regiment that passed through the area. I felt he needed to know, uh, how things were going."

Serenity paused, the flatware heavy in her hand. "Thank you for your concern, Mr. Bonner; but the decision to buy the mission was mine to make, not my fiancé's."

"I did what I felt best." Felix's eyes pleaded for her to understand.

"I know. And perhaps, in your situation, I would have done the same thing."

Felix strode across the room and placed a hand on hers. "I am your friend, you know, even if you do want to have another man's baby."

"Felix!" She snatched back her hand and flushed with color. "That was uncalled for. A gentleman would not have brought up my earlier indiscretions!"

The attorney smiled. "Are you joking? My mind is a steel trap. I never forget a thing."

Serenity whirled away, swishing her taffeta petticoats as she hurried to the stove. "The soup is ready. Let me slice the bread. Becca's bread simply melts in your mouth."

They sat down to the table. Serenity bowed her head for the blessing. So did Becca. Awkwardly, Felix and the sheriff did the same. A long pause followed. Serenity expected one of the men to offer the blessing, and they expected her to do so. When it was obvious to her that no one would, she took a deep breath and prayed. Her list of gratitude went far beyond the food sitting on the table before them.

" . . . and thank You, Father, for friends that care. Amen."

The conversation flowed smoothly during the meal. Serenity would have preferred that Becca not tell about the frightening experience with the two outlaws, but the child would not be stopped. When Felix heard about her bold behavior toward Savage, he looked at her in horror. Serenity shrugged and smiled weakly.

To change the subject, Serenity asked, "So, Sheriff, when do you expect the telegraph to reach Independence?"

Felix started at the mention of the telegraph. "Oh dear, I forgot." He rushed from the table to the suede coat he'd hung by the door. Reaching in the pocket, he drew out an envelope.

"This came for you last week." He handed it to Serenity. "When I mentioned to the postmaster that I was coming out here today, he asked me to deliver it."

Serenity stared at the envelope. The return address, a New Orleans location, sported the gold embossed seal of Josephine Van der Mere. Serenity's fingers trembled as she broke the wax seal and removed the linen pages from the envelope. As an afterthought, she glanced toward her guests. "Forgive me, but—"

Felix laughed. Picking up on his thoughts, Serenity chuckled aloud herself. After all the social gaffes she'd committed that evening, reading a letter at the table seemed insignificant.

"It's all right, Serenity. Go ahead and read your letter," the lawyer said.

Serenity blanched as she scanned the first paragraph. She looked up at her guests, her eyes brimming with tears. "My father . . . my father's alive." Her voice came out in sharp gasps. "He was reported lost at sea, but he's alive!" She squeezed shut her eyes. Her face distorted. "My daddy's alive!"

Dabbing her eyes with her dinner napkin, Serenity tried to focus on the rest of the letter: "Your father was beaten and robbed. The thief used your father's identity to board the ship, which later sank. Talk about justice!"

Serenity felt light-headed. Her breath came in short hiccups as she continued reading: "In serious condition after the beating, it was weeks before your father could tell anyone who he was and what had happened. When he did, the authorities contacted me; and here I am in New Orleans, nursing him back to health."

Becca and the two men watched in silence as Serenity continued reading the letter.

"I don't believe it," she whispered. "Josephine says that she and my father are planning to take the first riverboat available in the spring." Her eyes danced. "They're coming here! To Independence!" She covered her mouth with one hand, trying to catch her breath before she dissolved into tears, muttering, "My daddy's alive. My daddy's alive!" She slid to her knees beside the table and buried her face in her lap. "Thank You, Lord. Thank You. You are so good to me."

Serenity once again seated herself at the table. As she recovered from her shock, Becca busied herself with clearing the table and heating water for washing the dishes.

"Becca, let me help you—" Serenity tried to stand, but her knees refused to support her.

"I can take care of everything," the ten-year-old assured her.

"Sheriff Prior and I'll dry the dishes," Felix volunteered. Serenity laughed, in spite of her weakness, at the sheriff's nonplussed gaze. Felix helped Serenity to her feet and guided her to the sofa. He carefully covered her lap with the quilt and adjusted one of the sofa pillows behind her back. "You rest. You've had enough excitement for one night. A weaker woman would have fainted."

"I came close to it," Serenity laughed.

"Don't worry. We won't leave until we're sure you'll be all right. No more hysterics and definitely, no vapors." Felix leaned over the sofa and smoothed the quilt around Serenity. "You just take it easy—"

Suddenly the cabin door swung open, banging against the wall. A man bundled from head to tow in winter garb filled the doorway. Only his dark eyes peered over the plaid woolen muffler wrapped around his neck. Becca and Serenity screamed. Sheriff Prior and Felix reached for their guns.

"Oh, Lord, no more," Serenity whispered. "I can't take any more."

The man's gaze swept across the set table and the faces of the two male visitors. "What is going on here?" he demanded. "Bonner, what are you doing here?"

Recognizing her fiancé's voice, Serenity started to her feet. "Caleb? Is that you?"

The man laughed. "Who were you expecting?"

"Caleb!" Serenity flung the quilt from her lap and leaped into her fiancé's arms. "You're home! You're home!" She buried her face in his neck. Becca ran to her older brother, who scooped the little girl into his arms.

Wrapping his free arm about Serenity's slight waist, Caleb eyed the attorney and the sheriff. "Since when did the local law enforcement make house calls?"

"Who cares?" Serenity snuggled into his arms. "The important thing is you're finally home!"

She helped him remove his heavy wool coat and hat as he explained: "I've been traveling day and night since I got the letter about the Dorans. My mother insisted that you needed me more than she and Daddy. By the way, they send their love."

Serenity took his jacket and hung it on one of the coat hooks behind the door, then snuggled into his arms once again. "I've missed you so much."

Caleb glanced at Felix. "I want to thank you, Mr. Bonner, for notifying me. I really appreciate it." He kissed the tip of Serenity's nose. "What's this I hear about you buying this place?" He gazed into her glistening eyes. "And whatever for?"

She threw back her head and laughed. "To open an inn, of course, Serenity's Inn."

~20~
Satin Ribbons
and
Crocheted Roses

THE WEEK AFTER CALEB RETURNED HOME flew by quickly as Serenity prepared for the wedding. Waiting any longer to marry seemed unwise since it would be improper for Caleb, as a single man, to live at the mission. Recognizing the potential problem, Fay and Eli had given their blessing to an immediate wedding. Neither Caleb nor Serenity minded the haste.

When the Baptist minister, Robert Rich, and his wife, Louella, heard of the couple's dilemma, they invited Serenity and Becca to stay at their home while Caleb stayed at the mission to care for the animals. In the mornings, Serenity restyled one of her new gowns for Becca to wear to the wedding while Becca helped her stitch the seams. Each afternoon, Caleb rode into town to see his bride-to-be. Mrs. Rich kept herself and Becca busy in the kitchen while the couple sparked in the parlor.

The December sun rose bright and beautiful on their wedding day. Serenity blushed with happiness as she studied her reflection in the freestanding mirror in Mrs. Rich's bedroom. She held her breath so the pastor's wife could tighten the strings on her corset.

"As if you need one of these contraptions," the woman sputtered. "You have the waist of an ant."

Color shot through the young woman's cheeks. Changing the subject, she asked, "I wonder how Becca's coming with her dress."

"My daughter Esther is helping the child. You did a fine job redesigning that gown to fit her. You are quite a seamstress, young lady." The woman dropped the ivory lace gown over Serenity's arms and shoulders. The cool silk dress lining slid down over her body, followed by the delicate lace overdress.

"My mother insisted I learn tailoring skills. She said that even the humblest frock could look fashionable if designed and assembled well." Serenity smiled at herself. The high color in her cheeks accented the delicate nature of the dress's design. She turned to see herself from a different angle.

"Stand still." Mrs. Rich tugged at the dress from the back. "It's going to take me hours and hours to fasten all these buttons."

Serenity giggled. She knew the minister's wife enjoyed playing mother-of-the-bride. The thought of her mother and Aunt Fay missing this moment saddened the young woman.

"No woolgathering today, missy. Such thoughts will give you permanent worry lines." The older woman ran her index finger gently over Serenity's forehead, then returned to her task of fastening the tiny silk-covered buttons down the back of the dress.

During a lull in the conversation, Serenity wondered what Caleb might be thinking as he dressed in the minister's guest room. *Is he nervous? Is he thinking about his family missing this most important day in his life?*

The pastor's wife latched the last button and straightened. "There! I think we have it. Forgive me, but as your mother twice removed, I must ask. Do you know what to expect in marriage, especially the physical side?"

Serenity blushed and swallowed hard. "My mother explained all that to me a few years ago."

"A wise woman. Too many young women have no concept as to what a man—"

Serenity patted the woman's hand. "I understand, honest. I understand."

"Good! Let's do something with that hair of yours." The older woman opened the top drawer in her dresser and removed a crown of crocheted roses and creamy white ribbons. "I hope you don't mind, but I made this for you, if you like it. . . ."

Serenity inhaled sharply. "Like it? It's perfect!" She placed the wreath on her head.

"If we pin back your hair—" The woman demonstrated her idea to Serenity. The girl cooed with pleasure. "Now I look like a real bride." Tears glistened in the older woman's eyes as she stepped back to admire the beautiful young bride. A knock sounded on the door. "Are you ready in there?" Felix asked. "Everyone's waiting."

Serenity took several breaths before answering. "Yes. You can tell Mrs. Bishop to begin playing the organ."

Mrs. Rich planted a kiss on Serenity's cheek. "Thank you for letting me share this day with you."

"Thank you for letting us get married in your parlor," Serenity added. "And for caring for Becca during the next few days." She blushed again. "I hope she's no bother."

"Bother? Hardly. She's a delightful child. She'll help Esther string the popcorn for our Christmas tree. My

husband's family came from Germany where they always
. . . What am I doing going on about Christmas trees while
you are waiting to join your young man at the altar?"

Taking one last look in the mirror, Serenity adjusted one
of the crocheted roses on her crown, then tugged at a curl
spiraling down one blushing cheek. "All right. I'm ready,"
she whispered.

Felix and Becca waited for her outside the bedroom
door. Serenity gave Becca a quick kiss before the girl took
her place beside the organ. The organist pedaled the pump
organ as fast as she could, but with all the organ's wheezing
and squawking, the hymn didn't sound like any Serenity had
ever heard.

"Here goes," Serenity whispered, placing her hand onto
Felix's arm. The attorney patted her hand gently.

Walking down the hallway to the parlor, Serenity saw a
young man standing beside Caleb. If it weren't for his neat,
clean appearance and clean-shaven face she'd think it was—
Aaron! Seeing the recognition in Serenity's eyes, Aaron
smiled and mouthed the words, "Forgive me." Serenity
nodded, then turned her gaze toward her groom.

From the marble fireplace at the far end of the parlor, the
two Cunard men watched as Serenity, on the arm of Felix
Bonner, approached. Pastor Rich stood to one side of the fireplace; his wife and daughter stood on the other with Becca.

The moment Serenity's gaze connected with Caleb's,
everything and everyone disappeared. Her "I do" came
out barely above a whisper. Serenity studied the contours
of Caleb's face as the pastor read the vows and Caleb
repeated them.

"Serenity Louise Pownell, repeat after me. 'I, Serenity,
take thee, Caleb Elijah Cunard' . . ."

A smile crinkled the corners of her mouth. *Elijah,* she thought, *I didn't know your middle name was Elijah. How many other things will I learn about you in the years we will share together?*

It wasn't until Caleb kissed her lips soundly that Serenity emerged from her daze. Suddenly she realized, *I'm married—I'm Mrs. Caleb Cunard!* The thought both pleased her and terrified her.

A cheer went up. Mrs. Rich, Esther, and Becca rushed to her. Serenity quickly found herself caught up in the celebration of the moment. Her hostess guided the newlyweds over to the dining room table where a burnt-sugar cake waited to be cut and devoured. Felix toasted the couple with a teacup of apple cider. "To you both, a remarkable couple indeed." He turned and handed Serenity a needlepoint carpetbag. "A present for your new home."

She unlatched the latch on the bag, peered inside, and gasped. "The kaleidoscope! Oh, Felix, you shouldn't have."

The man shrugged. "You'll get more pleasure out of it than I ever will. Enjoy."

Serenity's eyes misted. "Thank you so much. We'll treasure it always."

"Thank you, everyone!" Caleb said. "Pastor and Mrs. Rich, Esther, Felix . . . Serenity and I feel so wealthy having made such good friends as you folks."

Felix grasped Caleb's hand. "Talk about happy endings! I don't understand, with all that's transpired . . ." He paused. "If I were a believing man, I'd have to say someone is certainly watching over you two."

Caleb slipped his arm possessively around his bride's waist and grinned at the lawyer. "My wife is a woman of faith, Felix. The wisest man who ever lived once said, 'A good wife is worth far more than rubies.'"

Felix laughed. "Sounds like luck to me."

"Not luck—God." Serenity gazed lovingly at her husband's strong profile. "God brought us together and He will keep us together."

Felix scratched his head. "I don't know. God and all, I find that hard to believe."

Caleb laughed and kissed the top of his wife's head. "Hang around Serenity's Inn awhile and you'll become a believer too."

"Serenity's Inn?" Serenity peered up into Caleb's face. While she hadn't forgotten the idea she'd whimsically thrown out at him the night he returned home from Kansas, she imagined he had.

"Yeah. I've been giving it a lot of thought. It's not such a bad idea. We need to talk about staying in Missouri. My folks want to continue west to California, but I'm not sure that's what we should do."

"There's lots of work in these parts for blacksmiths," Felix reminded. "And Independence could use a decent boarding house with less, uh, worldly influences." He reddened.

"Looks like we have a lot to talk about, honey." Caleb squeezed Serenity about the waist.

"You'd really want to run a boarding house of some kind?" She searched his face for answers.

He shrugged and grinned. "We have to fill all those bedrooms somehow." He nuzzled her neck.

"We could fill them with babies." Serenity laughed at the startled expression on her husband's face.

"Don't get her laughing, Caleb. You'll be sorry, I promise you," Felix warned. "Never set her to laughing!"

"Felix!" Serenity's eyes flashed. She straightened Caleb's suit lapel. "Don't pay any attention to him, Caleb."

The young groom observed the strange glances passing between his bride and his friend but chose to ignore them. "And now, if everyone will excuse us, I am taking my bride home." He scooped the surprised Serenity into his arms and carried her to the door, where Mrs. Rich met them carrying their coats, hats, and mittens.

Caleb set Serenity down long enough to help her with her coat and to kiss Becca good-bye, then swept his bride into his arms again and carried her to the waiting sleigh.

"I put a hot brick on the floor of the cutter for you," Felix called, but the couple didn't hear him.

Eager to go, the horses snorted and blew steam as the couple climbed into the sleigh. Caleb covered their laps with a thick rabbit-fur blanket.

Serenity snuggled close to her husband as he flicked the reigns and the horses moved forward. They waved good-bye to their friends and turned their faces toward the sunset and toward the adventure of a new beginning.